LOVE COMES HOME

A COLLECTION OF SECOND CHANCE SHORT STORIES

KRISTI ROSE

VINTAGE HOUSEWIFE BOOKS

Vintage Housewife Books

PO BOX 841

Farmington, Mo 63640

www.kristirose.net

Book Layout © 2014 BookDesignTemplates.com

Cover Design © 2015 Paper and Sage Designs

Love Comes Home/ **Kristi Rose**. -- 2nd ed.

ISBN 978-0-6925071-8-6

❀ Created with Vellum

SECOND
≶ A Coming Home Short Story ≷
CHANCES

KRISTI ROSE

Vintage Housewife Books

PO BOX 841

Farmington, Mo 63640

www.kristirose.net

Book Layout © 2014 BookDesignTemplates.com

Cover Design © 2015 Paper and Sage Designs

Edited by Paige Christian

Second Chances/ Kristi Rose. -- 1st ed.

❀ Created with Vellum

DEDICATION

This is for all those that needed a second chance and to those that gave them one~

L orelei glanced at the clock and stifled a yawn. She was definitely not a morning person and, in her opinion, anyone who thought five hours after midnight was morning was sadistic.

The door banged open and Andee, her business partner, backed into the diner's kitchen lugging a large crate loaded with groceries and fresh flowers.

"Morning, sunshine," she said in her typical cheerful singsong voice. Her dark hair swung in a ponytail.

"Bite me." Lorelei continued to beat the whisk against the bowl of eggs in the crook of her arm.

"Yay! You're in a good mood." Andee slid the crate onto the counter and began to unload the cartons of fresh eggs, gallons of milk, bags of spinach, scallions, red peppers, and fresh strawberries from the next town over.

Lorelei finished the eggs and poured them into a pie plate, completing her third quiche for the morning, this one a ham and Gruyere combination. "What did I say about talking to me before I've had my coffee and the clock hasn't struck noon?" She teased.

"To not to. But I haven't listened to you since we took tap lessons at Mrs. Becky's dance studio when we were six years old and you told me to try out for the skunk part. Who'd want to be a skunk?" She shook her head while pulling down a large mixing bowl and handed it to Lorelei.

"I was a skunk," Lorelei said.

"Exactly, and you said it was terrible. Remember how Buck teased you about stinking for all of first grade? Terrible."

Lorelei paused as she measured out the flour for her waffle mix and curled her upper lip at the woman who'd had been one of her closest friend for the last quarter century.

"And you still ended up marrying him. You're a true friend," Lorelei said with as much sarcasm she could muster, considering the early morning hour. Roosters were still asleep.

"And don't you forget it." Andee blew her a kiss before she turned to leave the kitchen.

Lorelei finished the waffle mix and pulled the scones out of the oven, replacing them with the quiches. Running a breakfast diner, a popular one at that, was exhausting work and Two Chicks and Bacon closed their doors every day at noon. Lorelei couldn't imagine how bone weary she'd feel if they ran a lunch and dinner service as well.

"Oh my God," Andee exclaimed as she barged into the kitchen, the daily special's chalkboard in her hand, the swinging door crashing against the wall.

Lorelei, who'd been checking on her croissants, jumped and burned her hand on the searing hot oven rack. "Ow." She rushed to rinse it under cold water. "What in the hell?" she asked, closing the oven door with her foot.

"I'm sorry. I totally forgot to ask if you saw the paper this morning." It was an explosion of words, as if Andee couldn't contain them any longer. Which she probably couldn't considering secrets leaked out of Andee faster than water ran through a colander. Her intentions never ran toward malice; she simply had a knack for inadvertently spilling the beans.

"Ah, no. I haven't seen the paper yet as I was here before they were delivered." Lorelei pulled an ice cube from the fridge and rubbed it over the red welt running across her wrist.

"Guess who's moving home? Well, not home exactly but back to Florida and crazy close, too." The smile on Andee's face was large and laughter bubbled from her lips.

It didn't take a genius to figure out whom she was talking about. There was only one person from Lakeland, the prodigal son, whose homecoming would make the papers.

"Why would you think I'd care one fig about Cole Williams moving back to Florida or moving anywhere for that matter?"

"Oh come on, Lorelei, it's Cole. We've all been friends for a million years. It'll be great to see him again. I bet Buck's planning all kinds of man fun for himself and Cole—or he will be once he sees the paper."

"Y'all didn't know he was moving back?"

Andee shook her head.

"Didn't y'all just see Cole a few months ago at the Sugar Bowl?" Lorelei tossed the melting cube into the sink and checked the list of items she needed to make and bake. She had no more interest in talking about Cole Williams than she had in getting a gynecological exam. Though both were unavoidable, at least one was in her best interest, the other...not so much.

"Yeah, we saw him at the Sugar Bowl but he was working. Coaching a top SEC football team requires a lot of his attention," Andee said and rested the chalkboard against her hip.

"He's not the coach, he's the offensive coordinator."

"Ah-ha, you do pay attention to Cole's career," Andee stabbed a finger in Lorelei's direction.

"No, I just overhear his momma every day when she comes in for her tea and crumpets. He's all she talks about. And speaking of crumpets, if I don't get back to this"—she swept her arm wide, indicating the kitchen—"we'll be hearing more complaints than gossip." Lorelei slid a bowl toward Andee and removed the towel she'd draped across it over an hour earlier.

Andee sighed. "I'll never understand how the two of you fell apart. You were so close."

Lorelei looked at her friend, the woman who knew nearly everything about her. "Things were never the same for us after he left for college. Once he got there he never looked back. So much for all those promises of love and forever." Truth was things changed for them the night he graduated from high school and she gave him her virginity in the back of his truck bed.

"Lorelei—"

Lorelei laughed. "Seriously, Andee. He forgot about all of us. I can't believe you and Buck even give a shit he's coming back to town. He showed his true colors. Ugh, how many times are we going to have this conversation?" She knew it would be a different conversation if Andee knew all the facts but she was also aware of Andee's bleeding heart and proclivity for forgiveness. The last thing Lorelei wanted to do was rehash her past. Heaven forbid she mention the letters she'd received from Cole every year, marking the anniversary of an event that only made her melancholy. Fourteen letters. Fourteen years. She'd never bothered to read any of them after the first one. She'd held them in her hand, thought about reading them several times, but could never muster the courage to reopen a wound that had long ago scarred over. Reading the first one had left her sad and confused.

Lorelei rolled out the dough with such vigor the handle on her German rolling pin snapped. "You have got to be kidding me," she said, tossing it in the trash bin. She took a second one from the hanging rack and continued her work.

"Maybe him coming home will give y'all a chance to put the past behind you. Maybe even become friends again."

"Doubtful, I've taken a page from Cole's playbook and moved

on." Lorelei gave Andee a pointed look and a half shrug. To her, Cole Williams was the past and she'd no sooner live in the past than she'd drive a Chevette or go a day without her smartphone.

They finished the food prep and morning set up in relative silence. Though they'd done most of the work the night before, bringing in the papers, making the food, cutting and arranging the fresh flowers, and booting up the computer was all done during the wee hours of the morning before they opened.

Twenty minutes before Andee was scheduled to turn the sign to OPEN, Lorelei loaded the front display with her homemade fruit Danishes, scones, crumpets, doughnuts, croissants, and biscuits. She flipped the newspapers open and laid them out for her customers to enjoy while they ate and stared down at Cole's face. Amazing how age had only made him look better. He still kept his dark hair cut short but his laugh lines had deepened and given his strong face more character. Lord, how she loved that cleft in his chin but looking at him now only made her angry.

The picture showed him on the sidelines talking to a player. The intensity of what he was saying was clear by his furrowed brow and how he leaned close to the other guy, his head bent toward him as if telling a tremendous secret.

How many times had he leaned toward her like that? To tell a joke, whisper his love for her, or share a secret. More than she could count. But that was high school, when she thought she knew everything, could have anything, and deserved it all. And this was now, when the only thing she was certain of was that everything came with a price.

"Morning all." Kylie, the young college student they'd hired as their barista, came in from the kitchen and took an apron from the rack.

"Mornin' Kylie," Andee called from across the room.

"Morning," Lorelei said, and pulled her own well-used apron off and donned a new, cleaner one.

"This place is gonna be all abuzz over Cole Williams moving

back. It's all my daddy can talk about." Kylie pointed to the picture in the paper before turning to fire up her large magic machine that could turn coffee into dessert.

"God help me." Lorelei glanced at the large clock that hung in the restaurant. It was going to be a long five hours.

"I wonder how long we'll have to wait before Mrs. Williams shows up. I bet she can't wait to hold court. My daddy says he wants me to bring home any good info she might give out." Kylie rolled her eyes and pressed a button that shot steam out a long stem.

"I'm turning the sign," Andee called out. "Two Chicks and Bacon is officially open." She'd been saying the same thing since the first day they'd opened for business six years earlier.

"I'm hiding in the kitchen," Lorelei replied but she didn't get three steps toward it before several locals flung open the front door to the restaurant and came bustling in. Thankfully, Mrs. Williams was not among them.

"Did y'all hear?" Mr. Thompson, a mail clerk, asked as he grabbed a seat at the bar.

"Oh, yeah. We heard. It's excitin' isn't it?" Andee answered.

"So proud we are. So proud." Mr. Thompson said.

"Of what?" Lorelei asked, one hand ready to push open the door to the kitchen. "He's an assistant coach for college football. He hasn't cured cancer or anything."

"But he's gonna be a head coach with this new move. Not right away, of course, but he's setting himself up for the job," was the reply from one of the others.

"Oh, well, I stand corrected." Lorelei backed out of the room. There was no point in disagreeing with a mob of football fanatics. She turned on the stove and prepared to make omelets and eggs over easy. They would gush about Cole and football all while ordering the same breakfast and going about their day in the same predictable manner. Who was she to be the sour apple of the group?

Lost in her work, Lorelei jumped when Andee came through the door. "Mr. Jenkins says your ham and cheese croissant doesn't taste as good as it normally does. Says you used the wrong cheese." Andee arched a brow, her lips twisting into a grin.

"The hell he did." Lorelei checked on the frittata in the oven before she tossed her oven mitts onto the counter and pushed through the kitchen door, heading straight for Mr. Jenkins.

"What's this nonsense I hear about the wrong cheese?" She stuck her hands on her hips and stared up at her old Driver's Ed teacher.

"What in the Sam Hill kinda cheese did you use?"

"It was Gruyere."

"Groo-what? What is wrong with good old American cheddar, Lorelei?"

"Nothing, but today it was Gruyere. You want American cheddar? Come back on a day when I decide to use that cheese."

"Some things don't change, do they Cole?" Mr. Jenkins said, looking over Lorelei's shoulder.

Lorelei sucked in air and tried to steady her suddenly shaky hands. Her heart skipped at least four beats before it took off at an erratic pace. She wasn't sure if she felt anger or surprise. Slowly, she turned to see the face that only a short time earlier stared at her from the paper. Fourteen years of unanswered questions, sadness, and longing pressed against her.

"Oh, I don't know Mr. Jenkins, I imagine a fair amount of things have changed." Cole briefly met her eyes and gave her a tentative smile. He shifted slightly, leaning closer, and whispered, "Sorry, Lore. My mom made me come. She wouldn't take no for an answer."

Though his aftershave was a scent she was unfamiliar with, she knew it would forever be a memory associated with this moment. She tried to focus on something other than Cole but her eyes were drawn to the small nick just below the dimple in his chin. It was astonishing how familiar yet foreign he was to her.

"I'm here to tell you that most things to do not change and Lorelei Parker's temperament is true and constant. She's a feisty one, has been and always will be. How in the Hades are you, Cole?" Mr. Jenkins asked, extending his hand, a smile larger than the Mississippi spreading across his face.

"I'm all right, Mr. Jenkins." Cole reached around Lorelei to shake the older man's hand.

"We're right tickled you're back, son."

"I'm pleased to be back in Florida as well," Cole said, before adding after a small pause, "How ya doing, Lore?"

Slowly, she turned. Feigning confusion she squinted as she scanned him up and down.

"Cole? Cole Williams? Is that you? Lord, I sure can't tell. Turn around." She waved her hand in a circle to emphasize her desire for him to turn, which he did, slowly, with a puzzled look on his face.

"Ah, there you are! I recognize you now," Lorelei said to the back of his head.

He turned back to her with a frown.

"I mean, *that is* the last thing we saw when you left for college. Did you even look over your shoulder or did you drive away as fast as that old pickup truck could take you?" She wanted to punch him in the solar plexus or kick him in the shin. She wanted to run away as fast as she could. She needed air, fresh air, far away from the air that Cole was breathing.

"Excuse me, gentlemen. Good morning, Mrs. Williams." She waved to Cole's momma as she stepped from between the two men and quickly made her way back to the kitchen.

Lorelei spent the remainder of the morning behind the scenes and away from the mob that had taken over their small diner. Though Andee accused her of hiding out in the kitchen, Lorelei certainly had enough cooking to justify her absence and the distraction of filling the orders kept her from spying on him. But it wasn't the overflow of customers flocking to see Cole that had

In hindsight, Andee designing the t-shirts for the Spring Fling Super Bowl had been a mistake. The team now sported hot pink t-shirts with the diner's logo—two fluffy chicks with long eyelashes sharing a piece of bacon—pressed on the front and the words TEAM TWO CHICKS on the back. On the women, the front logo's two chicks lined up across the chest in such manner that Lorelei had difficulty meeting the gaze of anyone in the crowd, much less her teammates.

"I say we just go with plain white t-shirts. Someone can run to Walmart and pick up a few packs." Leo wiped his glasses clean with the edge of his pink shirt.

"If we only had time, we're the first team up. In Andee's defense, her concern was that we'd blend in with all the others on the field. At least there's no mistaking who our teammates are." Lorelei shrugged.

"It happened one time. *One. Time,*" Mr. Jenkins defended.

"I wasn't saying anything, Mr. Jenkins." Lorelei held her hands up and began backing up only to collide with a wall of man behind her.

Cole caught her by her shoulders and steadied her before

sliding his hands down her arms and moving one to rest on the small of her back.

"All right, someone give me the scoop on the first team, Jamison Chevrolet. What do I need to know?" he asked, his thumb stroking her back.

Lorelei took a tiny step away from his hand and the distraction it brought with it. Even in the hot pink shirt, he was a fine specimen of a man. The fabric stretched across his defined chest and shoulders. When she touched him, the years and distance between them seemed to fade and the familiarity of years together was back, wrapping its arms of time around them, and pulling them together.

The flash of a memory transported her back to Cole's seventeenth birthday and the party his mother had thrown for him.

They'd spent the day tubing behind her parents' boat with several of their high school friends. Cole, riding the tube beside her, had dared her to switch places with him, a stunt he favored as it allowed him to demonstrate his physical strength. But on this day, as Lorelei was letting go with one hand and reaching for the other handle, the tube caught a wave and bounced high and landed hard, slapping the water and tossing her off, sending her ass over teakettle and her bikini top floating away.

Coming up for air, trying to tread water while simultaneously keeping her chest below the water line, Lorelei was not surprised to see Cole swimming toward her. Though it was typical practice for the guys to leave those that fell off the tube to tread water or swim their way in.

"Nice flip, Lore."

"I lost my top," she answered and watched Cole look around for the lost fabric. He pointed to some reeds, the top floating against the tall stalks, and flipped onto his back to stroke his way over to it.

"Careful. Watch out for gators." She scanned the water, hoping not to see any swimming toward him. He grabbed the cloth and swam back toward her and when he was close enough, tossed it to her.

"Thanks. For getting my top and not leaving me out here alone."

Tying on the top as quickly as she could, she swam toward him and home.

"No sweat. I plan on getting some mileage out of this, like on a day I let you down. I'll be sure to remind you of this."

"Don't be stupid. You could never let me down," she told him before splashing him in the face.

But he had let her down, at the worst possible time.

"What's the plan, coach?" Leo asked, nudging her back to the present.

"What? I'm not the coach. Cole is." She handed him the armband coaches were required to wear.

Cole shook his head. "You or Andee should be the coach. It's y'all's business."

"For God's sake, man, take the band, though saying Andee should coach makes me wonder whether you're in your right mind or not," Buck mumbled.

"Hey, I heard that." Andee punched him in the arm.

"I love you," Buck said, patting her on the shoulder. "You're my wife. You're my life. But you'd be a terrible coach."

"Whatever." She turned her back to him.

"Are you sure, Lore?" Cole asked, still not reaching for the band.

"Why fight the inevitable. People will listen to you before any of us."

"Smart woman." Leo gave her a nudge with his elbow.

"My daddy didn't raise no dumb-dumb," she replied under her breath and the two shared a laugh before she called, "Huddle up."

"Hey, I'm the coach." Cole snatched the band from her hand.

"Well, start coaching."

"I was waiting for you to turn your attention back to the game." He gave her a pointed look.

Lorelei cocked her head to the side and searched his face. A flutter of something she hadn't experienced in years tickled her stomach. For a moment, she thought she might be sick, until she realized what it was she was feeling.

Could it be possible that Cole still had feelings for her? More than just remorse for his actions all those years ago back? More than obligation or a need to gain her forgiveness?

Cole leaned forward and brought the whistle that hung from her neck up to his lips. He gave it a quick blow before dropping it, winking at her, and turning to the team.

"Listen up, here's how we're going to run the first game." He delivered a strong strategy against an unknown opponent and fifty-five minutes later, they emerged victorious.

With breaks scattered between games, several bottles of water downed, layers of sunscreen applied and more trash talk spoken than in the history of the charity, Team Two Chicks and Bacon emerged a contender for first place. Their opponent? Miller's Auto Body.

The game was tied, only minutes were left on the clock, and Cole had called a time out.

"You want a win?" Cole asked, his voice raspy from hours of yelling.

"We want a win!" the team yelled.

Cole nodded, his eyes swinging from each player. "Then let's take the win." He brought his gaze to hers. "Lore, Classic William's play. Think front yard, go long to left side pocket and—"

"Zing around the tree. Old School. I like it." She put her hand out for the team cheer.

"Wait, what do the rest of us do?" Andee asked.

"Watch my moves. I'll fake a pass to Buck and you all run it like that's what's happening. They'll be trying to anticipate you. Lorelei and I will cover the rest." Cole put his hands on top of hers and when their eyes met, he winked.

"Team Two Chicks," they yelled in unison.

"Break." Finished Cole.

Buck and Cole pounded fists and they scattered back on the field seconds before the ref blew the whistle. Lined up for the snap, Cole called bogus plays and Buck tossed him the ball. Cole stepped back and faked a throw toward Buck who'd gone right, pivoted quickly on his heel, and locked eyes with Lorelei who was nearing the end zone, her arms raised, a player on her tail.

Cole took two seconds before he launched the ball, a smooth spiral landing right in the cradle of her arms. Lorelei ran forward before making a sharp turn and heading for the end zone. Buck and Leo ran to cover her, Andee screaming for her to run.

Lorelei crossed into the end zone seconds before the player behind her reached out to snatch her flag, tripped, and flew into her, taking them both down.

The air horn sounded and Team Two Chicks erupted in cheers. They'd won by a touchdown. Cole ran to Lorelei, who was lying on her back still on the ground, the football clutched in her arm across her chest. The other player sat next to her.

"We did it. We won." He came to a stop, standing over her, his arm extended to help her up.

"Of course we did. That move never failed us before." She winced.

"You ok?"

"Yeah, though I think I might have broken my arm."

"I'm sorry. I tripped," the player said.

"It's all right. It happens," she told him.

Cole knelt beside her. "What? Are you kidding me?" But he could tell by the crinkle of her eyes that she was hurt. "Are you in a lot of pain? Where's it broken? Don't move. I'll call an ambulance." He waved for the volunteer paramedics to join him and then started patting his pockets looking for his cell phone.

"Cole, stop. You're freaking me out. Help me sit up."

Gently, he moved his arm under her shoulders and eased her up, pausing with each wince.

"I don't need an ambulance, but I think I need to go to the ER. Can you take this football from me? Gently though, that's the arm."

Cole could see splotches of color and a slight deformation near her wrist.

"Looks like it's your wrist." He eased the football from her grasp, wincing himself when she gasped.

"What's going on here?" Andee plopped down next to Lorelei.

"I think I broke my arm," Lorelei told her.

Andee's eyes grew wide as she glanced down at Lorelei's arm. "Oh no, it's your whisking arm, too."

"I know," Lorelei said. "But more importantly, I think I might pass out."

And she did just that.

6

"Cole, I broke my arm, not my leg," Lorelei said as he bent to lift her from the front seat of his truck.

"I know that, I saw the X-ray. I also saw how much pain medicine they gave you and I'm surprised you're as coherent as you are." He carried her to her steps and waited while she dug her house key out from her purse.

"Just drop me on the couch. I'll be good." She fit the key after several tries and pushed the door open.

"Really? You're good. You planning on sleeping in your grass-stained t-shirt for the next couple of days?" He kicked the door closed and elbowed a light switch, casting her living room in a soft glow.

"I hadn't thought about changing my clothes."

"I figured. Wow, you've changed a lot in here." He set her on the couch and took in the updated living room kitchen combination.

"Yeah, well I don't know if you remember or not but my momma wasn't one for cooking." She stretched out on the couch and the pain that was creasing her face seemed to ease.

Cole snorted. "I used to think you were the luckiest person in the world getting pizza once or twice a week. Then I started going on the road with the team and later scouting I would have killed the next man for a home-cooked meal."

He went into her kitchen and started opening and closing cabinet drawers.

"What are you looking for?" she asked, never opening her eyes.

"Scissors. The only way you're getting that shirt off is to cut it off. You know how I told you my mom would send me some of your food? Sometimes, many times, that was the only quality food I'd get. Half the time I was too tired to bother looking for a place to eat and I'd just down a Cup of Noodles or something." He found scissors in the drawer next to her flatware and came to stand by her. He lowered himself to sit on the edge of her wood coffee table, the scissors resting in his palm.

"The owners of Two Chicks and Bacon thank you and are glad they could provide a bit of comfort to you on your travels," she said and yawned. Pushing up with her left hand, she sat up and took the scissors from his palm.

It took a few moments of her trying to figure out how she was going to use her non-dominant hand to cut off her shirt without bringing further harm to her body before she gave up and fell back against the couch.

"I give up. I'll just be stuck in this shirt forever." She threw an arm over her eyes and sighed wearily.

"I can cut it off." Cole said.

"No, call Andee."

"I'm not calling Andee to have her drive all the way over when I'm sitting right here." He was determined to wait her out. "Besides, you freaked her out with that crazy long list of things she needed to do before y'all open tomorrow. She'll probably sleep at the diner tonight."

"There's no way I'm letting you cut this shirt off me. No sir."

her twisted in knots, it was knowing what waited for her when she got home. After all, if Cole Williams was in town, eating at her diner at the ungodly hour of nine o'clock in the morning then it was likely he was staying in town. At his momma's house. Right next door to her own.

Cole stood at the large picture window that overlooked Lake Gibson. Coming home, to Lakeland, had been something he'd put off for a long time. A very long time. And seeing Lorelei again, well hell, he knew the length of his absence had only made the already strained relationship even more so and the likelihood of a happy reunion impossible. He wondered if he'd ever be able to garner her forgiveness.

He caught site of her weaving down from her parent's deck and leaned toward the glass in surprise.

"Mom," he called over his shoulder, "does Lorelei live with her parents?" That was something he'd never imagined. He knew everything about her, at least everything his momma knew. Including details about every guy she'd dated and the many theories the townspeople had on why she wasn't married with children. But last he heard she was living in the central part of town not next door.

"No, honey. The Parkers moved to North Carolina. Let's see, it was right after you took that job in Texas—"

"Eight years ago," he mumbled. He hadn't stepped foot in his hometown in over eight years, preferring to invite his mother and friends out to visit him. At first, while in college, he'd come home every chance he got which was pretty limited with football training, practice, games, and attending classes. He tried repeatedly to reconnect with Lorelei but her father was a mighty foe and once she left for college those opportunities ceased to exist. It was near impossible for him to get from the northern part of the state where he went to school to the southern part where she was. It's not like she'd ever responded to any of the letters he sent either, and, like with all things time became the great divider. Once he graduated it was easy to find a million reasons why he could never make it home.

"Was it eight years? Well, if you say so. You remember me telling you that they lived in Maggie Valley part time, so her dad could teach at the seminary. Recently, they decided to stay for good. Lorelei bought their house a few months ago. They plan to continue to come down in the winter and stay with her. In fact, you just missed them. They left a couple weeks ago."

He watched Lorelei amble toward the dock, a basket swinging from her hand. She looked just like she had in high school, only prettier. Same long blonde hair that reminded him of the fresh honey his momma always set out with the breakfast biscuits. Same large greenish brown eyes that reminded him of campfires and pine trees. Only this time those eyes no longer looked at him with mirth and mischief but a coldness born from her anger.

She nestled into a chaise lounge on the dock and settled back with a book, taking from the basket a small yellow carton and a wine glass.

Funny, how she still preferred her wine from a box instead of a bottle. Likely acquired the taste after all those times of swiping wine from her parents believing they couldn't tell it was missing because it was from a box.

"I'm gonna step outside for a bit, Mom," he called, already unlocking the sliders and pushing one open. He didn't wait for her reply but stepped out onto the deck and quietly slid the door closed. Tucking his hands into his front pockets, he crossed over his folks' lawn onto hers and wove his way down to her dock.

"How are you Lorelei?" he said when he reached the first plank and stepped onto the creaking wood.

Without looking over her shoulder, she replied, "Do you really care?"

"Listen, I'm sorry about coming to the diner today. I know you don't want me in your space—"

"Like you are right now."

Cole stifled an audible sigh. The last thing he needed was her misinterpreting it for impatience. He knew coming home would be difficult; that he would have to face his past. It was long overdue and the obstacles that needed to be overcome looked insurmountable.

"I'm gonna be staying with my mom for a few weeks while I get settled and look for a place. I don't want that to be a problem for you. I know you don't want to see me. I'll try and be mindful of that but—"

"But I've never had my wishes granted before so I guess I shouldn't expect anything now."

"Why are you busting my balls, Lorelei?" He knew why and maybe now was as good a time as any to clear the air.

"Why are you and your balls standing on my dock asking to be busted?" she asked, this time looking at him over her shoulder. "Go away, Cole."

"Do you really hate me that much?" His voice was soft, nearly lost in the breeze.

She dropped her head briefly before placing her book on the table and turning to him. "I used to be so very angry with you, so yes, I probably did hate you 'that much' for a while. But that was years ago. Now, I just can't be bothered."

He pulled his hand from his pocket and swiped it down his face, sighing heavily before shoving it back into the pocket. "I never meant to hurt you, Lore."

She gave a bitter laugh and sat straight up. "Oh really? Because where I was standing it sure looked like you didn't give a shit about me and that hurt an awful lot."

"I was scared." He took another step forward.

She jumped up from the chaise and came toward him, her finger pointed at his face, her hand quivering.

"You were scared? You? Imagine how I felt. While you were at football practice at your big university and hanging out with all the lovely co-eds, I was telling my parents—alone I might add—that their only child who was just a week away from starting her junior year in high school was pregnant. You can imagine how that went over, considering my dad's a preacher and all. So forgive me if I don't feel all that sorry for you." She stood in front of him, poking her finger into his chest.

"I asked you to give me a few days to wrap my mind around it. To figure things out. You could have waited."

"I was throwing up all the time. My mom was bound to figure it out sooner than later. I didn't have the luxury of giving you time to figure things out."

"I'd have come, you know that." He caught her eye and held it, pressing his point.

"And when I lost the baby, why didn't you come then?" She moved her hands to her hips and stared up at him, eyes fuming, shaking her head.

"I told you I was sorry a hundred times in the letters."

"Because that's the same thing. I mean, you could have tried saying it to my face." Her voice was heavy with anger and hurt.

"You told me in an email that you lost the baby. How is one better than the other?" His voice quivered.

"At that point I thought you didn't care anymore and I was just telling you out of obligation."

"I *did* try to see you. Several times." It took everything he had not to shout.

"Oh, sure you did." She crossed her arms and pressed her lips together.

"I came here, skipped classes and everything, and tried to catch you right after school. Your dad was home and he told me that the best I could do for you was to never come back and leave you alone."

Lorelei eased her shoulders back slightly and stared at his face.

"I tried again that night, but your dad, he must have slept on your porch or something. He caught me trying to sneak up to your window. So I went back to Gainesville and came back a few weeks later and tried to get to you at school."

"I never saw you at school."

"No, that's because the principal came out and said your dad had been called and was on his way. I tried, Lore, I really did."

"So you wrote a letter."

"I tried email but you never answered those. Your mom gave me the idea about the letters. She saw me outside, staring at your house and told me one thing she liked about her day was checking the mail and seeing if anything good was waiting." Cole laughed. "It took me a few hours to figure out what she was telling me."

He searched her face. For years, he'd been looking at her in old pictures, the only current one he had was the newspaper article about her and Andee opening the diner. Seeing her now made him itch to know her again. To know how she'd spent the last fourteen years.

"Would you even have accepted an apology from me? Face to face?" He took a step closer.

Cole wanted to pull her into a tight embrace and never let her go. Force her to forgive him through a bear hug like he used to do when they were kids. He'd royally screwed up the one good relationship he'd ever had. The one person he wanted to share everything with could barely stand to look at him. To say he was sorry now felt more like another tear in their relationship, rather than the first stitch in mending their bond.

Lorelei shrugged. "It might have been nice to have one. But you're right. It's too late for apologies." She turned back to the chaise and her book.

"You know, Cole. I wasn't the only one affected by your actions. I swore my parent's to secrecy and it was really hard on my mom trying to maintain her friendship with your mom knowing what she knew." Lorelei plopped back down on the chaise and stared up at him.

Several times Cole had listened to his mother questioning what had gone wrong between her and Mrs. Parker, blaming it primarily on jealously because of Cole's success. Knowing that Lorelei had never told anyone made him ask, "Why didn't you tell my mom?"

He tried to picture how his mother would have reacted. It would've devastated her. Since his father's unexpected death the year before he graduated high school, Cole's momma had put everything she had in making sure that her son was successful. To insure that he would have a different life than the one his father led.

He looked at Lorelei stretched out on the chaise and thought of all the times they'd tossed a football around in his front yard. Football had been his lifeline, his way out from under his father's thumb, and his path to a different life. If anyone wanted to be close to him, they had to do it through football and Lorelei had. He'd taught her how to throw a spiral and to catch a long pass. She'd taught him how to laugh at himself and about patience, showing him that good things came to those who knew how to pace themselves. A practice that had paid off for him and in fact landed him the coach-in-waiting job.

"I've always wondered why you didn't just tell anyone who'd listen." Cole stepped forward and came to stand at the foot of the lounger.

"I wanted you to do the right thing because of who you were, not because your mom made you. Plus, I figured if you made it to the NFL, I could file a paternity suit and take all your income."

Cole laughed and sat on the edge of the lounger. "I knew you had to be beyond mad at me. I know I let you down, Lorelei. I think about it every day and for what it's worth, I'm sorry. I'm sorry I wasn't the man you needed me to be, or the friend you thought I was. I'm sorry." He looked at her, their eyes holding and though it was ever so slightly, hers soften and he wasn't about to let the opportunity go.

"When you called to tell me you were pregnant, all I could think about was how would I ever be able to support you and a baby? I could hear my father ranting about how much he hated his job and how terrible it was to be stuck in a job you hated. And with you still in high school, I didn't see how I could make it work. I couldn't picture myself working for Publix, stuck in a grocery store. I'd be like my dad and probably have a heart attack on the warehouse floor just like he did—"

"Lots of people work for Publix and are really happy. It's too bad that your dad didn't have the courage to change his situation either."

"I know that now. I know my dad's unhappiness came from his poor decisions, but all I could think about was how we'd end up hating each other sooner or later. I didn't want to work for a grocery store, even if I could work my way up to management, and the alternative was... What? A high school coach? I wanted more than that for me, for you. Especially in this town."

"What exactly does that mean?"

"You know how people talk here. Once you're out of earshot, people would've been lamenting, 'Look at Lorelei Parker, got herself pregnant in high school. She had so much potential.' Or 'poor ol' Cole Williams, he had a shot at the big leagues until he knocked up Lorelei Parker'. I didn't want that for either of us. I didn't want to resent you and Lord knows I didn't want you to hate me any more than you already did. At least you still had control of your life."

Lorelei's smile was wistful. "Well, it's irrelevant anyway. I had a miscarriage and no one is the wiser. You got everything you wanted and your momma... well, you're all she talks about." She drained the remains from her wine glass and tucked it, along with her book, back into her basket.

"Have you gotten everything you ever wanted, Lore?" he asked, curious as to why this enchanting woman was not attached to someone. Why any dumb ass, other than him, would be stupid enough to let her go.

She moved off the lounger, careful not to touch him, and picked up her basket before she answered, "I can't complain. I'm doing what I want with my life. Congrats on the new job, Cole. Good luck."

With a swing of her basket, she walked back toward her house, never looking back. For Cole, it was a start. One he'd readily take.

S leep was fitful at best and elusive at worst. Lorelei continued to replay the conversation with Cole and thought about the box of letters buried deep within her closet. The letters her mom had left waiting for her on the desk in her bedroom instead of on the kitchen counter. She thought about how she'd deleted his emails without a second thought, so angry that he hadn't even bothered trying to face her. She didn't need to call her daddy to confirm Cole's story. It made sense and explained why her dad would unexpectedly show up at school.

Seeing Cole brought up so much emotion and confusion and as she watched her clock click down the minutes until her alarm would go off, Lorelei stared at her closet doors and wondered what would have become of them had she not had a miscarriage. Would they have found their way back together, she more open to forgiveness for the sake of their child? Or would she be lying in bed, like she was now, pining away for a love she'd never got over. But, for all the happiness walking up to Cole and telling him how she felt might bring her; what was love without trust? Lorelei certainly didn't trust Cole. Not anymore at least.

At a time when she'd needed him the most, when her life had

changed forever, the only thing she had from him were letters. What could he say that would make it better? Nothing could give them back the innocence of their hope before she found out she was pregnant. She knew one of his greatest fears was to become a slave to job he hated like his father had been. He feared becoming his father, of not seeing his lifelong dream of playing football come to fruition, of being stuck forever in their small town. Apparently more than he feared losing her. Certainly, it had been sage advice from her mother to do nothing until she passed the twelve-week mark and when she'd miscarried at ten weeks, all of Cole's problems had been resolved.

And the best he could do was to write a letter.

Lorelei turned off the clock, beating the alarm by twelve minutes, and shuffled to the shower.

Did she really hate him *that much*, he had asked. No, she hated herself more for still loving the boy, now man, who out of fear made a decision that was less than she expected. Forgiveness was a concept harder to practice than one could ever have imagined.

At the diner, Lorelei went through her make and bake check-list and began the process of getting the diner ready for the day.

She'd finished the crumpet dough and set it to rise, diced all the vegetables, and began setting out pie plates for her quiches when Andee walked in toting her crate.

"Morning, sunshine. Whoa, you look like crud." She kicked the door closed.

"Gee, thanks."

"Are you getting sick?"

"I didn't sleep very well."

Andee's eyes widened. "No kidding."

"It's not *that* bad." Lorelei walked over to the mirror by the back door and gasped at her reflection. Her eyes were bloodshot, not terrible by themselves, but the pallor of her complexion made the red of her eyes stand out. Dark circles rested heavily under her eyes.

"You want to talk about it?" Andee asked before handing her a large coffee cup that she'd just topped off.

"Not really," Lorelei said, returning to her quiches.

Andee poured herself a cup and quietly went about emptying the crate.

"Remember how people used to call me a goody-goody just because Daddy was a preacher?" Lorelei asked.

Andee nodded, "I do."

"Or if they weren't saying that, then they were accusing me of rebelling because of what Daddy did?"

"You could never catch a break, that's for sure. My momma always said that preacher kids have it harder than other kids because they're always being scrutinized." Andee began trimming the flowers under running water.

"Cole never did that. Neither did you, for that matter." Lorelei looked at her friend and smiled.

"Well, of course not, honey. Anyone who knew you knew you had a mind of your own and weren't prone to doing things out of spite."

Lorelei stopped whisking eggs and thought about her friend's words. Had she held onto her hurt to spite Cole?

"Hey, Bucky and I got to reminiscing last night. Remember that time—we were in seventh grade I think—Bucky had a party and Shawn Fields picked you to spend seven minutes in heaven with him?"

Lorelei laughed. How could she forget? That night was the first time she'd been kissed and by two boys nonetheless. Those minutes in Bucky's hall closet had been life changing for her.

"Yeah, you all started banging on the door early and Shawn got mad." Lorelei remembered how Cole had hollered through the wood that their time was up not seconds after they'd closed it. Shawn had quickly pressed his lips to hers and Lorelei had felt nothing. Not a single butterfly of excitement.

"Remember how when y'all came out, Cole announced it was

his turn and pulled you into the closet? We were laughing because I remember you telling Cole he better know what he was doing because Shawn Fields had set the bar pretty high."

Lorelei tossed back her head and laughed. "I had completely forgotten about that." Not the kiss of course. The kiss, a simple press of Cole's lips to hers, had made her knees wobble and her stomach turn inside out. But she'd forgotten she'd challenged Cole like that, knowing it would make him crazy.

"Later that night when we were lying in bed, I asked you what it was like, remember? I was desperate to be kissed but scared I was gonna make a fool of myself and not know what to do and you said—"

"That I was gonna marry Cole Williams." Lorelei sobered instantly. Andee hadn't been the only person she'd mentioned her aspirations too. She'd told Cole, of course, to which he'd responded, 'All right, Lore. Just let me play football, too.'

"Some things just can't withstand the burden of distance, I suppose." Andee shrugged.

Lorelei stepped back to look at the assortment of food ready to be baked or prepped, yet all she could think about were the what if's. So much about her had changed that summer, enough that even though she dated now she'd never been willing to risk the remaining half of her heart.

Andee came up from behind and wrapped her in a hug. "Sometimes even when food tastes good, it could always taste a little bit better with seasoning or trying a different ingredient. Isn't that what you always say?"

"I have no idea what you are talking about." Lorelei clasped her hands on her friend's arms and gave them a squeeze.

"I'm saying it's time to be happy, Lorelei, and it's ok to change the ingredients."

With a final squeeze, Andee was off to set up the dining area, leaving Lorelei with her thoughts. Until Cole walked into her diner yesterday, Lorelei had thought she was happy. Or content at least. She had a very full life.

Lorelei chuffed at that last thought. Yeah, she had such a full life that two conversations with Cole and she was rethinking her actions of the last fourteen years.

4

"Now this is how you make a croissant, Lorelei," Mr. Jenkins said as he cut open his second ham and cheddar croissant.

"God forbid you stretch out your palate." She topped off his coffee.

"Don't you think the croissant is real good, Cole?" Mr. Jenkins shouted around her to where Cole was sitting and had been fielding questions for the last two hours.

"Oh no. I'm not getting in the middle of this. I think anything Lorelei makes is delicious."

"What would you know about what I make? This is the second time you've eaten here." She turned to face him and quirked a brow.

"Not true. My mom has been overnighting me crumpets and scones and all sorts of pastries since y'all opened the diner." He returned her expression with a matching one.

"For the last six years, your momma's been mailing you my food?"

"Yup. Though I have to confess. Those goji berry granola bars were not my favorite."

Mr. Jenkins exploded with a larger than life laugh. "No one liked those, did they Lorelei? You couldn't even give them away. Even the ducks at the lake wouldn't eat them. I tried."

Lorelei slid the coffeepot onto the warmer and threw her hands up in defeat. "Why are you even here, Cole? Don't you have a football to throw, a house to buy, or a cheerleader to woo?" She hated that she was probing into his personal life but her search of the Internet had given her nothing about him but his stats as a coach.

"Let's see if I can answer those in order. I'm doing an interview for The Ledger. I'm tossing the football later with Buck. I plan on renting at first to figure what area I want to live in, and I prefer pastry chefs to cheerleaders."

The restaurant was suddenly quiet and Lorelei wished she could stop the heat spreading up her chest by sheer willpower alone.

"If I gave you a free croissant, would you promise to shove it in your mouth and not say something so stupid again?" It was all she had.

Cole laughed, but before he could say more the ringing of bells indicated the front door opening and Leo, the sports reporter for the local paper, walked in. Lorelei leaned over the counter to give him a high five.

"I see you signed up for my team again, Leo. We're gonna take it this year."

"That's the plan, except I have some rather bad news." He held up his hand quickly. "I don't want anyone to panic, but I'm actively seeking alternatives."

"What's happened?" Lorelei filled a cup with hot water and offered Leo an assortment of tea bags. He was a regular in her diner and she sometimes thought she might like to date him. He was only two years older, the same age as Cole, and attractive in the smart and literary way. It had always surprised her that he covered the sports beat, but behind his tortoiseshell glasses and oxford shirt was a die-hard fanatic of all sports.

"Mitch, the guy from my department that we used as the QB last year, quit a few weeks back and I haven't had any luck in finding a replacement yet." Leo put a voice recorder and small notebook on the counter before he slid into a seat.

"Poop." Andee came up from behind Lorelei. "I'll have Bucky start looking, too. I really thought we'd take Miller's Auto Body this year."

"What are y'all taking about?" Cole moved to the seat next to Leo.

"The annual Spring Fling Super Bowl," Andee answered. "Don't you remember? Oh wait; you were gone by the time it got started."

"Spring Fling Super Bowl?" Cole asked.

"It's something the city organizes," Lorelei said. "Fifteen teams sign up and have to be sponsored by a business. It's an all-day round-robin flag football game and charity event. Each year the city selects a charity to receive all the proceeds. This year's charity is…."

"Juvenile Diabetes Research Foundation," finished Leo.

"And you sponsor a team?" Cole asked Lorelei.

"*We* sponsor a team." She put her arm around Andee.

"Wow." Andee blinked. "I just had a flashback to high school. Even then you could never see past Lorelei." She turned to Leo. "Everyday world events happen and these two—clueless." She turned back to Cole and rolled her eyes.

"So you two have history?" Leo asked, flipping open his notebook and setting up his voice recorder.

"I'll make it real simple for you, Leo. We all grew up together. That's it. Cole and I lived next door to each other and more from convenience than anything we just stuck together. Until Cole left for college."

"Hey, Buck left for college the same time I did," Cole said.

The room was quiet and Lorelei knew everyone was waiting for her to answer. Stuck together was the understatement of the century, and convenience? Who was she kidding? They'd been inseparable. Lorelei had even tried out for the dance team in high school so she could be on the football field when he was.

She pressed her lips into a thin line, picking her words carefully before she said, "Yeah, but Bucky came home every chance he got. Isn't that right, Andee?"

Andee nodded and smiled. "Just for those first two years when I was finishing high school. I didn't even bother applying to a different college."

Lorelei pointed her gaze at Cole. Their mutual friends had done what he'd thought was impossible. They'd made it through high school and college in love and intact.

She swung her gaze to Leo. "You hungry, Leo? You want the usual?"

"That'd be great. Thanks." He turned to Cole and flipped on the recorder. "Let's talk about those college years," he said as she left the dining room.

In the kitchen, she took a towel and wet it with cold water, wrung it out, and pressed it to the back of her neck for a few moments before dabbing it up and down the column of her neck.

Thinking of high school always made her remember the endless nights she and Cole had spent parked off some back-country dirt road or down by Lake Morton, in the bed of his truck making out or talking about the life they wanted after college. Cole dreamt of coaching an NFL team and Lorelei dreamt of... well, whatever Cole wanted.

Man, she'd been so pathetically consumed by him. With a shake of her head she forced the past back where it belonged, in the past, and set about filling the orders.

She carried Leo's spinach omelet, home fries, and a plate of strawberry scones into the diner and slid Leo's plate toward him.

Reaching under the counter, she snagged a bottle of Tabasco sauce before he could ask for it and handed it to him.

Cole looked at her and then Leo. "I was thinking, Lore—"

"Well, please don't keep us waiting." She put the plate of scones in the display before coming to rest her hip against the counter.

Cole sighed and leaned back in his chair, one hand on his hip. "You all need a quarterback for the Spring Fling Super Bowl and I happen to have some experience throwing a football."

"He's got one of the best records for passing yards and you've wanted to beat Miller's Auto Body for the last three years," Leo said.

"I feel like this conversation has already happened and if I went to check the website it would show Cole has signed up for the team." Lorelei picked off a corner from one of the scones and popped it in her mouth.

"Well, there is that," Cole said, his finger resting on the screen of his smartphone.

Lorelei shrugged and swallowed. "Not much I can do now. But we should have someone waiting to take his place in case he doesn't show." She gave Cole a pointed look and a smirk.

"Let's finish up this interview, Cole." Leo flipped on the voice recorder. "How about you tell us why you turned down that offensive coordinator position with the Cowboys for the same job with a smaller university than you've been with so far."

Lorelei paused, the bite of scone halfway to her mouth, and waited for his answer.

Cole met her eyes, "I was honored to be offered the opportunity to work for the Cowboys but the chance to grow a team and become the head coach appeals to me more. It's about the bigger picture and, quite frankly, I've been awfully homesick. So this job was darn near perfect."

Lorelei put down her scone and walked into the kitchen. How many nights had she listened to Cole dream about a future with the NFL, player or coach? He ran scenarios like plays leaving no room for failure. Yet when he finally gets the chance he turns it down? Homesick he said while looking at her with such sincerity it left her breathless.

She spent the rest of the morning avoiding Cole and Leo, who appeared to have become the best of pals, bonding over her scones and sports stats. In the quiet moments after she and Andee closed the diner, it was not lost on Lorelei that her life had taken an unexpected turn. With Cole now living in the same state and working not fifty minutes away, it was inevitable that their paths would continue to cross. Could she function in the same town with Cole? Become friends again? Watch him date? Marry? Certainly, she'd been dreading listening to his momma talk about it, but listening to talk and watching it happen were two different things indeed

He ducked his head, sighing heavily. "You've got to start trusting me again. Let's start with this. I know me helping now does not even begin to make up for me not being here last time. But let me start making it up to you, Lore. I have to start somewhere."

"It's over. It's in the past."

He gave a wry chuckle. "Sure it is. That's why it's always the elephant in the room. I'm sorry; I can't say it enough times. There's nothing I regret more in my entire life. Nothing. And if it takes the rest of my life to do it, I'll spend it making it up to you."

She uncovered her eyes and stared at him. Cole didn't blink or waiver.

"Until you meet the future Mrs. Williams and move on with your life—"

Cole jumped up. "Don't you get it? There's no future without you. I may have had great success in my professional life but that's mostly due to not having any other sort of life whatsoever. Just football and memories of you."

"Cole—" She sat up all the way and swung her legs over the cushion to sit on the edge of the couch.

"At first I tried to get you out of my system." He started to pace in front of the couch, "I had football to take my mind off everything in the fall and winter but spring and summer were hard. After I sent the first few letters and emails and heard nothing back from you, I was angry. Angry with you, our parents, this town, and myself. Mad at everything I could be mad at. I tried to blame you for setting high expectations of me—"

"That part is true."

Cole paused. "Excuse me?"

"I said that part is true. The thing about me having high expectations. That's true."

His mouth gaped slightly.

"You're high right now, aren't you? It's the painkillers talking."

She laughed and leaned back against the cushion, staring at the ceiling. "It's the painkillers giving me the courage to say this. Remember your seventeenth birthday party when I got thrown from the tube?" She didn't wait for him to say whether he did or didn't remember before she continued. "You knew then that my expectations were always too high. I never thought you could do any wrong. To me, you were perfect. You said you'd let me down and I didn't believe you. I mean, I really didn't think it was possible at all. I said you could never let me down and you said—"

"I said, 'I'm human. It's gonna happen. But that doesn't mean I don't love you.'" Cole sat down next to her and wiped the lone tear slipping out from the corner of her eye.

"What a mess," she said and looked at him.

Cole nodded. "But it doesn't have to stay a mess. Give it a second chance. Give us a second chance to see what happens. Friends, more than friends, who knows? But man, I'd love to see how it plays out. We'll take it slow, one day at a time."

"Why now, Cole? Why not last year or the year before?"

"Because now my job has more stability. I'll still be on the road a fair amount but less than I used to be and I'm close by. I've never felt like I could ask you to travel to see me and leave the diner. I'd already taken so much."

She searched his face. "I'm scared."

"So am I," he said softly. "So. Am. I. But we'll start slowly. One trust exercise at a time."

She laughed and held her hand out to him, palm up. He took it in his and entwined his fingers with hers.

"One trust exercise at a time," she repeated.

"We'll begin with this shirt. I promise to do the least amount of looking humanly possible. Besides, we both need to get some shut-eye. We have to get up early because you have to teach me how to bake scones and croissants and—"

"You don't have to do this. Andee can—"

"It's not about what I have to do. It's about what I want to do."
He gave her hand a squeeze.

"I really missed you," she whispered.

"Not half as much as I missed you," he bent his head down to
gently place his lips to hers.

EPILOGUE

SIX YEARS LATER

Dear Lorelei,
   It's been twenty years since we lost our first child, our innocence, and ourselves. Today marks that loss and in my arms, I nuzzle the sweet face of our third child, Eliza Jane. Though I will always wonder what our first child would have been like and it hurts that we will never know, I find comfort in the faces of our son and now our daughter and know that our lost one is in them both.

   My love, you continue to give to me in ways that I can never reciprocate. Why I have been gifted this blessing of a second chance with you and these little people that make up our family, I will never know, but will always be thankful and will endeavor to show you all how much you mean to me on a daily basis.

   You are my light, my love, my hope and I am the man I have always wanted to be because of the love you give me.

   Forever yours,
   Cole

Lorelei folded the letter and tucked it behind the one he'd given her last year and the year before and so on. She'd read them all, more than once and through them found forgiveness, acceptance, and love. She'd found Cole.

ONCE
A Coming Home Short Story
AGAIN

KRISTI ROSE

Vintage Housewife Books

PO BOX 841

Farmington, MO 63640

www.kristirose.net

Book Layout © 2014 BookDesignTemplates.com

Cover Design © 2015 Paper and Sage Designs

Edited by Paige Christian

Formerly titled: FOREVER HIM

Once Again/ Kristi Rose. -- 1st ed.

✿ Created with Vellum

CHAPTER 1

WORD OF THE DAY: GAMBLE- ANY MATTER OR THING INVOLVING RISK OR HAZARDOUS UNCERTAINTY

No matter how hard Evie Barker tried to manage each day, this one had gotten away from her. It had started as soon as she arrived at the nursing home where she worked, but before the actual paid portion of her day began. Like she did every day, she'd stopped by her momma's room to feed her the specially made oatmeal she picked up from her favorite diner, Two Chicks and Bacon. But momma had been out of sorts. Crying, refusing to eat, and escalating to such a state of inconsolability she'd required a sedative.

From there the day went to hell fast and included a patient falling in the shower—thankfully not while she was providing therapy—and a rampant, building-wide stomach bug, which made everyone, residents and staff, short tempered at best. The day's tone spoke of a foreboding of tonight's full moon or perhaps worse, an omen of "something wicked this way comes."

Pulling in her driveway, she forgot the disaster of the day and the state of her stained scrubs as she stared at the large U-Haul parked at the family-home-turned-frat-house next door. An old lobster trap, a telescope, an olive green trunk, and a lamp made from an old musket with a fringed shade were in the yard.

Those items could go either way. Was it possible her new neighbor was an old man and not a college student?

She wanted to cheer. A nice, quiet old man who would prune his bushes and keep to himself. Evie buried her face in her hands. What in the world was wrong with her that she was excited that her new neighbor might be elderly? She hated that after a year of neighbors who were frequently seen in the buff as they streaked down the street or hosted all night beer pong championships, she was desperate for the polar opposite. Yes, a nice old man who took advantage of the early bird special, played shuffleboard, and if she were lucky—after the day she had that was doubtful—one who would keep his eyes on the neighborhood would be a delight. Evie's gaze settled on the telescope. Yeah, keep his eyes on the neighborhood by using his telescope to look into other's windows?

She weighed the probabilities: creepy old man, nice old man, college student. The odds didn't look favorable.

Chewing the edge of her thumbnail, eyes narrowed, she considered her options and tallied the risks. Normally, Evie would go inside and hope for the best, but after two weeks of peace and quiet, she wasn't about to leave it to chance the new renters would be dream neighbors. Her hydrangea bushes were still suffering PTSD. Apparently, the last occupants thought vomit was fertilizer. She couldn't rely on the hope word had spread on campus that this neighborhood was unfriendly for all-night raves. She needed to make sure, in no uncertain terms, these new neighbors knew there would be no funny business happening in that house. This was a respectable neighborhood.

Today's pick on her word-of-the-day app, Gamble, was the ideal word for her, especially as her current resolution was to mix things up. This new neighbor situation was the perfect opportunity to do just that and stretch her comfort zone. But for Evie, a creature of habit, risk was a filthy, bad word, belonging in the same family as madness, hysteria, and turmoil, and it gave her heartburn. She took three deep yoga breaths.

Honestly, there was no better time to go against her normal inclination of hiding in her house and waiting to see what would happen. Hadn't she decided her life was dull and she needed to mix things up a little? Isn't that why she'd cut seven inches off her hair, broken up with her duller-than-dull boyfriend? Because she knew little things needed to change. If she was going to have a constant internal conversation about changing her life then she'd better start right now, with the opportunity that had nearly fallen on her doorstep.

After getting out of the car, she eased the door closed, paused, opened it and gave it a good slam before straightening her spine and rallying her courage. Evie adopted what she hoped was a good impersonation of her take-no-shit friend Lorelei's resting bitch face and, using long strides, walked across her yard and into the neighbor's.

Seriously, a lamp made from an old shotgun? Who bought that stuff?

"Hello," Evie called out and stepped into the opened garage. "Hello?" She felt her expression slip. The longer her calls went unanswered the more effort it took to keep the look going. She sucked in a deep breath and tried again, placing her hands on her hips for added emphasis.

"Hello," she said louder.

"Whatever you're selling, I'm not buying," a man yelled. His voice came from the cut out square above her on the ceiling. The attic space, she assumed. He sounded older than a frat boy, his voice deep, almost gravelly with the slightest southern drawl. The odds for creepy or nice old guy were fifty-fifty.

"I'm your neighbor," she said, using a tone she hoped matched her expression.

"Jeez, sorry. I'll be right with you. I was...." Strong tanned legs with just the right amount of dark hair appeared out of the hole in the ceiling. They dangled for a moment before the rest slowly came into view. Dark green cargo shorts and a navy t-shirt, the words *Semper Fi* scrolled across a chest deserving more than a cursory glance. The t-shirt hugged his body in such a way no time was needed to ponder what was underneath, but instead allowed the imagination to run free.

What a person could do to a body *that* defined. She came up with five things in that small flash of time and none of them required clothing.

He hung briefly from the ledge before dropping to the ground with an ease that made Spiderman look clumsy.

"...checking out the condition of the house. I heard..."

She stared into flint colored eyes. That combination of blue and gray could only belong to one person. At least, she'd never seen eyes that color on anyone else, ever, and try as she might she'd never been able to wipe those eyes from her memory.

Grady Duke.

How long had it been since his name drifted across her mind?

Years of memories flashed before her as she took in the face of the guy who was responsible for all her firsts. From kisses to sex, she'd done it all with Grady and all over the course of the summer before her sophomore year. Evie rubbed the space between her breasts with the heel of her hand, hoping to ease the sudden burn of indigestion.

Gamble.

Grady Duke had been a high stakes game on which she'd gambled and lost. She'd offered him her virginity and he'd taken it, only to end things by moving on to someone else a week later. She knew she'd been expecting too much, hoping he would want to be with her more than he'd ever wanted or had been with anyone else. But Grady had proven what others said about him to be true.

"Evie Barker?"

Same square chin, same long nose, which on another person would almost be too slender, but on Grady's slightly narrow face only made him look stronger. His dark brown hair was cut close. As she absorbed it all, she realized her resting bitch face had been replaced with what was probably mouth open, catching flies face.

Time had been good to him.

"Grady. What are you...?" The collision of thoughts left her brain addled. "How are you...uh...." She scrambled to gather her wits. "Lord help me," she mumbled.

Seeing him again came with a jumbled mess of emotions. Surprised, she found herself just as breathless as she'd been back then, her heart thumping erratically. Yet, the soured taste of disappointment at having something beautiful end the way it had, suddenly and stupidly, weighed equally on her. She'd long thought she'd gotten over their summer together.

"You look great. Wow. Check you out. You're the last person I thought I'd run into here."

"Here? Here like this house or—?" Sweet Jesus. She should shut up.

"Here in Lakeland. I always thought you'd blow out of town first chance you got."

"Kinda like you did." She hadn't meant to say it. Think it, sure, but out loud it sounded so rude.

She'd spent her entire sophomore year avoiding Grady Duke. It had helped he'd been a senior and they didn't have any classes together. Outside of the one incident at Shawn Field's party, she'd been successful. Nonetheless, when he'd left for the Marine Corps soon after graduation, she'd nearly wept with relief. Out of sight, out of mind and she'd tucked that chapter of her life was neatly away, for the most part, forgotten.

"The Marine Corps doesn't have a base in Lakeland so chances of staying were pretty slim." He laughed and reached across his chest to scratch his shoulder, and a large tattoo of the Marine Corps insignia on his bicep caught her eye. "I'd heard you left for college but didn't know you'd come back. I'm surprised you're still in town."

There was no derision toward Lakeland in his voice, just confusion. If there was one person, other than Lorelei, who had seen a true glimpse into her childhood, it was Grady. Not because she'd willingly shared that part, but hiding it had been difficult. There'd been more nights than she'd care to count when she and Grady, coming home from a night together, would find her father stumbling down the road, having left his car at the last place he'd been drinking. Grady would help her get him inside. Refusing to let their night end that way, he'd convince her to sit on the tailgate of his truck, tucked between his legs, and they'd wish on stars and talk about life after Lakeland.

"My momma's still here so..."

"Ah, that's right." Even though Grady had been long gone, serving his country, when the accident occurred, it was clear from his sorrowful expression he knew what happened. "For what it's worth, I'm sorry about your dad, too."

"Thanks." She was surprised. Folks never said they were sorry about her dad's passing, likely because he'd been driving drunk and colliding with the corner of their house had sent him through the windshield, killing him on impact. Her momma hadn't been so lucky. When her father overshot the driveway, crossing the grass, he never saw her momma standing in the yard, and pinned her between the car and house.

Evie'd been told, more than she'd been offered condolences, how fortunate they were not to have to go through the trial of watching the state convict her father. But usually those comments came from the same people who'd made it a habit of laughing at her family long before the accident.

"Looks like your yard gnome's been stolen," they'd said, when on the rare occasion her father actually passed out inside the house instead of on the lawn.

"So what are you doing here? I mean in this house, well...and in town... Is this the first time you've come home?" All these years and she'd never run into him.

"I took a position at Florida Southern. My dad's been sick. The timing of this job and the opportunity to come home and help coincided, so here I am, renting this house."

"A happy coincidence, I hope."

He shrugged. "I was eyeing something closer to where more Civil War events occurred. But this works for now. Look at you. I always knew you'd be successful. You're an occupational therapist. Sounds interesting."

"How did you know?" She tried to smooth her wrinkled and stained scrubs. She picked a patch of dried oatmeal off her sleeve and noticed a large, gross, brown spot on the cuff of her pants. There was no telling what other disturbing stains might be clinging to her. If she were bold enough to sniff her pits in his presence, she wouldn't be surprised if she smelled. Suddenly, she wanted to escape to her house and restart this moment as something less of a hot mess. Why did he always have to see her at her worst?

"I read it on your badge. Your hair is much longer in this picture." With a smile, he lifted the badge hanging from her lanyard and showed it to her. His fingers grazed the top of her stomach and a burst of heat flooded her chest. Her knees wobbled and the same butterflies that had fluttered nonstop that summer long ago revisited her. She stared at his fingers, willing them to touch her again, wondering if it was the newness of seeing him or the rekindling of the same old flame that left her unsteady.

Trying to find equilibrium, she sucked in her gut and forced out a steady breath and a nervous giggle. She grabbed her badge from him and twisted it in her hand. "Duh. Of course you knew that from my badge." She glanced at her terrible badge picture. She. Hated. It. With her fat braid and bland scrubs, she looked like a matronly resident and not an employee.

"I just cut my hair last week," she mumbled.

"I'm sorry?"

"Oh, you mentioned my hair." She showed him the badge picture, her thumb over her face. "I cut it last week."

Yes, she was looking for something new this week that she could change up, but as she stared at Grady's smiling face, she made a vow. There was no way in hell he would be her next *change*.

"I like it. Of course, I liked the braid, too. That's how I remember you." He shifted his weight to the other foot and stuck his hands in his front pockets. The change in position drew her attention to the span of his broad shoulders and how his t-shirt hugged his biceps.

Evie gave into her nerves and giggled. She sounded like a crazy, unstable person with her weird conversation skills and unexplained laughter. The need to escape before the heat from her chest crawled up her face propelled her into action.

Taking a step back, she said, "Welcome home. I just popped by to make sure more hooligans like those who lived here last time hadn't moved in. They were so loud. Always partying and being naked and...."

Oh. My. Word.

She took several more steps back. She had to get out before she sounded any more like a sixty-year-old woman. "I mean, not that I don't like parties or being naked—"

Shut. Up. This was going south, fast.

"Or both at the same time?" he teased.

"Ha." She pointed her finger at him, her badge still tucked in her palm. "Yeah, all the above. It was good seeing you." She backed out into the sun, gave a wave, and hauled butt home.

"See you around," he called.

When she got inside, she leaned against the door and tried to steady her pounding heart.

Wow, Grady Duke.

One thing was certain, making an idiot out of herself in his presence always happened. History certainly liked to repeat itself.

CHAPTER 2

WORD OF THE DAY: KISMET- FATE; DESTINY

She hadn't had another encounter with Grady since the incident in his garage. It'd been two days since his fingers brushed her stomach through her scrubs and consequently left her daydreaming about him, nonstop.

Yesterday, after work, she'd *noticed* him breaking down boxes in his backyard. She just so happened to be looking from behind her curtains out the window, which, coincidentally, gave her a sweeping view of the entire side of his house, front and back yards. He'd come out carrying boxes, wearing exercise shorts and another tight t-shirt that read "Seemed like a good idea at the time." She'd nearly drooled all over herself, which of course, left her wanting to punch herself in the face. As if anything would ever happen between them again. Yet, she was window stalking him just as much as she had the frat boys, only this time her thoughts were more along the lines of watching Grady mow the yard, shirtless, than protecting the neighborhood.

It was hard to guess what his schedule might be, but when she left that morning for Two Chicks and Bacon, there were no signs of life at his house. The moving truck was long gone, a large silver pickup in its place.

The second she arrived at the diner, she inhaled deeply as she slid onto the same chair where she sat every Monday, Wednesday, and Friday. The smell of comfort food did its magic and the tension of her job, Momma, and her new neighbor faded away. Picking up her smartphone, she checked her word of the day app.

Kismet, her ass. Kismet could go take a long walk off a short pier. If Grady Duke was fate's way of moving her forward, well then, fate could go—

"Morning," Andee said and poured her a cup of coffee.

"Morning." Evie inhaled the aroma and closed her eyes. Peace. "What's new?"

She opened her eyes and reached for a menu. "Um. Nothing. What's new with you?" She did not want to have a conversation with Andee about Grady. She wanted to joke with her friends and remember the Evie she was now and not the one from the past, the one she'd spent so much time thinking about these last few days.

"Everything here is the same as it was yesterday and the day before that, and the day before that." Andee flipped her hand dismissively. "You get the picture."

Evie ran her finger down the menu's list of specials and debated sharing her news. Andee would find out soon enough.

"Why do you even bother, Evie? You know you get the same thing every time." Andee laughed, took the menu from her, and put it back in the holder before she moved down the counter to help another customer.

"Today is a new day. I might actually go crazy and try something different," Evie said and snatched the menu back out of the holder.

"Weirder things have happened, I suppose."

The familiarity with which Andee teased warmed Evie from the inside out. Andee enjoyed poking fun at Evie about being so predictable, but truth was Andee was the same and that's why they got along so well, a mutual respect of their need to make lists,

61

have designated chore days, and leave spontaneity to the foolhardy.

Once she finished her rounds, Andee returned to Evie and, with great flourish, produced her order pad and pen. "You bringing anyone to Lorelei's wedding?"

"Nope." Torn between her desire to shock Andee by ordering something different yet craving the comfort of her favorite bacon and Gouda omelet, Evie waffled on her decision.

"So, what's it gonna be?" Andee tapped her pen on the page.

Darn it all, today was not about breaking out of her comfort zone, but about building up her reserves and now that Grady was her neighbor, she was going to need lots in reserve. "I'll just have the usual," she said, daring Andee to say anything.

Andee leaned against the counter. "You ever thought of trying one of those online matchmaking sites?"

"Are you gonna put in my order?"

"I did, when you got here. Have you? I know you don't have problems getting dates; I've seen the way some of the guys around here look at you. But I think the pond here's been overfished. You need to follow the tributary out. Maybe Orlando or Tampa."

"I'm taking a break from dating for a bit. It's so exhausting getting to know someone. I dread that point where they start asking about my family. It's hard being evasive all the time." Evie rolled her eyes, as if it were no never mind, but really, getting serious with someone was scary enough, telling them her dad nearly killed her momma was not a conversation she liked having. At all. Ever.

"Just so you know, I'm keeping my eyes open for you."

"Don't do me any favors," Evie said and glanced over at the kitchen doors as they swung open.

Lorelei Parker, co-owner of the diner, came from around the counter, slid Evie's plate before her then plopped onto the chair next to her. She poured herself a coffee and blew on it as a maintenance man walked by with his toolbox.

"What's that about?" Evie sprinkled more pepper on her eggs.

"The storage closet keeps sticking. Even when it's unlocked you can't get out. I discovered that the hard way. Freaked Cole out when he couldn't find me. Hence the handyman." Cole was Lorelei's fiancé. Their history extended back to high school but was finally coming full circle this summer when they would marry.

"How'd the oatmeal go?" Lorelei asked.

"Um, good." Evie pointed to her plate where little pats of butter shaped as chicks garnished the toast. "These are cute."

Andee took a step back, moving to stand behind Lorelei, and repeatedly waved her hand under her chin.

"Thanks, my momma's come to town to help with the wedding planning and she's driving me berserk. These butter pats were a little project to help me burn off some...."

"Feelings?" Evie offered.

"Yes," Lorelei said and pointed her finger at Evie for emphasis. "Feelings. I had lots of feelings to burn off."

Taking the cue from Andee, Evie backed away from the landmine and didn't probe further. "I'm sorry. If you need some help, just let me know."

"Thanks, but if my mother keeps it up, I might just elope. Listen to me go on. You don't want to hear about my momma. But I want to hear about yours. How's the special diet we've created for her going?"

"It's hard to say. She's had a rough few days, another infection." Evie found the frequency at which her momma continued to get sick worrisome. She'd been taking care of her for so long she didn't know what she'd do if she no longer had that.

"You still want me to make up some oatmeal for her?"

"Yes, please. At least I know she's getting the nutrients she needs. It's exercise and all the other stuff she's lacking."

Lorelei nodded. "I've been playing around with a recipe for a chia seed yogurt. That might be good for her, too. I'll let you know."

Andee moved to top off the coffee cups of the retired set who, today, were debating the merits of gator wrestling.

Though they'd graduated together, Lorelei, Andee, and Evie hadn't run in the same crowd back in the day. After the accident that killed her father and left her momma unable to care for her own basic needs, Lorelei and her parents had stepped up. They'd visited Momma every week, helped Evie complete her college applications, and became the foundation she'd needed to get the start into adulthood.

Evie never imagined she'd spend her senior year being fostered by a family from their church and trying to manage her wild sister or that when she turned eighteen she'd become the legal guardian to her sister, Shea. Parenting a teen while maintaining a full time college load had been far from easy but she couldn't imagine what would have become of them without the support of Lorelei's family.

"Evie," Lorelei whispered. "Isn't that Grady Duke?"

Her fork clattered to her plate as she turned to watch her neighbor come in the door. Apparently, cargo shorts and tight t-shirts were his signature threads. Though the expanse of his chest made the likelihood of a shirt not being tight slim. Today's t-shirt read "Civil War Buff" in bold letters

"Yeah. Yeah, it is." Evie looked away as quickly as possible.

"Wow. Nice. He sure filled out. He used to be so lanky but mercy, someone's been eating his Wheaties."

"That's because he was a soccer guy, not a football guy." She wanted to tell Lorelei he'd always had muscles, from stocking groceries throughout high school and working a second land-scaping job every summer. He'd always had a nice body.

"Well, I'll go do my job," Lorelei said and pushed off the chair, walking toward Grady. Evie watched him scan the place as soon as he came in, his eyes resting on her, a smile spreading slowly showing even white teeth.

"Holy cow, I swear you look like Grady Duke," Andee said, beating Lorelei to the door.

"I guess that's a good thing since that's my name and all. How you doing?" He let Andee fold him into a hug and then Lorelei. "I heard that y'all opened a diner. Thought I'd come check it out."

He slid into the chair next to Evie and winked. She forced her eyes to focus on her half-eaten omelet and steadied her hands by gripping the edge of her chair. She'd promised herself to approach Grady as if he were just someone she went to school with. As if she didn't have a history with him or know that on the body Lorelei had just admired was a long scar from when he'd had his appendix removed. A scar she used to rub her hand over. A scar she'd kissed.

"What brings you to town?" Andee asked.

"I took a job teaching over at the college."

Evie glanced out of the corner of her eyes and could swear his chest puffed out ever so slightly. She knew the feeling. Though she'd become good friends with Lorelei and Andee over the years, there were days she still felt like one of the poor kids, someone on the outside looking in. Grady may not have had any of the nonsense in his childhood that she'd had in hers but he'd still grown up one of the have-nots.

"Teaching? At Florida Southern? What subject? You want coffee?" Andee held up the pot.

"Yes, please. I'm teaching American History with a focus on the Civil War." He smiled before he took a drink of coffee. When he reached across Evie for a menu, his forearm skimmed her hand, and the force of her attraction for him nearly blew her out of her seat.

"That's right. If you all were as scholarly as I am you'd know that our Grady Duke is building quite a reputation among the history crowd as an expert in the Civil War." Mr. Jenkins, the driver's ed teacher back when they were in school, now ringleader of the retirees, said from behind them, laying a hand on Grady's shoulder.

"I didn't know you were into history," Lorelei said.

But Evie had known. She'd listened to him talk about it for hours.

"I don't know about expert, but I really enjoy what I do and don't mind sitting around debating the past. Thanks for the compliment, Mr. Jenkins." They shook hands briefly before Mr. Jenkins moved back to his cronies.

"Such a contrast to how you used to spend your days." Andee was never one to mince words.

There was no denying Grady's reputation as a player. Known for not having a type, a steady, or a second date, he'd cycled through so many of their school friends it had been embarrassing. The only reason he'd never been with Lorelei or Andee was because they'd been firmly attached to their beaus.

Then there'd been Evie. If others had known how much time she and Grady had spent together that summer, she'd probably be linked to his reputation as the girl he *dated* the longest. Grady might not think of what they did as dating, but Evie did. It had been so natural, so easy, being with him and laughing, flirting, and falling in love. With Grady, she'd been able to forget the mess that was her family. For Grady, though, she'd just been a way to mark time before he could leave town. Just another girl added to his roster of conquests.

"What have you been up to all these years, Grady? " Lorelei asked, while giving Andee the stink eye.

"I spent six years in the Marine Corps, did a couple of tours in the sandbox, went to school at night, and got my bachelor's. When I got out I did my master's and just last year finished my Ph.D."

"He's perfect for you," Andee whispered in Evie's ear.

She turned to give a snappy retort, but everything was stuck in her throat. The omelet, words, and sixteen years of emotions strictly associated with Grady, their summer, and the girl she'd let herself be. An astute student of life's hard knocks, her childhood had taught her well, Evie preferred not to repeat her mistakes.

CHAPTER 3

Evie Barker. As I live and breathe, his momma would say.
Gone was the makeup-free skin and her thick, long, red
braid, replaced by hair that fell to her shoulders and swung carefree with her every move. Evie had been the prettiest and smartest
creature he'd ever set eyes on back in high school but now she was
a knock-your-boots-off heartbreaker.

After leaving town, he'd thought—maybe hoped was more
accurate—to leave it all behind him. Getting out had been his
main goal and the Corps his solution when no college scholar-
ships came his way. He'd wanted more out of life and wasn't going
to get it in Lakeland. He'd craved something other than warm
Florida winters and sand between his toes. He wanted to learn to
ski on snow and watch the leaves turn shades of red, yellow, and
variegated shades of green.

Yet on those long days under the hot Middle Eastern sun,
waiting to kill or be killed, Grady had thought of home. He'd
laugh at the irony of how he'd been desperate to get away from
sand only to spend extended time in a country that left sand
between his toes and in crevices he never knew he had. He'd close
his eyes and try to recall the sweet fragrance of orange blossoms

or how his family would tailgate, claiming a good spot for watching fireworks at Joker Merchant Stadium every Fourth of July. He'd think of the corn bread, pinto beans, and collards his momma made every New Year and then, inevitably, his trip through the past would lead him to Evie Barker. She'd been just as driven to survive their childhood as he had been but whereas he'd done it by staying detached and leaving, she'd done it with grace and kindness, finding happiness in the space around her.

"Hey, Lorelei, can I get that oatmeal and a pecan roll? I have to be heading out," Evie said, pushing her omelet away and gathering up her purse.

Lorelei looked surprised. "So soon? Ok. It'll be a few minutes." She turned and gave his arm a squeeze. "You come back, Grady. I'm pretty sure Cole would love to catch up with you. He had an early meeting or he'd normally be here."

"I look forward to seeing him, too." Grady smiled at Lorelei and turned to Evie before flipping open the menu. "That looks really good." He gestured to her omelet.

She looked at it with longing. "It was... I mean, it is. Lorelei makes some great food. Her pastries are divine."

"Especially the pecan roll?"

"Yes, they're my favorite." She bit her lower lip and looked away.

Grady searched for something to say that would keep her beside him longer but Lorelei rescued her by arriving with a to-go bag.

"Here you go, Evie. Let me know how it goes. We'll see you Friday morning." Lorelei handed her the bag and a travel mug of coffee bearing the University of Florida emblem.

He caught Evie glance his way at the mention of Friday and made a mental note to be here as well. She was an enigma and he wanted to know why she hadn't taken her momma and escaped from a town that weighed her down with such heavy baggage. Grady used to think he had hurdles to jump in his endeavors to have a different life, but Evie, holy hell, she'd had everything against her and still beat the odds. He wanted to know that story.

At the time, he'd never believed happiness could be crafted from the fragmented pieces of her childhood. But he was a different guy now, thanks to time and seeing some of life's glorious wonders like the Great Wall of China and some of life's horrific tribulations like holding a buddy as they lay dying. That would change anyone. It certainly had Grady, who now understood that leaving never guaranteed an easy road or a better life.

Grady watched her leave and turned to find Andee staring at him. "What's your story? Got yourself a missus?" She glanced at his bare ring finger and raised her brows.

"Nope, I'm completely unattached at the moment. But that shouldn't surprise you." He winked at Andee and leaned back against the chair, draping his arm over Evie's now vacant chair.

"It doesn't—"

"It's hard sustaining a relationship when you're doing back to back deployments or you've got your nose buried deep into folds of old moldy Civil War documents and textbooks."

"We've all changed. A lot. I'm hoping you have, too," Andee said and gave the arm on Evie's chair a pointed look. "Be gentle with our Evie. She doesn't have it easy."

"She never had it easy," he said, remembering all those times he'd seen her dad stumbling down the road. "But it hasn't gotten any better for her?"

Lorelei sighed heavily. "Even though her momma's in a home, she still takes care of her and it wears on her. Her momma's not doing well and with Shea in Nashville, it all falls on Evie."

"That girl needs a fairy godmother, not a wolf in sheep's clothing," Andee added. "Now, what'll it be?"

He ordered, got pulled into a light debate regarding the military tactics of Grant and Lee with his old driver's ed teacher and some of his cronies, and left with a box of pastries including a free chocolate croissant. With a few more days of vacation left before he needed to report to work, he figured there was no better time to get to know thy neighbor than right now.

At Publix, where he saw more people from the old days than he had on any other visit to date, he bought some groceries for a cookout and managed to escape Melinda Bane's incessant questions and heavy flirting. It was ironic that he should run into the girl he used to break Evie's heart sixteen years ago considering his sole purpose at the store was to get back into Evie's good graces.

Using his Marine Recon training and subterfuge, Grady timed wheeling his garbage can to the curb with Evie's arrival home from work.

"Hey," he called as he parked the container at the edge of his drive.

She looked at him, eyes large and wide as if constantly surprised he'd talk to her.

"How was work?" He walked across the yard to where she stood, in her blue-checkered scrubs that were overly wrinkled, like they'd been wet and wrung out while still being worn, then leaned against her car.

"*My* work? Don't answer that. Of course you mean my work. It was...work." She tilted her head and smiled. "Thanks for asking."

"You like your job?" He tucked a hand into his pocket.

He put his other hand up to stop her from answering. "Hold that thought. I have an idea. Why don't you come over? I'm grilling out; I'll make you some dinner and you can tell me all about it. I'd like to know more about what an occupational therapist does." He'd researched it, of course, but knowing what had drawn her to the profession was what interested him. For a girl who cared for so many people, he'd have thought she'd have run away from something as demanding as a rehabilitative service.

She laughed, glancing away before saying, "You don't have to pretend to be interested in my job, but I appreciate the effort. You are under no obligation to be nice to me simply because we live next door to each other or because we used to da—, I mean, we...we went to high school together. But thanks for the offer."

With the press of her key fob, she locked the car and turned to go inside.

"Wait." He cupped her elbow to stop her. "I'm not pretending to be nice to you and certainly not because we went to high school together. There are a lot of people I went to school with that I couldn't care less if I never see again. I like you, I always have. I've only been home a couple of times over the years. Life's been hectic. Now that it's finally slowed down, I can't imagine anything better than spending time with an old...friend. Come on. It's just food and iced tea. Maybe some of Lorelei's éclairs."

She hesitated.

"And a few cream puffs, too."

"You're killing me." She sighed.

"Come on. Do it for a veteran."

She laughed and rolled her eyes. "Oh all right. What time?"

"How does now strike you?" Now that she was hooked, he wasn't letting go.

"Now?"

He nodded.

"Let me change and I'll head over."

"Just come on into the back yard." He watched her walk away before heading back home. Leaving the back gate open, he lit the citronella candles with hopes of keeping the mosquitos at bay.

He could tell Evie really didn't want to come, it was evident by her inability to make eye contact, but her good manners and gentle nature wouldn't allow her to be rude to him. He'd been counting on that and if the opportunity presented he was going to try and mend the bridge he'd burned between them. Life had shown him that for all the people there were in the world, finding someone to connect with on a deeper level was a rare gift. Evie had been someone he'd connected with. Hell, even now he used any opportunity he could find to touch her and loved the zing of excitement he got when there was physical contact between them.

Truth was, over the years he'd thought about her often. Joining the Corps had been a deliberate act, his way out, but when he'd spent more than four months on a ship with not a single letter from anyone but his folks, he'd wondered if the town where he'd grown up had left more of a mark on him than he did it. After several longer deployments in a country where he wasn't wanted, it was thoughts of home that helped Grady hang on and get through the tough times. Though deployment days were busy, there were always lulls when his mind would drift to the small central Florida town and Evie. He'd wonder if she was happy, wished he could change the events of the past.

Grady made no apologizes for who he was and what he'd done in the military. He understood the simple fact that in order to save lives, he had to take some, and he'd paid his dues with the night-mares, relentless survivor's guilt, and volunteer work he'd done at the VA. Maybe Evie being the first person in his path was the Universe's way of giving him a second chance to square things there, too. Maybe it was also a sign that his slate was being wiped clean.

There were lots of things that he remembered about Evie: her laughing face, the way she closed her eyes as if she was holding on to the moment a little while longer, how she'd slowly raise her lids after he'd kissed the breath out of her, or how her eyes would glisten with unshed tears as she'd try to steer her drunken father into the house after he'd stumbled home. What he wished he could forget was her look of mortification mixed with straight up hurt when she'd found him with Melinda. He'd wanted to scare her off, hell, he'd been scared witless by the vast weight of emotion he'd felt around Evie. But none of that compared to the self-hate he'd felt when he'd seen her face. It had nearly done him in, almost convinced him to forget all about his plans and dreams.

It had made him consider ways he might bring her along with him.

Pushing the sliding door open, he brought out the jug of iced tea and tall glasses filled with ice. Glancing at his watch, he set a cut off time when he'd go retrieve her if she hadn't shown up and stepped back inside to get the food from the fridge.

"Knock, knock."

She was wearing a loose, blue-striped skirt and white t-shirt with matching blue tennis shoes. With her hair in a short ponytail, she looked breathtakingly innocent and triggered his need to protect her. He want to wrap her in his arms and be that fairy godmother Andee had spoken of earlier today. Hell, he'd even take being the warty frog she might kiss hoping to find a prince.

"I thought you might stand me up." He slid a plate of steaks onto the counter.

She stood at the sliding door and waited.

"You can come in," he said and took a salad from the fridge. "You eat meat, right?"

"Did you not notice how much bacon was on my omelet today? Lorelei always doubles my order." She stepped in and stared at his musket lamp. Boxes still cluttered the area. For a guy who'd been overseas and in school, he'd sure accumulated a lot of crap.

She went immediately to the photos he'd set out on the table, waiting to be placed around the house or hung on the wall, and picked up several, most of him and the brotherhood of men he'd served with.

"You look so different in uniform. More intense, I suppose," she said, holding one frame in her hand. It was one of him decked out in his dress blues, graduating from Parris Island, his parents flanking his sides. She replaced it with another of him in uniform, only this one he was wearing his fatigues, his gun slung across his back, the hot Afghanistan sun in his eyes, and an arm flung around his friend.

"That's Daniel. We were in boot camp together. He was killed in action four days after that photo," he said.

"I'm sorry." She rubbed her thumb over Daniel's laughing face and gently put the frame down.

"Me, too."

She moved away from the photos and toward the musket lamp.

"What's this? I mean, I know what it is but... It's interesting." Her fingers played with the fringe on the shade.

He shrugged. "I teach history. You know I like the Civil War."

"I don't think this really has anything to do with the Civil War. Like this wasn't in Lee's office or anything."

He laughed. How did one respond to that?

She picked up a few books, looked at their spines, then made her way over to a hat and turned it over.

"That's a Hardee hat. Worn by both sides. Usually enlisted."

"Is this one an original?"

"No." He moved the pastries Lorelei had sold him onto a platter.

"I knew you were into the Civil War but not to this extent. You dress up and geek out to musket balls and old movies about the Civil War, don't you? Read Whitman and Beecher Stowe over and over?" Her lips teased at a smile.

He held the platter of treats over the trashcan. "Are you making fun of me?"

"Oh, of course not." She pointed to the platter. "Don't be wasteful. Think of all those hungry soldiers who would have killed for something to eat. Anything."

Hesitating, wondering if he could call her bluff, he couldn't stop the smile from taking over his face. This was the Evie he'd spent one of the best summers of his life with. Her lips twitched but she retained her serious look.

"Lorelei would never forgive you," she added.

"How would she know?"

Evie shrugged and picked up another book. "She's crazy like that. Psychic almost. Oh, *North and South*. I *love* this book."

"You loved the movie," he guessed.

"Yeah, Patrick Swayze as Orry Maine. Duh. But I actually did read the books."

He moved the pastry platter away from trashcan. "Let's take this outside. Any more time looking at my stuff and you'll be running out of here."

Her smile was slight. "You're ok. I'm a bit of a book nut."

"You were more than a book nut in high school. I would have called you a—"

"Book connoisseur?"

"Yes, connoisseur. That's the word."

He stepped aside so she could precede him. Once outside, he held up the jug and offered her tea. "I'm glad you came over."

Nodding, she took the glass he poured for her. "It's not like I could really avoid you if I didn't."

"True. Make yourself comfortable." He indicated the patio set he'd purchased earlier today.

"That's unlikely," she mumbled.

The moment to clear the air had come. "Listen. At risk of ending this night sooner than I'd like, there's something I have to say. I'm sorry I was a douche and ended things the way I did back then."

CHAPTER 4

After everything between them had gone sideways, Evie had spent endless amounts of time wondering why and how they could make things right, if they wanted to. But life had given her other things to focus on. Her sister had started rebelling long before the accident and she could see the erosion of her family was gaining momentum. Thoughts of her time with Grady had been pushed back and filed under fond memories as her energy was spent elsewhere.

An apology was a good start. It didn't fill in the blanks but it felt right and the simplicity of the act left her speechless. Though she'd believed she'd long since moved on, the truth was she wanted more. She needed an explanation.

"You don't like me much, do you? Not that I blame you. But you don't like being around me," he said, his hands tucked in his pockets, his shoulders drawn in.

Evie put her glass on the table and reached for her braid only to remember she'd cut it off. Instead, she clasped her hands before her and with the long intake of air, gathered her courage, the truth on her tongue.

"It's more that I don't like who I am when I'm with you,"

she said.

He looked surprised. "I'm not sure I understand."

She looked away, using the moment to organize her thoughts, and decided to go for broke. "That summer we spent together, I'm not sure if you remember it—"

"Evie, I could never forget that summer."

She smiled. "Anyway, that summer I...became someone I always wanted to be or maybe *thought* I always wanted to be." Memories of their time together filled her mind's eye. "We had a good time. At least I had a good time."

"I did too. The best." His thumb stroked the edge of the glass.

She forced herself to look away, recalling how he'd stroked her arm in the same fashion. "When I was with you, I felt like anything was possible. That the future was bright and mine, the options were unlimited. Something about being with you made me feel reckless and carefree and it was beautiful."

"Until I ruined it," he said matter of fact.

She gave a sad laugh. "Yeah. You certainly burst the bubble."

"And yet you still don't want to be around me."

Because she had nothing to lose and because it had been sixteen years, these things were surely in the past. "It's not only you, it's more the heady feeling that comes when I'm around you. It's the crazy notion that I can do whatever and it doesn't matter. Thankfully, we're old enough to know that's not true at all and having feelings like this are useless."

"You used present tense."

"I beg your pardon?"

"Present tense. You said, 'when I'm around you' like you still get that same feeling now."

She coughed on her panic, breath stuck somewhere between going in and coming out. The last thing she wanted was for him to know she still felt like a sixteen-year-old girl when he was around. "What? No, I guess I was just...you know...remembering how it felt then, now."

"It was pretty good, between us," he said.

Evie laughed. "And yet."

It was his turn to struggle for words, his mouth opening with false starts only to snap shut again. She watched the filmstrip of emotions cross his face.

"You know I wanted to see the world," he said.

"Yeah, I did know that. I get it now, Grady. I didn't then. I wish you had simply come to me to say that we weren't going to hang out together anymore." Her fingers traced the bumpy surface of the treated wicker outdoor table.

He shot a glance at her but quickly looked away, toward the grill. If he'd been a guy who'd spent his days indoors and his skin hadn't been tinted by the sun, she would have sworn he blushed. She stared at him, waiting. The moment was suspended between them. Whether they would continue forward as neighbors with a history or strangers with an embarrassing past was up to him.

"I was a dumb, selfish kid."

She searched his face, pleased that he met her gaze.

"Can you accept my apology?" he asked.

She nodded. "I think I can manage that."

His smile was so wide and bright she couldn't help but return a matching one of her own.

He took a step closer.

"I've thought about you for years and that night we spent on the bank of Lake Gibson. Sometimes when I close my eyes I can hear the sounds of the waves lapping against the shore and I feel you under my hand."

Evie's heart stuttered. She was lost in the flinty pools of his eyes as their gaze held. But she had so many more questions that needed answers.

"Why did you end it that way? Why did you tell everyone at Shawn Field's party that you couldn't bear to touch me?"

"I said I couldn't do it. When I drew your name for seven minutes in heaven, I knew I couldn't go in that closet and not touch you. But, I had no right. Not after what I'd done." He took a second step toward her. "I didn't know what to say or how to react. I hadn't expected you to be at the party. I don't even know why I went. Jeez, I was an asshole. But when I saw your name on the paper all I could think about was kissing you again. I already hated myself for what happened at the lake. Adding to that would have done me in." He pulled his hands from his pockets, ran the heels of his palms down his face, and then palms up and arms extended said, "Again, I'm sorry."

It wasn't a play, a move, or pretense to put her at ease. The sincerity of his words was reflected in the broken gruffness of his voice and sadness she found in his eyes.

"Grady," she whispered.

"I really want to kiss you right now, Evie. But I need to know if that's ok with you."

She wanted to be kissed by him. She wanted to know if it was as good as she remembered or if she had built it up in her head. If it sucked then maybe all the window stalking and headiness she felt around him would go away. What harm could come from one kiss? She was older and wiser and had no expectations. What were the odds that he was still the player from high school?

"Maybe just one," she whispered, holding up her index finger. "A little one." Anticipation buzzed around her, making her light-headed and short of breath. Being near Grady brought an excitement she'd forgotten existed.

He grinned and closed the distance. When she stood before him, a wisp of space between them, he cupped her face in his hands and brushed his lips against hers in a gentle rediscovery.

"One," he whispered before exploring her lips again.

Evie entwined her arms around his neck and met his gaze. "You call that a kiss?"

He chuckled, slid one arm around her waist, and the other arm behind her, his hand splayed against her back. Slowly, he pulled her toward him, closing the tiny space and fitting her perfectly against his frame. She fit against him as well as she had all those years back and became just as scattered as soon as his lips touched hers.

Evie'd had her fair share of relationships, yet none seemed to reach the bar Grady had inadvertently set. It was hard to find the right combination of headiness, butterflies, and companionship that left a lingering satisfaction coupled with a subtle craving. Something was always missing and yet Evie harbored no illusions that just because Grady's lips were on hers and every nerve ending in her body was buzzing and vibrating through her, things between them would be any different or better.

Certainly not. They were different people, after all. One thing hadn't changed however and that was Evie's craving for him.

He backed her up, pushing her against the wall of his house, and she pressed against him. She wondered if there was a word of the day for time travel because it was as if she straddled the line between the girl she'd been that summer and the woman she'd become and both were at the mercy of Grady.

"I'm sorry for ending things the way I did," he said in her ear right before he blazed a trail of kisses down her neck.

Was it possible that after all this time she actually missed his touch? That all these years she'd been longing for him? Or was she perhaps an addict like her father except Grady was her vice? Either way she'd need to tread lightly here. There was no room in her life for the havoc hooking up with Grady, the player, might bring. She'd have to watch him closely and use all her self-discipline to not get lost in him again.

"Let it be in the past." She slid her hands down, caressing the peaks and valleys of his toned chest, an urge she'd had from the moment he dropped out of the attic. "Saying no to you is incredibly difficult." She rested her hand on his waist, his lips hovering above hers.

"You're telling me. Even back then I had to sabotage us in order to get you to stay away. Stopping cannot be left to me and me alone." He bent to kiss the hollow space between the curve of her neck and her collarbone.

"What?" She pushed him back slightly.

"What?"

"What do you mean you sabotaged us?" It was one thing to think Grady had been off playing fast and loose with her feelings and something completely different to know that he'd orchestrated her seeing him with Melinda.

With a small shrug, he said. "After our night together I wanted you again. I couldn't stop thinking about you. It scared me. I had plans and I knew the more we were together, the deeper we got involved, those plans would change. So I did the unforgivable and got with Melinda. I figured word getting to you wouldn't be enough, that you'd have to see for yourself." He went in for another kiss but she blocked him with her hand.

"Wait, you planned it all? You planned to use Melinda?" she asked.

"I wouldn't say I planned it. I mean I was out at the old pasture partying with everyone and Melinda came on to me. That's when I got the idea. Until then I didn't have a clue as to how I was going to handle things. It was an asshole move. I was a coward."

"Yes, that was a coward's move. What if Melinda really—"

"Please don't think about Melinda," he said, resting his forehead against hers.

"But what if she really liked you and she felt used and—"

"We kissed a couple of times, that's it."

"I saw your hand up her shirt." When Evie stepped away, a cold breeze washed over her.

Grady pushed off from the wall. "I doubt Melinda had any great expectations."

Unlike me. I had romantic dreams and an innocent notion that I might be enough.

"I'd like to try this again," he said.

"Try what, exactly?"

"This." He gestured to the space between them. "There's something here and I'd like see where it takes us."

"I don't know. What was between us back then was overwhelming—"

"We're different people now," he said.

"Who don't know each other at all."

"Maybe we don't know the everyday things about each other but those little nuances that make us who we are at our core, we know that."

"Sweet Jesus," she said and stepped forward to caress his cheek. "I think you could talk me into just about anything. But I owe it to myself to not get carried away here. I'm not the same girl. I'm more complicated. My life is complicated more so than before. My mom is ill, my sister is distant, and my job is wearing on me. I need more than this to trust you, much as I want this." Briefly, she pressed her lips to his, almost got pulled under again by her desire for him, and stepped out from his arms.

"I can give you—"

"Woohoo. Grady? Are you back there? I've been ringing your bell."

Evie looked over her shoulder and watched in shock as Melinda Bane came through the open gate of the fence, a covered dish in her hand. She swung her gaze back to Grady's.

"Melinda?" he said and stepped beside Evie.

"You said you were grilling out tonight so I thought I'd bring over some of my dad's famous wings. I tried texting you." She handed him the plate.

Evie looked between them both and digested the information.

"Evie? How are ya? How's your momma? You hear much from your sister?" Melinda asked as she plopped into a chair.

Melinda Bane was a beauty queen. Tall, blonde, perky in all aspects, and, if rumors were true, a man-eater. She went through men like she had a subscription service to them. As if they were on a rotation, lent out to her based on her preferences and moods.

"Um, fine. Everyone is fine. How's your family?" Evie didn't harbor any ill will toward Melinda. She'd been played, too, after all.

"Oh, you know. The same. Busy with the diner. I know you enjoy Lorelei and Andee's establishment but you should pop over to ours sometime. We serve breakfast, too."

Melinda and her father owned a cafe a few miles down the road called Bert's. Where Lorelei and Andee had specialized in more eclectic fair and creative merging of flavors, Bert's was a straight-up greasy spoon.

"I might just do that," Evie said and turned to Grady. "I've got to get going." She needed space to sort through all her thoughts. To deal with the fear that she'd nearly been done in by Grady again. To try and find the reason for why she cared so much that Melinda had shown up.

"Evie." Every time he said her name, her knees went weak. He looked so freaking vulnerable yet strong as he tucked one hand in his pocket and reached for her with the other. "Don't go."

"Am I interrupting something?" Melinda asked.

"No. No, I just need to get home. It's an early day for me tomorrow. You all have a nice night." She waved away Melinda's concern.

He took a step toward her and she turned on her heel and fled.

"I'll see you later. Sorry about dinner," she called over her shoulder, not daring to look back.

"It looks like it's just you and me, Dr. Duke. Oh, I like the way that sounds." she heard Melinda say, ending on a giggle.

Evie knew she was doing the right thing. Without a doubt, she was scared. Terrified by how she felt when she was with Grady and that she had to draw on every ounce of self-discipline to not be ruled by impulses and desire and want. For her, the risks were too great. No matter how amazing the time with him might be, she needed a whole lot more to open herself up to him again.

CHAPTER 5

Grady knew the only way he'd be able to catch up with Evie and finish what they'd started, the discussion first and foremost, was to run into her at Two Chicks and Bacon.

She'd spent yesterday avoiding him and he had been forced to spy on her from the window in his upstairs loft. Only the opportunity to talk to her never came as she stuck to her backyard. But he'd enjoyed watching her. She'd come outside to water her plants, so cute with her blue watering can and bouncy ponytail. Her cut-off shorts showed her long, lean legs and he was reminded of when they'd gone swimming in the lake and he'd watched her rub lotion on her fair skin, laughing. The moments where she forgot all about what waited for her at home.

He pulled into the parking lot of the diner right behind her on Friday and she gave him a look, hesitating in her car before getting out.

"What are you doing here?"

"Eating. You?" He held the restaurant door open for her.

"The same. Is this going to be your thing? Eating here?" She automatically went to her seat at the counter and he took the one next to her.

"If it means I'll get to talk with you, then yes."

"You live next door."

"And yet I never see you."

"It's been one day."

"Hey y'all. You come together?" Andee asked as she poured their coffee.

"Nope," said Evie and folded her hands in her lap.

"What? You don't want to look at the menu?" asked Andee.

"I'll just go with the usual," she said.

"Gotcha." Andee winked. "You like what you like. What about you, Grady?"

"I'll have what she's having," he said and waited for Andee to leave before starting the conversation.

"I've been thinking a lot about the other night and that summer we spent together." He turned his chair to face hers.

"I have too, actually." She didn't look at him, instead adding creamer to her coffee and stirring it slowly.

"I haven't been very honest with you, then or now."

That caught her attention and she looked at him, her hand no longer stirring. "Go on."

Grady looked around, wondering what the odds of keeping this conversation private were. He was going to do his best. "Where do I start?"

"You can start with her." Evie nodded toward the front door and Grady turned to see Melinda Bane come in.

"Hey y'all," she said. "Just coming to check out the competition."

"Oh my word, Grady Duke. We meet again and so soon," Melinda said and came to stand in front of him. "Thanks for dinner the other night," she added with an exaggerated wink for flair.

"Thanks for bringing wings. Wish you would have stayed, Evie." he said.

"Yeah, it was nice catching up. We talked about the diner and Grady's job and—"

"Devouring men," Andee said in a low voice as she walked by.

"Excuse me," Evie said and pushed away from the counter.

"Oh, Evie. You should have stayed with us the other night. We had a good time." Melinda's effort to be bubbly and chatty was over the top.

He watched Evie walk toward the restrooms and saw the opportunity for what it was, a private moment.

"Listen, Melinda. It's good seeing you. But you'll have to excuse me for a minute." He stepped around her and caught up with Evie as she vanished into the long hallway leading to the restrooms. After opening a door marked EMPLOYEES ONLY, he pulled her into what looked like a storage closet and closed the door behind him.

"What in the world—"

"Hold on, I'll find a switch" It took a few pats along the wall before his fingers brushed the light plate and he switched on a light.

"What are you doing?"

"I'm finishing a conversation that we should have had years ago."

Evie shifted on her feet and moved to lean against a wall. "Well," she said with a flick of her hand. "Go ahead."

"It's true that I wanted out of this town more than anything—"

"I know this part."

"Let me talk, please." He paused and waited until she pressed her lips together. She made like she was locking her lips with a key and then tossed it over her shoulder.

He laughed. "Thank you. As I was saying, getting out was all I had thought about since I was twelve and heard my dad complain about how he would live and die in Lakeland. I didn't want that to be me. I didn't want to get serious about a girl because I didn't want anything to get in my way. And then you came along." He stood before her, one hand resting against the wall over her shoulder.

"At first I thought we'd just be like all the others. A little flirting, some kissing, and maybe a couple of dates but the days went into weeks and the weeks became months and I couldn't get enough. Then that night when we went down to the lake, school was getting ready to start up and I kept telling myself I needed to cut you out. I had one chance at college with no student loans and needed to focus on my senior year. That was my excuse. That was my plan for that night."

"You took me down there to dump me?"

He shrugged. "Yeah, I guess. But then we got to laughing and you bumped my shoulder with yours and I got lost. I told myself I'd get one more kiss and then say goodbye but one thing led to another—"

"I actually think I'm mad at you more for taking my virginity knowing you wanted to dump me."

"You took mine."

"What?" Her mouth fell open and she shook her head. "What are you talking about?"

"You gave me your virginity and I gave you mine in return," he said. "I never thought we'd go that far, but once it started, to stop it would have been torture and by then I had sold myself on the belief that it was the one little keepsake I would take with me when I left. It was and still is one of the best moments of my life."

"How is that even possible that you were a virgin? You were such a man-whore."

"I let everyone believe I was a man-whore. A few of the guys started speculating and spreading rumors and I let them. It worked to keep things at a distance with girls."

"And Melinda the other night?"

"I saw her when I was getting groceries. She came over to hit on me but after you left, she clued in quickly that I only had eyes for you. She said I needed to be honest with you now. That I shouldn't waste time. Whad'ya say, Evie, you think there might be something left from the old days? An ember? Spark?"

"Kiss me," she said. "Kiss me now."

And he did. He kissed her slowly, letting his lips linger on hers, breathing in the taste of her. Together they found their something old and embraced the something new.

"It's just like it was when I was a kid. I can't get enough of you." He slid his arms around her and pulled her close. "I'd like to take you out. Get to know you better." He winked.

"I'm afraid I'm going to make you buy me dinner and a movie first." She wrapped her arms around his neck and cupped the back of his head as she'd done that night on the bank of the lake.

"Oh, I had planned on it. Dinners, movies, and so much more. I want to make it up to you, Evie. Do it right this time."

"Well, we're off to a bad start. We're in a storage closet."

"Nah, this is right where we need to be—"

The door to the storage room swung open and Lorelei stood in the entryway, mouth agape, Melinda behind her, smiling.

"Care to explain what's going on here?" Lorelei said.

"We're having our seven minutes in heaven, Lorelei. I believe I owe it to Evie. So if you don't mind," Grady said.

"Oh, I don't mind at all. Just let me grab this bag of flour and we'll be on our way. Oh, and when you two are ready to come out, just pound on the door. It still sticks. We close at one." She flicked on a flashlight, switched off the overhead light, and closed the door with a quiet click.

"Mood lighting," Evie said, grateful the dim light would hide her blush.

"I don't need anything to help with the mood. All I need is you." Grady dipped his head and teased her lips with his. "What are the odds I can convince you to call into work and stay in here till noon?"

"Pretty good, if you know what you're doing with those hands and that mouth."

"Excellent. I think I remember a few of your sweet spots." He slid his hand under her top.

Evie wondered what the word of the day would be to describe the second chance and good fortune they'd been given. Maybe it was all the words combined or maybe it came down to being open and willing.

Either way, she was thankful.

EPILOGUE- ONE YEAR LATER

WORD OF THE DAY: SERENDIPITOUS: GOOD; BENEFICIAL; FAVORABLE

"**Here's your bacon and Gouda omelet,** Evie, and for you, Grady, the vegetable frittata." Andee placed the plates in front of them and stood there, grinning like a crazy person.

"What's up with you today?" Evie asked, staring at her.

"Nothing. I'm just very happy. Lorelei is over the morning sickness and finally more bearable to be around and you two..." She shot a look to Grady. "Well, you two are just so stinking cute."

"Why don't you go fill some cups with coffee, Andee," Grady suggested.

"Aw, do I have to?" She stared at Grady briefly before giving in. "Fine." She snatched up the coffee carafe and shuffled off.

"What's up with her?" Evie asked and went through the motions of sprinkling copious amounts of pepper on her eggs.

"She's probably wondering why you aren't paying attention to what you're doing," Grady said.

"I don't have to pay attention. I always do the same things. First, I put pepper on my eggs and then I spread the little butter pats on my toast... Oh my word. That's not butter."

Evie stared at the large sapphire ring sitting upright in a butter pat shaped like a heart.

"Yes, the intention is for it to be an engagement ring. I'm hoping for a yes here. A hell yes would be even better."

"You want to marry me?" It wasn't that she doubted his love for her, but the timing. Her life had become definitely more difficult with her momma's worsening medical state. He would be making a permanent commitment to her at a time that life wasn't all unicorns and butterflies.

Grady laughed. "Well, it's not from Andee or Lorelei." He pulled her chair around to face him and dropped to one knee before her.

"Evie Jane Barker, will you marry me? You know you're my world and I can't imagine a day without you in it. I want to be there for you. Good times or bad. If you'll let me I'll help you carry this weight. Please say yes. I'll even throw out my musket lamp."

"Say yes," Andee called from across the restaurant. Lorelei stood in the door of the kitchen and wiped her eyes.

"Of course I'll say yes. Yes, I'll marry you. I loved you then, I love you now, and I'll love you forever," Evie said and threw her arms around his neck.

It had forever been him.

REASON TO STAY

A Coming Home Short Story

KRISTI ROSE

Vintage Housewife Books

PO Box 841

Farmington, Mo. 63640

www.kristirose.net

Publisher's Note: This is a work of fiction. Names, characters, places, and incidents are a product of the author's imagination. Locales and public names are sometimes used for atmospheric purposes. Any resemblance to actual people, living or dead, or to businesses, companies, events, institutions, or locales is completely coincidental.

Book Layout © 2014 BookDesignTemplates.com

Cover Design by Paper and Sage Designs

Reason to Stay/ Kristi Rose. -- 1st ed.

❀ Created with Vellum

Dedicated to my loves.

Do not brood over your past mistakes and failures as this will only fill your mind with grief, regret and depression. Do not repeat them in the future.

— **Swami Sivananda**

1

Sister tries to keep it real, clothes are washed and house is cleaned but hearts are broken and heads hang low~ "WHISKY AND WATER."

Home.

Being here was nothing like she'd feared.

What had she expected? She wasn't sure. Would it be awkward? Yes. Did she feel like a stranger? Absolutely. Was there a heavy weight of guilt pressing down on her? Without a doubt.

She'd never imagined she'd *want* to be here; she'd worked so hard to get out and stay away. But being near Evie filled her with a sense of familiarity that actually was good and comfortable. Trouble was, she didn't know if she'd be welcomed by anyone other than her sister.

She should have come back before today. Even for a short visit.

She discarded that idea as quickly as she'd had it. Coming home at any point until now would have been stupid. Toxic.

Good grief. Isn't that what momma would say? There was so much negativity rattling around in her head, too much doubt and uncertainty.

Standing next to her sister, Evie, with Evie's husband, Grady, on the far end, she wondered if the people behind them were thinking about her momma or how she, Shea, had been the worst daughter in the world.

She should have stayed away.

Evie reached out her hand and entwined her fingers with Shea's.

"I'm glad you're here," Evie whispered.

At least someone was.

"Let us pray," said Reverend Parker.

Shea bowed her head. Whether it was from the pull of the earth's gravity or the realization that goodbye was coming soon—they would be officially laying her momma to rest—the unshed tears that had pressed against her eyes all day slowly began to fall.

Evie handed her a handkerchief, the cotton soft and worn, her momma's initials embroidered on the corner, and Shea began to cry harder. It used to infuriate her that while their father was out drinking and spending money they could've used, her momma had sat quietly in her rocking chair, humming and embroidering fabric squares.

Now she was gone and Shea would never get to say goodbye. Or that she was sorry for causing her so much grief. Or that she loved her. She would never be able to tell her momma that she was finally turning things around and success was at her fingertips.

She buried her face in the soft cloth and tried to breathe in her momma's scent but all she could smell was Evie's light perfume. Her chest burned with need to take in more oxygen, for all Shea could manage were little gasps as she held back her hysterics.

Shea'd been a terrible daughter. She'd been a terrible sister for that matter, leaving Evie to deal with the day to day. But no one was under any different illusions. No one expected Shea Barker to be good, upstanding, or hell...anything. They saw her as they expected someone with her troubled childhood to be. Evie may have broken the cycle, but no one expected Shea to.

At least she'd been able to afford giving her momma a nice funeral with an abundance of Gerbera daisies in all colors. Her momma's favorite. She already had enough bad karma to atone for; making her momma's funeral the best it could be was a no brainer.

One hit song, the equivalent to hitting the lottery, and this quarter's royalties were enough to cover the cost. She figured Evie would be worried about the expense Shea had gone to. When they had a quiet moment, she'd try to soothe her sister's worries—she'd tell her about the song. Though, superstitious to a fault, she'd wait to tell the rest of the story until everything was set and in motion. But any conversation about her life was a loaded topic requiring courage, and right now Shea's emotional bucket was depleted.

"Shea?"

She looked up to find Evie staring at her and she broke, her once contained sobs set free.

Evie wrapped her in a hug. "Talk to me." Her voice was low, a whisper in her ear. She rubbed up and down Shea's back.

"I didn't get to say goodbye." She tried not to wail, her sobs ragged and gasping. She'd started the day short of breath, afraid a deep one would set free her tears, and now she couldn't get ahead of them to get control.

"I didn't either. Come on." Evie wrapped her arm around her shoulder and led her from the pew out through the side of the church door. Shea was relieved to have her sister's support, her legs unsteady beneath her.

She hiccupped, sucked in a deep breath, and wiped her cheeks with the handkerchief. "But you were there. I wasn't."

"Neither was she. It'd been a long time since momma was really with us. I think she'd been slowly slipping away each day. I didn't realize that until it was too late."

A black town car waited to take them to the graveyard. The crowd of mourners made their way to their own vehicles. She saw so many familiar faces, so many friends of her momma's. Some Shea couldn't look in the eye—too afraid all they'd remember were her teenage antics.

Her eyes met those of a tall, handsome stranger who gave her a friendly smile. It was nice to see many of Evie's friends come out to support her.

Grady held open the car door and Shea slid in, followed by her sister.

"I'm sorry for sticking you with all the responsibility, letting you do it all, Ev. I'll never be able to make it up to you." Shea took three deep, ragged breaths, trying to steady herself and contain the hot mess that she was.

This was certainly a conversation for a different time. Had she arrived as early as she'd hoped yesterday, maybe they would've had it. But planning and timeliness had never been her strong suits even when they needed to be. She covered her wrist with her hand, hiding the pink tint of emerging hives that was beginning to speckle her skin.

"Stop, you didn't stick me with anything. I stayed because I wanted to. You have your path to follow and I have mine." Shea watched Evie and Grady share a look and thought she might burst out in a second round of tears. The way her brother-in-law looked at her sister, with such longing and love, the way he stood behind her as if he was prepared to catch her should she fall— Shea had never experienced anything remotely similar to that unless she were to count the unconditional love of her dog, Roscoe. She scratched a spot on her wrist.

Lord, if her momma were to see her, she'd call her a sad sack. She'd tell her self-pity was as useful as hen shit on a pump handle —though her momma would have found a different word rather than use an expletive.

"After the burial, lots of people will be coming by the house. Are you up for that?" Evie asked.

"I have to be. Just tell me how I can help." Shea wound the handkerchief through her fingers as she rolled her shoulders back.

With a weary sigh, Evie nodded.

"Here." Shea reached up and wiped away the smudge of mascara on her sister's cheek.

"So much for waterproof." Evie laughed and returned the favor by dabbing a tissue under Shea's eyes.

Because she and Evie looked so much alike, every time Shea looked at her sister she was struck with a sense of belonging. For all the twisting in the wind she'd done as a child, hating her home and the hand they'd been dealt with their father, there was no denying this was where she was supposed to be. As horrible as it had sometimes been, today, looking into Evie's brown eyes, so like her own, she found comfort. A unity with their red hair—though Shea's was a tad more strawberry—the smattering of freckles, and very pale skin. Their shared history, ironically, gave Shea the sense of being tethered as if she'd found her way back on the map. A feeling she'd lost long ago. Truth was she'd turned her back to it years ago and drifted so far off course she'd been unable to find true north.

The burial was gut-wrenching. Watching Evie break only made it worse and she felt so helpless as she watched Grady hold her up. Somehow they made it through.

As she stared down at the fresh mound of earth, Shea found herself wrapped in the arms of Lorelei Parker—Williams now, she supposed, having married her high school sweetheart last summer.

"Remember that summer my parents took us to Steinhatchee?" Lorelei asked.

Remember? How could she forget? Even the constant smell of the sulfuric waters the town boasted had done nothing to diminish the greatness of her first and only summer vacation.

"Your daddy made us eat rattlesnake," Shea said and let out a deep exhalation.

Lorelei gave a small laugh. "That's right, I'd forgotten that. Daddy thinks things like gator and rattlesnake are delicacies. It's no wonder I like to experiment with my food. Anyway, after that trip, when we dropped you all back off at the Crawford's, I started to cry on the way home. When daddy asked me why, I said I was sad, sad that nothing seemed to be turning out all right for you all, sad that everything had been so difficult. And daddy told me a story. Said he got to talking with your momma one day, asked her how he could help her..."

Shea scratched a new welt on her upper arm. "I wish he could have talked her into leaving my dad."

Would their life have been any different had their momma left their daddy? She'd likely be alive today and would've been someplace other than standing in their front yard when he came home one evening, drunk, overshot the driveway and crashed into the house. Pinning their momma between the house and car. He'd died instantly in that wreck and she hadn't, living the rest of her days in a nursing home.

"I bet a part of him does as well, but he asked her what she needed help with and she told him that her one wish was for you two to have a good life, to be able to chase your dreams. She spent her days setting you up for that journey, building you up so you could fly. She loved you, Shea, and would be so proud of who you've become and what you're trying to achieve."

There was no way Lorelei could know that she'd not only embedded a knife deep in Shea's chest, but had twisted it as well. Until now, what could her momma possibly have been proud of? In true Shea fashion, she was once again too late to show she'd changed. Several years of trying to break into the country music industry, and what did she have to show for it? More broken-up bands than she could count, a handful of bad relationships, a suitcase of broken promises, and proof that she was slow to learn lessons and change her ways. Sure, she'd written a few songs, sold them, and one had done well, but she'd been an absolute failure at what she'd set out to do and holding on to it was killing her from within.

"Thanks, Lorelei."

"You may not think this is true, Shea, but you have friends here. Just reach out. We care about you and your sister." Lorelei gave her another hug, rubbed her hands up and down her arms before slipping away.

The drive back to Grady and Evie's house went by much too quickly and Shea had only a few minutes to catch her breath, cover up with a light sweater, and reapply her makeup before the first mourners rang the front bell. She spent a long moment hugging her dog, Roscoe, finding comfort in his unconditional love.

With a glance at her cell phone, she saw Kimberly, her agent, had called. No matter how hard she tried, she couldn't convince herself that she wasn't a flash in the pan and might actually be talented enough to warrant an agent.

With shaky fingers, she pressed the button to listen to the voice mail.

"Hi, Shea. Again, my condolences about your mother. I hope the funeral went as well as these things can. I don't expect you to call me back. I just wanted to touch base with you about the interview. They're really excited to meet you. I was able to postpone it until Friday but they head back to LA after that. I've sent an email about what they're looking for; an original song is essential. I know you're not interested in writing children's music but this is a step in the right direction for building your name. Call me if you have any questions. Being a songwriter for a TV show is a great opportunity, one that doesn't come around often, if ever. I'm here, day or night. Reach out. Bye for now."

She had six days to get her tail back to Nashville. Surely that would be enough time to do whatever else was needed for her mother's estate, or lack thereof. The hardest part was today and she was half way through that. She would get out of Lakeland, head back to Nashville where she could secure her future. She would finally be something more than the havoc-making, troubled teen. She'd be more than her childhood.

One Billboard number one song had done more for her in the year since she'd sold it than nearly twelve years of trying to break into the industry had even hinted toward. She was not about to let this chance to pass her by.

Shea stared at her phone. She didn't want to go downstairs and make nice with people who still judged her for her past. She wanted to get lost in the now with the people who were emailing and calling her agent, people who wanted a product from her. Who she knew how to respond to. It was far easier to give than the emotional commitment needed downstairs. Jumping out the window and escaping in her pickup was more like her. But she wouldn't leave Evie to handle it all. She'd done that for far too long.

Her guitar and banjo rested against the wall and she promised herself she'd spend some time with one of them tonight. Maybe she'd have a breakthrough on a new song, either way she'd find some comfort.

The turnout was larger than Shea expected and she saw a whole new side of her momma. She was able to look past her anger that her momma had never left their drunk father. Instead, she saw a woman who had given repeatedly at her church, helped fundraise and taught Sunday school. She saw a woman who'd sat on the PTA while she and Evie were in school and whose friends were not just the lunch ladies she'd worked with in the school cafeteria. She saw a woman who had been well liked by her community, who had a stream of friends that were standing out on Evie's deck near her hydrangea bushes holding handmade handkerchiefs, gifts from her momma, laughing, crying, and telling stories that simultaneously warmed Shea's heart and broke it.

"What a tribute," the guy next to her said. It was the same guy from the funeral, the one with the sympathetic smile.

Tall, with dark blond hair cropped short except for the top, which flopped over his eyes no matter how many times he pushed it back—he'd done it twice since she looked over—he was not the sort who normally chatted her up. He looked too scholarly for them to have anything in common. Dark brown, round, tortoise-shell glasses gave vision to light blue, laughing eyes. He sported a beard that at first glance looked to be the result of a busy life and a few days growth but upon closer inspection was actually mani-cured enough that she knew this was part of his look.

And what a look it was.

He was fine, if one liked the Indiana Jones type. Which, honestly, who didn't? At his root, Professor Jones was a player and all women liked a guy they could chase and reform. Shea certainly did. But she liked guys who were easy to figure out. This one she couldn't get a read on.

"How did you know her?" she asked. He looked to be a few years older than her sister, which made him too young to be a friend of her momma's.

"I didn't. Not really. I knew of her through your sister."

"Oh, you went to school with Evie?" That would explain why she didn't know him. By the time Shea got to high school, Evie was in her senior year; this guy was probably a class or two ahead of her.

"No, I know Evie through Lorelei and Cole. It's a winding trail, I'll explain on another day. I hope you don't think I'm being too forward, but you look like you could use a break. I brought Krispy Kreme donuts hoping sugar might help. If that doesn't work—" he tapped his suit jacket breast pocket, making a soft *thunk* "—I've brought with me a liquid painkiller."

She raised her brows.

"Sounds like I have a problem, doesn't it? Does it make it worse or better if I told you I was a writer?"

Shea wasn't sure how to respond.

"Benjamin Franklin said, 'In wine there is wisdom. In beer there is freedom. In water there is bacteria.'"

"That might be a nice line. If I drank. If my dad hadn't been an alcoholic." Normally, at this point, she'd turn and walk away, shutting out any further attempts at a second conversation or more, but today she stood firm and waited for...something.

"Cripes. I'm sorry. I totally forgot. I didn't mean to offend you or your sister. Shit, I'm really sorry." He scrubbed at his beard, his eyes darting to hers.

"Did you say 'cripes'?"

"Yeah, my mom says it all the time. It's kinda stuck."

"My mom said, 'good grief.' It's kinda stuck as well." She gave him a watery smile.

"I'm Leo. Leo Marshall. You're Shea, right? Evie talks a lot about you." He held out his hand. The nails were chewed and small dots of ink stained his fingers.

She smiled and put hers in his. "Nice to meet you. Thanks for coming." She pointed to the fluffy hound at her feet. "This is Roscoe."

Roscoe lifted his dark head, sighed, readjusted his front paws, and laid his head back on them.

"He seems very loyal," Leo said, giving Roscoe's head a brief scratch before standing up to face her. "Nice to meet you, Shea. Your sister says you're in from Nashville. What do you do out there? Wait, your sister said something about writing songs. You're a songwriter, right?"

"Yes—"

"That's got to be a whole lot better than a wanna-be country star. I bet those are a dime a dozen." His smile and raised eyebrows spoke of the levity he was attempting.

"I was gonna add that I moved to Nashville to break into the country music business as a performer. Songwriting has been another way to pay the bills." Until now. Now, songwriting meant something more to her. It was therapy and healing. It was comfort and acceptance. It was the success she'd been chasing.

"You're kidding me, right?"

She shook her head and drew her fingers over her heart, crossing it.

Leo closed his eyes and groaned. "I should quit while I'm ahead."

"Who said you're ahead?" She threw him a bone. "You said you're a writer? Let me guess, satirical greeting cards? Op Ed pieces?"

"Satirical greetings cards, that's funny. I'm one of the sports writers for the local paper."

He had to be kidding. He was wearing a button-down, oxford shirt under his—obviously tailored—suit jacket. He wasn't wearing tennis shoes and didn't flex his arms every chance he got. A writer? Yes. A professor? Absolutely. Working in the field of sports? Not a chance.

"Do you play sports?" At the risk of offending his delicate male sensibilities, she posed the question with a modicum of disbelief. She figured she was due a gimme.

"Yeah, tons. Football's my thing. Your sister and I play on the same charity team."

"Aw, I see. You play on the girls' team." She stifled her snicker.

"All right, you can tease me. But I want one chance at a defense and that's to say it's a co-ed team."

"Sure." This time her smile did break.

"On that note, I'm going to leave while I *am* ahead. My objective has been achieved. It was nice meeting you, Shea Barker." He stuck out his hand and waited.

She cocked her head and narrowed her eyes. "What objective?" she asked as she raised her hand to take his.

"My one goal was to see you smile. Even for just a moment."

Her hand slid into his and he clasped it tightly between both of his, leaned in close and said, "As the great Shakespeare said, 'Give sorrow words; the grief that does not speak knits up the o-er wrought heart and bids it break.'" With the slightest squeeze, he slid his hands from hers and walked away. She glanced at her arms, surprised that she hadn't scratched once while talking with Leo.

She wondered what it was about herself that drew the attention of oddballs. Could they smell her chaotic childhood on her and assume she'd be more understanding? Tolerant? She'd had one decent conversation, well, as decent as one can have considering she was at her mother's wake, and it was with a booze-toting, dead-guy-quoting, oddly dressed jock who hadn't known the teenage Shea.

Shea sighed and Roscoe looked up at her.

Though she found herself curious about Professor Jones, football player and journalist, and the dichotomy that he was, she couldn't go there. This was not the time for that. Besides, she no longer trusted her perception of people. For the last ten years, she'd been so heavily surrounded by naysayers and takers that negativity had become her normal, her instrument for decision-making and a broken one at that.

Today was about the future, about getting it right from here on out, and she was more determined than ever. She'd never get over the regret of the lost time with her momma or even Evie. Her only silver lining on this dark and cloudy day was knowing she had at least changed her direction or rather, was grabbing for a new one. She'd finally figured out that the bigger picture was not about making it in Nashville, about being famous. That was not what was going to make her happy. Help her overcome her past. Nope. But a respectable job like song writing for a TV show might. A steady income, investments, even healthcare would be her markers for having arrived. Like Evie, she would show everyone that she was not the sum of her parents.

Earlier, when she'd stood over her momma's grave, she'd promised her she'd get her act together, that she'd become the person her momma had always hoped her to be and letting herself get distracted by an attractive guy was not the way to achieve that. She would not get in her own way. She was going to use those wings her momma had worked so hard to give her.

2

MOMMA WORKS TO BUY US EXTRAS, SHOES FOR CHURCH AND RICE AND BEANS~ "WHISKY AND WATER."

Shea adjusted the muter on her five-string banjo and picked out the melody again. Roscoe was sniffing the fence line, looking for all the places he could mark. The hour was early and she hadn't wanted to wake Evie, though Grady had left for work a bit ago to teach an early class, so she'd come out to the backyard to work on the thread of a song that had been teasing at her mind since the wake.

The business of the funeral was behind them and all that was left was the healing. A darn near impossible task considering she was already broken into so many tiny fragments. She had no idea where to start. Normally people, or should she say normal people, grounded themselves at home. But she had no home, just a small studio apartment in a less than desirable part of Nashville. Not even a houseplant.

The squeak of the French door opening drew her attention.

"Hey, I brought a peppermint tea. I'm assuming you still don't like coffee." Evie sat on the deck stairs next to her, two mugs of steamy amber liquid in her hands.

Shea shrugged. "It reminds me of dad in the mornings trying to combat his hangovers."

Evie nodded.

"I didn't mean to wake you," Shea said and continued to pick the chords. It was how she worked through the hang-up of finding the melody

"You didn't. I couldn't sleep."

"Me either."

"Is that a song I know? It's beautiful." Evie blew on her tea and watched.

"No, something I started last night." It had come out suddenly, moments before she was about to drift off into sleep. Knowing she'd never find the thread again, she'd gotten up and written it down. Sleep after that had been limited.

"You're really good at this song writing thing."

"You think so?" She really hoped so because she liked it so much more than performing and standing in front of a crowd, baring her soul. Writing was still a wonderful way to exorcise the demons but if people didn't like the song then they usually blamed the artist and not the writers. She knew people would find it hard to believe she didn't like the attention performing in front of a large crowd brought her, considering her antics as a teenager. But honestly, she'd rather stab her eyes out with a hot poker than do one more gig, fight one more time with the band about the set, scramble to find a bass player, and smile with fake appreciation as some Nashville big wig talked down to her about all the things she needed to change.

But writing songs, that came naturally. Having a screwed up childhood helped to add depth to the well.

"You still have daddy's old guitar?" Evie asked.

Shea nodded. "In a case upstairs. I don't play it much since I learned how to play the banjo but it's still in great shape." Unlike anything else her father had touched. Including them.

Apparently, Evie was thinking the same thing. "At least he was a happy drunk."

"There is that."

"You know, momma left a life insurance policy. You and I are about to come into a fair amount of money. So, you'll get back what you paid on the funeral."

Shea's fingers stilled, her picks suspended above the strings. "Seriously? How did she manage that?" Money had always been tight and a policy would have to have been created before the accident.

Evie shrugged. "I dunno. Maybe she had some sixth sense or something. She must have had it taken out of her paycheck. We have an appointment with the lawyer on Tuesday to review the will. That's the first step. I can show you all the papers."

Shea shook her head. "I trust you. I don't even need to go to the appointment if you don't want." She picked up the mug of tea, sipped. "This is nice."

"Of course I want you to come to all the appointments. But I think you have to be present for the reading of her will." Evie paused to sip tea then continued, "Any idea of when you're headed home?"

Home? Did such a place exist? "Ready for me to leave?"

"Are you kidding? I want you to stay forever but I figured you're really busy. It's nice having you here. I don't know how I'd be coping without you."

"You have Grady."

"Yes, but you're my sister. It's your loss too."

Shea put down her mug and took her sister's hand. Just like Evie had done all those nights when they were children, lying in bed listening to their father stumble through the house and their mother trying to coax him into bed.

"I miss you. I know you love it in Nashville and I can't express how proud of you I am that you're sticking to your plan and how determined you are. It can't be easy. That's what makes it easy for me with you so far away, knowing you're chasing your dream. But if you could stay a bit...."

Shea searched her sister's face and could tell by the way she bit her lip that it had been hard for her to ask. "I have no timeline," she said.

"Good. You hungry? Come on, I'll treat you to a fabulous breakfast."

"Are you cooking?" Shea looked up as Evie stood.

"No, I said fabulous. I'm a pretty decent cook, if I do say so myself, but Lorelei...wow. Roscoe, come on. Inside. Check your bowl," Evie called to the dog and patted her legs. He ran to her and stuck his head into her hand.

Shea left her banjo leaning against her sister's living room wall and her dog stretched out on her kitchen floor. Evie's home was everything Shea imagined a home to be, right down to the tacky musket lamp with the fringed lampshade in Grady's office.

They sat in Evie's SUV in silence for the first mile before Shea reached out, "How's married life?"

Having eloped only six months earlier, Evie and Grady were still in the newlywed stage.

"I don't want to gush before you have something solid in your stomach but it's better than I'd ever hoped it could be. I think a lot of that has to do with Grady. He's pretty spectacular."

"Well, you're no slouch yourself." There was no denying that Evie was nothing less than amazing. Shea wouldn't have had half the chances she'd had if not for Evie. "I mean, how many sisters take on the job of being a parent at eighteen, and while they're in their first years of college? I didn't make it easy for you. That's for sure. You're pretty magnificent and he's lucky to have you."

Evie smiled, her cheeks slightly pink. "It was hard for all of us. I hope you know that all those things you did when you were a teen are long behind you. What kid wouldn't do what you did?"

Lots of kids might roll houses with toilet paper, steal shopping carts and crash them into the lake, but she'd taken it further with

KRISTI ROSE

shoplifting, graffiti on cars and buildings, underage drinking, smoking...hell, the only thing she'd managed to hold on to was her virginity and she'd wasted that on some stupid drummer and a promise of stardom.

"You didn't." Shea pointed out.

"Yeah, but I had a different daddy for the first few years. It was around your third birthday that he started to really drink."

"I remember him playing the guitar when I was younger. Momma would sing along."

"Then it all stopped," Evie said. "I never understood why and unless you know, I guess it's buried with them."

"I have no idea. Maybe life was just too hard for him. Maybe he tried to do what he thought he was supposed to do and it didn't fit and he didn't know how to fix it." Shea had no idea where those words came from. She'd always been so angry with their lot in life. But, now at her own impasse, struggling with who she wanted to be and finding who she really was, the fear and uncertainty were overwhelming.

"Maybe." Evie shrugged and pulled into a spot outside a diner with a red and white gingham awning. Two Chicks and Bacon was stenciled on the door. A cute, artsy sign hung in the door telling the world they were open for service.

Shea followed her sister into the diner and the aroma of freshly baked bread, caramelized sugar, and chocolate made her mouth salivate. Even the aroma of coffee didn't bother her, the place was that welcoming. They sat at the counter and Shea pulled out a menu.

"Morning, hon," said Andee, a woman Shea recognized as one of Evie's high school classmates. Andee poured her sister a cup of coffee and gestured to Shea.

"No, thanks. But I'd love a hot tea if you have any."

"Oh, we have plenty of tea." She put the coffee pot back on the burner, pulled out a large wooden box, flipped open the lid, and presented Shea with an assorted display of teas.

"If I might suggest one, the Lady Earl Grey is nice and Kylie makes a mean London Fog." A guy slid into the seat next to her and plucked out a packet of Lady Earl Grey.

Shea turned to find Leo.

"Kylie?"

"The college kid who works here as a barista. She's only here for another hour so if you want something steamed or frothed, you have to order it now."

"You getting a London Fog, Leo?" Andee asked and took his tea packet.

"Make that two." Shea picked up a tea bag and handed it to Andee.

"You won't regret it," Leo promised and folded his hands together, resting them on the counter. The tips were still covered in ink and he was dressed much like she'd seen him yesterday, an oxford shirt, this time tucked into jeans.

"I hope not or you'll really be batting zero," Shea deadpanned.

"Sports metaphor. I like it." He winked. "Morning, officer," he called over her shoulder.

Shea turned to see Officer Carlson walking toward them. She'd had many run-ins with the police, specifically Carlson. He'd hand delivered her to her momma more times than she could count with the spray paint still evident on her hands, or with another report of vandalism. One time he'd busted her drinking and she'd thrown up in his patrol vehicle. It was his quiet story, a cautionary tale delivered with the same avuncular attitude he'd always shown her that made her realize she could be an alcoholic like her father. She hadn't taken a drink since.

"Morning, Leo. Evie, Andee." He looked square at Shea. "Welcome home, Shea. I'm really sorry to hear about your momma."

"Thanks, Officer Carlson. I see you're still keeping the city safe." Shea tried to smile. Part of her wanted to thank him but the other diners in the restaurant gave her pause; she was unwilling to air her dirty past for everyone.

"It keeps me busy," he said.

"Probably not as busy as *she* used to keep you, huh, Carlson? That girl is a troublemaker. She actually graffitied the side of my building. Remember when I owned that pizza shop? People like her don't change." Mr. Hubbs, one of the retirees, who was as acrimonious now as he'd been back then, chimed in.

Was a troublemaker. She had been but no longer was and she hadn't graffitied the entire wall. Just one small spot. She'd only wanted to leave her mark on one tiny spot.

"That was a long time ago, Mr. Hubbs," Officer Carlson said.

"I got my eye on you, missy. I'll be locking my doors," Mr. Hubbs said, pointing to Shea.

She scratched at a small pink spot blooming on her wrist.

"Again, my condolences to both you girls. Your momma was an exceptional woman." Officer Carlson gave a quick nod before walking out of the diner.

Shea faced ahead, afraid to look at her sister or Andee or even Mr. Hubbs with his stabby finger and sharp words. Would she never shed the shame of her past? If it weren't for the reading of the will or the way Evie had looked so forlorn, she'd leave today.

"I have it on good authority, Mr. Hubbs, that your son, Mike, was also known to draw pictures on buildings around town. I believe he spray painted a devil face on the side of my daddy's church," Lorelei said as she delivered plates of hot food to a table.

The diner was quiet with the exception of a few snickers. Mr. Hubbs grumbled something under his breath, pushed back from his chair, and stomped out of the restaurant.

Andee cleared her throat. "Now, I know what you two want." She pointed to Leo and Evie. "But how about you, Shea? You had a chance to look at the menu?"

She smiled sheepishly, happy to have something else to focus on, and pulled the menu from the holder. "Not yet, sorry."

"No worries. I'll get your London Fogs and be right back."

"I like the Gouda and bacon omelet," Evie said.

"I get the spinach omelet," Leo said.

Andee placed two frothy mugs in front of them and Shea reached for hers, took a small sip.

"Wow, very good."

"Home run?" Leo asked.

"Yeah, home run," she said without looking at him. Purposefully focusing on the mug, she took another sip.

"All right. Ready to order?" Andee placed a pecan roll in front of Evie. "It's the last one and I was saving it in case you came in."

"Thanks." Evie stood then reached across the counter and hugged Andee. "I need this."

"I figured as much," Andee said.

Shea watched the exchange, her breath stuck in her tightening chest.

"I'll take the southwestern frittata." She wasn't really paying attention to food but the community that had become her sister's family. Leo played on the same charity football team. Andee knew what her sister wanted for breakfast and held back the last pecan roll 'in case she came in.' A fair amount of people at the wake yesterday had come to support Evie as much as they had come to say goodbye to their momma.

For the first time in her life, she wanted what her sister had. She'd been aware of how empty hers was but never felt the vast echo of nothingness until now. No one had called to check on her aside from her agent and that was her job. No one was wondering where she was, if she could come perform. The only calls she got were because someone wanted to capitalize on her talent and hoped she'd sell them a chart-breaking song. The only person who even gave a fig about her was sitting next to her. One person, her sister, and wasn't there some sort of law that required Evie to care?

"Ohh, have you heard this song? I love it. It's crazy popular." Andee reached below the counter and the country music quietly playing in the background got louder.

"It is a good song. Pretty sad though. I think it's called 'Whiskey and Water.'" Leo said.

Shea looked at her sister. "Have you heard it? Do you like it?"

Evie shrugged. "It's not a bad song. It just doesn't do it for me. But that does." She reached across the counter and picked up a magazine Andee had been looking at when they walked in. She and Andee started oohing and aahing over organizational containers.

Shea had to force the air from her lung and focus on bringing more in. The diner around her blurred as she watched her sister talk about the variety of ways to organize a laundry room.

She didn't like the song.

Yes, Evie had said it wasn't bad but that was her version of saying she hated it. For Evie, hate was too strong a word to use. Not one to hurt anyone's feelings, even someone she thought she didn't know; Evie would never say she hated it. But she did. She hated the song.

"I'd like to introduce myself," Leo said from behind her.

She turned to face him, confused, the diner coming back into focus. "What?"

"I'd like to introduce myself. I'm Leo. Leo Marshall. I'm a friend of your sister. I tend to put my foot in my mouth so I'm giving you advance notice."

"I'm confused," she said, pushing all thoughts of Evie and the song aside. Disappointment was too much to add to her grief.

"I'm going for a do-over here. I can't get yesterday out of my head and I feel like an ass."

"Listen, I'm not interested. I just thought I should tell you that up front."

Leo shrugged. "You're not interested in making a new friend?"

Friend. "You think we could be friends?"

Leo pressed his lips together in what she thought was his way of processing her words. "Jane Austen said something about Mr. Darcy and how at first appearance his address was not striking and his person was hardly handsome but he turned out all right in the end. I hope you give me a second chance."

"Because you're like Mr. Darcy?" Shea said, ignoring the vibrating of the phone in her pocket.

"I'm misunderstood like he was." Leo put on a false air of disdain.

Shea laughed. "As a person looking for a second chance from a lot of people, I can hardly not grant you one. But that's it. All I'm saying is that I won't hold your first few attempts at conversation against you."

"You'll be open to the friendship?"

She shrugged. "Sounds like it's inevitable."

He searched her face. Typically, she'd be uncomfortable with his non-verbal query but with Leo she was more at ease, as if he understood her or maybe was just really empathic. Either way, his quick smile and the way he leaned toward her when he quoted books, as if he didn't want anyone else to hear, made her feel like maybe Leo could be the first person in her new community.

If she were to stay.

"You know, if you're looking for a place to get away, something quiet where you can clear your head, Hollis Garden is nice, but there are some really good benches at Lake Morton. There, I find...inspiration," Leo said in a quiet voice.

"Inspiration. How?"

"I find it a good place to gather words. Since you write songs. I thought, maybe, it might help you, too."

"Thanks for the tip," she said. She wanted to reach out and take his hand. To bond with him through ways other than words, funerals, and food. She wondered if he felt as adrift as she did, for the need to tether her line to his was overwhelming.

"Here you go," Lorelei said and placed a tray on the counter. She unloaded plates in front of each of them and Shea looked between their dishes.

"Ok all. I just want you both to know that I *will* be sampling what each of you ordered." She poked her fork at Leo. "Starting with you. Each of these dishes looks amazing, Lorelei."

Leo pushed his plate toward her and she took off a corner of his omelet. The bite was divine. The flavor burst incredible.

"Good, right?" He pulled the plate toward him and started eating.

"Here," Evie said. "Before I cover it in pepper." She pushed her plate toward Shea and pulled Shea's toward her. They each took a few bites.

"I'm gonna eat here every day," Shea said. "Every day. What was your daddy thinking when he made us eat rattlesnake when we could've been having this stuff? So good."

Lorelei laughed, a blush on her cheeks.

"I'd forgotten all about that," Evie said. "Remember that time he wanted us to try gator tail?"

From there the conversation wove its way through memory lane and their shared experiences. It was not lost on Shea that in addition to the lows she'd shared with her family, she actually had some fond moments to recall. Not everything was about alcohol, a police car bringing her home, or the desperation she often felt as she tried to navigate even the simplest hurdles of life. She actually had memories where she'd considered, for a moment, turning down food. Gator tail, who ate that stuff?

But Daddy starts each day the same. Always full of regret and shame. He
tries to cleanse himself with water but the whisky's call is always to
blame~ "WHISKEY AND WATER."

L eo hoped she'd come out to the park. He knew sitting quietly among trees wasn't for everyone but he thought it might be a place that worked for her. One look at her during the wake a few days ago, shoulders slunk low but her head held high, he'd recognized a kindred spirit. Everyone changed as they grew up. Either they matured, became angry, found happiness, or whatever. But he'd never met someone who was just as they were in the past.

Shea was no different.

Caught between who'd she become and proud of it but unsettled with her past, she'd stood on the outskirts watching her momma's life being retold through different eyes.

It caused her pain. She'd nearly chewed her lip off while simultaneously trying to shred the hankie. He'd wanted to rescue her then and there. Unable to stop himself if he'd wanted to, and he hadn't, he'd gone over and inadvertently made an ass of himself. At least she'd smiled and for a small moment, relaxed.

Leo didn't know much about loss; he was lucky like that. But he knew a helluva lot about reinventing oneself. He was the master at such a feat. Or so he hoped. Either that or he was the master of disguise. Sharing with her his place of peace, where muses traipsed between the trees, was the least he could do.

He heard the banjo before he realized she was singing along with it and he paused to listen, his hand resting on the messenger bag slung across his chest. Her voice, though sad and wistful at times, was soft and calming and he not only enjoyed the tune but found a new understanding in its melody and lyrics.

The right thing to do would be to clear his throat or walk out from behind the trees, but he stood rooted. His eyes closed, listening as she hummed to fill in the space void of words before starting all over again.

"I've searched high and low for the path, checked the map. There's no trail of breadcrumbs to guide me back. When I look around nothing is familiar but everything is the same. Have I walked in circles? Why do I continue to miss my aim?"

With her words and voice around him, he pictured Shea doing the simplest of tasks while humming: arranging flowers, rocking a baby, and holding his hand.

His eyes sprang open. Who was he kidding when he'd said he wanted to be her friend? There was something about this girl that he dug.

She stopped and he held his breath, waiting, letting it out slowly when she restarted from the top, this time adding a line.

"I'm only trying to get back home, someone please bring me home."

Leo watched her bend over the banjo, her body moving with the melody, her light red hair casting rainbows of light as she moved between beams.

This girl knew his soul. Her words spoke to the deepest part of him. Bits that he'd thought he'd left behind when he finally learned how to be more than his disability. When he no longer believed in the can't but started living the cans.

He pushed off the tree, hesitating, wondering if he should move toward her or slip away, back in the direction he'd come. Clearing his throat, he stepped toward her. When she didn't turn he took another step and called her name.

She looked over her shoulder, surprised, a pencil stuck behind her ear, her hands still on the banjo.

"I'm sorry. I wasn't trying to sneak up on you." He came from around the bench and stood beside where she sat.

"It's not you. I hadn't realized I was so lost in my own world." The hollowness and desperation of her lyrics were etched on her face. He may want something more than friendship but right now, this girl needed a friend like people needed air. He was consumed with a prodigious need to ease her pain and offer a shoulder to lean upon.

"Where's Roscoe?"

"He's at home with my sister. He doesn't like the heat."

"Do you mind if I join you, for a moment? I don't want to interrupt your process." He gestured to the open seat next to her and she shifted to allow him space.

"You're good. Once I've built a foundation it's pretty easy for me to get my groove back," she said. On her thumb and first two fingers were quirky little slide-on picks she twisted around her fingers as she talked.

"You're lucky. Sometimes if I lose the thought it's hours before I can get back my direction. Writing is labor intensive for me."

"Sports writing? How so? Figuring out who's on what? I'd have thought that would be brainless stuff." As soon as she finished her sentence, she covered her hand with her mouth. Through her cupped hand she said, "I'm so sorry. That was awful of me to say. Anything creative, whether it's painting, writing, or whatever, is still an art and I should not make fun of your art."

"I appreciate that. Thanks. But I wasn't actually talking about my pieces for the paper. I actually write books." He took a chance and told her part of his secret. He'd never told anyone, outside his parents, about the short pieces of fiction he wrote. Not since third grade when he'd mentioned he wanted to be a writer and his teacher told him he'd have to learn to read and write first and chances of that were unlucky.

"That's great. You're more than just a pretty head full of sports stats." She wagged her brows. "What kind of books?"

He paused, wondering how much more he should share. "Mostly action and adventure. Guy stuff."

"Now the button-up shirts and glasses make sense. You're a novelist. Though I would've gone with something more literary."

"I like being unpredictable." He winked, something he found himself doing often with her. "I figured you for a guitar player, but a banjo?"

"Yeah, I worked part time in the Country Music Hall of Fame Museum and we had a lot of Earl Scruggs and Lester Flatt stuff... You know who they are?" She continued when he shook his head, "You ever watch Beverly Hillbillies?"

"Yeah, they were the musicians." He snapped his fingers in recognition.

"Right. Well they were musicians long before they were on the show and Earl Scruggs invented a whole different style of banjo picking. Working at the museum, I got to watch lots of videos of him and the music and I fell in love. I taught myself how to play five string Scruggs style. I aim to write songs that use lots of banjo."

And songs that twist a soul up.

"Is this where you write?" she asked.

"Yeah, this is where I come to get unblocked when I'm having trouble writing." He flipped open his messenger bag and pulled out a laptop. "Do you mind if I share space with you?"

"Can you write with all this?" She gestured to the instrument.

"Yeah, I think I can, actually. Listening to you helps clear my head and that's what I need."

She gave him a skeptical look and began picking the banjo fast. "This helps you clear your head?" She laughed and picked faster and louder, her fingers working so quickly they blurred.

"I was thinking more along the lines of what you were doing when I walked up. Not that that isn't crazy amazing or anything."

She laughed again and slowed her fingers, returning to the melody she'd been working on earlier and began to hum.

"Cripes, something about the way you sing makes me want to cry or laugh or..."

"Run away screaming?" she sang.

"Are you kidding? No way, it makes me feel a part of something. Something bigger than all this."

"That's how I feel about music," she sang to the melody. "Always have."

"'If you stop long enough to listen to the song of your soul, you will always find your path.'"

Her fingers stilled. "Who said that?"

"Ah, I just read it in a book somewhere I think." He'd written it in his third novel or perhaps the fourth. He couldn't recall.

"I love it."

They stared at one another and a soft whisper of a smile pulled at her lips. "I have felt so out of sorts since I came back. Being here, at this park, is the first in a long time that I've felt like I'm where I'm supposed to be."

Leo nodded in understanding and looked around. The lake, the ducks, the trees giving shade from the hot sun, somehow it all felt like life had slowed down a little and a person could pause long enough to get their bearings, to catch their breath. He elbowed her and when she looked at him, he indicated with his chin to Mr. Hubbs walking along the lake feeding the ducks.

"Afternoon, Mr. Hubbs," Shea called.

The sour-faced old man looked at them both, frowned, but called out a greeting before moving on.

Leo watched her look down at her arm, rub her smooth, creamy skin, and smile.

Shea went back to working the melody. He flipped open the top and read through the outline he'd drafted and felt just as stuck. Something wasn't working and he didn't know what. Glancing at Shea, he watched as she picked a new set of chords and searched for words to finish the line, scratching out entire lines or words along the way. He longed to have words flow again and the fear that he couldn't even start his first draft because he didn't know what the hell he was doing made finding his muse all the more difficult.

"What's wrong?" she asked and he snapped his eyes away from her paper, bringing them to her face.

"I'm sorry? What?"

"You looked like someone had sucker punched you. You were staring at my paper and I thought you might cry." She stretched her fingers and waited patiently.

Leo looked back at her paper, at the progress she'd made. "I'm just blocked, that's all."

"So walk me through it. Blocked how? Like, need a new idea or not sure where you're going on the page?"

He opened his computer again. "I have an idea. I just don't like it and I can't think how to fix it."

"Don't fix it. Get a new idea. Let that one sit for a while but in the meantime work on something else. I have books with song lines and chords that just don't work with anything yet. But their time will come. It's just not today."

He nodded and closed his computer. "But I can't even come up with a new idea." He didn't want to add that he felt like a hack at best, a failure at worst.

She began to strum the banjo like a guitar. "I've often thought the same thing. But all you need is some distance. To step away from what you think you can't do. So, let's come up with a new idea. You said it's adventure, right? Tell me about your characters."

He didn't know how he was going to have this conversation without tipping his hand. He'd kept his writing a secret from everyone because of what he wrote. He wanted the work to stand on its own and not be judged because of him. He may not look it, hell he'd done everything to make sure he *didn't* look like it, but at his core he was the epitome of a dumb jock who was a slow reader and a bad speller. Technology was the learning disabled kid's friend, it certainly had been his.

"I need a mystery—"

"Someone found a mythical unicorn," she blurted.

"What?"

"I think unicorns should be in every book, and ninjas. Someone says that they were taken down by a ninja but all signs look like the ninja was a unicorn. A NINJA UNICORN!"

"Ninja unicorns?"

"Yes, and no one believes them—"

"What possible signs could a ninja leave behind that lets everyone think it might be a unicorn?" He couldn't believe he was having this conversation; yet, he couldn't stop himself from asking for more or laughing.

"I don't know. You're the writer. Maybe it's a trail of banana slugs."

"Banana slugs?"

"Sure, they're real. I saw a documentary of them on TV last night. I couldn't sleep and was flipping through the channels—"

"And you stopped on one that was doing a documentary on banana slugs."

"Yes, sometimes when the mind is bored it's free to be creative. I think I saw a study on that or something."

Leo laughed. "Ninja Unicorns. Banana Slugs. This is the best conversation— That's it!" He snapped his fingers and jumped up from the bench, clutching his computer.

"What? What just happened?" She looked up at him with large brown eyes, laughter on her lips.

"Shea Barker, you're brilliant. I just figured out the next story. I've got to get home and get it all down before I forget." He tucked his computer back into his bag.

"I'm glad I could help," she said as she flipped her hair over her shoulder and then reached back to pat her back.

"You did more than help. You...you...cleared everything up. Thank you. Thank you." Exuberance poured from him.

Maybe it was something in her smile or the way she looked up at him, her face alight with pleasure. There was no stopping him; momentum and desire pushed him headfirst and he wrapped his hand around the back of her neck and planted a firm kiss on her lips.

Shea gasped against his lips but as he moved to step back, she pulled him toward her, deepening the kiss. When they separated, she giggled. Leo brushed his thumb over her bottom lip, his smile big.

He stepped back. "Thank you," he said again. "I can't wait to start writing. I owe you." He turned toward his car, ideas running at full throttle, desperate to get on paper.

"You're welcome. Any time," she called after him.

Leo turned and walked back to her. "Let's meet tomorrow for breakfast, at the diner. I'd love to see you again."

"Sure. I can be there around eight." Pink tint colored her cheeks.

Leo's lips continued to tingle from their kiss and he stepped closer. "Eight sounds great."

"You going to kiss me again?" she asked.

"You want me to?" He'd been thinking about it.

She shrugged. "I wouldn't stop you if you tried."

Taking the invitation for what it was, he bent toward her, slid his hand around the back of her neck for the second time, and pulled her toward him. This time their kiss was gentle and full of exploration. When she parted her lips and his tongue touched hers, his body pulsed.

They pulled apart slowly and Leo felt as if he were resurfacing, or better yet, coming alive.

"Thanks for your help," he said.

"Anytime."

He backed away, smiling. "Don't forget. Tomorrow."

"Eight a.m. I'll be there."

"I can't wait," he said.

She blushed. "Go write your book."

"Until tomorrow," he called before he turned and jogged off to his car. Ideas were all around him. Most about the book but others about Shea and he felt like a schoolboy who'd just figured out how to ace a test and win the girl. He felt like a champion.

Lying in bed, I stare at the ceiling, there are no glow-in-the-dark stars to carry away this scared feeling. There are no monsters in the closet, no boogey man at the door. Just a broken father who is drunk and passed out on the floor.~ "WHISKEY AND WATER."

"Do you want to go to the diner with me?" Shea asked Evie, who was suited up in yoga clothes.

"Actually, I would love to go with you but I think I'm going to take this chance, while I'm off work, to try this hot yoga thing." Evie laced up her shoes.

"I'll be home in time to go with you to the attorney's so we can tie up the loose ends with momma's will." Knowing that their momma had gone to such lengths, had the foresight to plan beyond her death, still baffled Shea. Being in her small hometown had her constantly reexamining her childhood. It was shitty, without a doubt. Stressful, absolutely, but maybe it had also had its good times too. Maybe.

"Ok, I'll see ya then. Get me a pecan roll, please." Evie hugged her briefly, gave Roscoe a scratch on the hindquarters, and was gone in a breath.

She had to leave in two days at the latest if she wanted to arrive for her interview in the best possible shape, well rested and put together. She and Kimberley had gone over the day ad nauseam in an effort to get her mentally ready. She didn't have a new song geared toward kids ready, like they'd stipulated, but the song she'd started working on after the funeral was really coming together beautifully. She was just going to go with what she knew and hope for the best, it was what drew their attention in the first place. Time to write a kids' song was evaporating quickly.

Roscoe ambled over to the large picture window, circled a sunbeam three times before he stretched out across it. He sighed happily, his tail giving two thumps.

"You like it here, don't you, boy?" Shea bent down to give his belly some rubs.

His tail thumped again.

"Yeah, I do too. But don't get too attached, we're not staying." Shea glanced at her arms, surprised that hives were not blooming, even though she was planning to venture out into a place where people still remembered her past.

The large clock on the wall chimed the half hour, prompting Shea into action. Discarding her robe, she changed into a flowy, white summer skirt, a navy blue tank top. With a quick swipe of gloss across her lips, she ran a brush through her hair and sat on the hall bench to pull on her navy cowboy boots. Grabbing her banjo case and purse, she jumped in her truck and drove to the diner, arriving a few minutes before eight.

"Hey, girl," Andee called and pulled out the box of teas.

Shea sat in her sister's seat and smiled. "Hey."

"Where's Evie?"

"She's off trying hot yoga. But I'm to get her a pecan roll."

"Hon, she'll want two of them after she's done with hot yoga. I tried it once. I didn't pee for days. I think I was so depleted of fluids that my body just reabsorbed it. That's a true story." She poured hot water into a mug.

Shea laughed. "I tried it once and all I could think about was that wicked witch from the Wizard of Oz. I kept wanting to call out in class 'I'm melting.'"

They shared another laugh. Further conversation was cut short when the door chime went off and Andee said, "Oh my word. Would you look at him? Leo! What in the world happened to you? Were you mugged?"

Leo staggered into the diner wearing running shorts and a tight, white, stained t-shirt. Except for his glasses, he looked like the jock sports writer he was. His hair flopped over his eyes and his beard looked scragglier, if that was even possible. Shea stared at his arms and chest, her eyes gliding over the subtle definition of muscles.

Damn, he had a body that could make a girl forget she was in mourning or, at the very least, ease some of the ache.

"Are those orange stains from eating Cheetos? Did you wipe your hands on your shoulder?" Andee asked.

He looked at one shoulder, then the other, sniffed the first one, and scratched his beard. "I think it's from Dorito's. I haven't had sleep or any nutritional food since I saw you last," he said to Shea and fell into the chair next to her. He took off his glasses, turned his blood shot eyes to her, and smiled.

"Did you drive here?" Shea asked.

"I think so. I don't remember."

"What happened? Last I saw, you were running off to..."

"Plot."

"Plot your story. Today you look like you've been on a bender." She leaned in close and sniffed. "Have you been drinking?"

"I had a beer but only because I was out of milk, energy drinks, and Coke. I wrote the first half of my book." He rubbed his eyes and yawned. "After I talked with you I was all pumped up. I sketched out my plot and then sat down to do the first chapter. The story just poured out of me and I couldn't stop. I've been up all night. I stopped so I could meet up with you."

"You should've gone to bed," Shea said.

"I can't. I'm still really pumped up." He yawned again.

"I can see that. Come on. I'm taking you home. You're going to crash here and be bad business for this diner."

"At least let me get some food. I'm starving."

Shea waved Andee over and placed a to-go order. Even with Lorelei rushing the order, the wait was agony. Leo's cycles of up and down as he fought off sleep might have been funny if she wasn't so worried he might pass out right in his seat, collapse forward, and bash his head on the counter. Once his food was complete, she pushed Leo out of the diner and asked for his keys.

"I can't let you drive my car," he said.

"Why not."

"Because then you'll be stuck at my place."

"I'll call Evie to come get me. Keys." She gestured with her hand.

He dug in his pocket, put the keys in her hand, and took the to-go bag from her other one. "I'm gonna eat in the car."

"You do that."

Between bites, he gave her directions to his house. She pulled into the driveway of a cute Craftsman-style house on the south side of town a few streets away from Lake Hollingsworth, an area Shea used to think of as the rich side of town.

"Don't hate me because I didn't grow up on the north side," he said scarfing down toast.

"I used to want to live on this side of town. I thought that it was far enough away from people who knew what my dad was like and we could all start over. I could go to the performing arts high school and Evie could go off to the University of Florida. Something about that dream felt right. Doable."

"Why didn't you go to the performing arts school? I bet you would have gotten in."

"I did get in. But then the accident happened and everything changed."

He nodded in understanding, his eyelids fluttering.

"Come on, sleeping beauty. Let's get you to bed."

She followed him into the house and starting turning down the blinds. His place was homey, comfy leather couches and chairs made of tweed. His desk, a large, heavy wood piece, sat in a room off the living room and was covered with books and paper. A large kid's dictionary sat on a chair, as did an even larger thesaurus.

"I'm going to call Evie and I'll let myself out when she comes," she said as he fell onto the couch.

"Just take my car," he mumbled from the cushions.

Shea pulled out her phone to text her sister but paused when she saw a pile of books, all with the same cover, stacked on the floor. Three similar piles were next to it. Four different books, each stack the same height. They looked to be books for kids. She picked one up.

"Hey, Leo. What's this?" She stood next to the couch and showed him the book. Why would he have stacks of kid's books? Her mind ticked off the possibilities. Some were not good.

He cracked an eyelid open. "It's mine," he mumbled and just as quickly closed his eye.

"Yours?"

He lifted his hand and wrapped it around her calf then opened one eye again. He looked at the book then back at her and she saw a slight lift to his mouth.

"You are the prettiest girl I've ever seen. I wanted to tell you that at the wake but thought it might be inappropriate."

She laughed softly and bent to brush the hair from his forehead.

"When I listen to you sing I feel like I can beat any odds. That everything is fixable." His voice faded off as he closed his eye.

She was grateful his eyes were closed and that he was unaware of the impact his words had on her. If she were to look in a mirror, she was one hundred percent positive her cheeks would be flaming red. No one had ever said such a lovely thing to her without wanting something in return: sex, to mold her into what they thought a country star was, to steal her songs.

"Leo, did you write this book?" she whispered.

"Mm-hm." His hand dropped from her leg and the beginnings of a soft snore came from him.

She scanned the cover and flipped open the book to the back page looking for the author information.

Leo Davis lives in the South where he enjoys watching sports and pretending he's a famous quarterback. As a child, he had a difficult time learning to read, and writing was just as hard. Catching a ball came easy to him, but like the boys in his adventure stories—sometimes doing what's easy does not lead to happiness. With a lot of hard work and determination, Leo was able to improve his reading and, since he wrote this book, his writing, too. If you have a hard time with writing, reading, or even math, just know, you're not alone. Ask someone for help. Make time to practice and review what you know. Leo Davis was able to do it and you can, too.

Shea opened the book and read a few of the pages. It was clearly written for the enjoyment of all levels of readers. With her phone, she researched his pseudonym. Although no picture came up, there were several articles about high interest, low-reading-level chapter books, and Leo was one of the bestselling authors in that market. Parents were raving about how his books appealed to a wide variety of kids who weren't able to read at their grade level yet weren't embarrassed to read these books because the cover spoke of a content that wasn't geared to the developmentally younger child.

Taking a sheet of paper off his table and a pen she found on the floor, Shea wrote *Call me* and left her number. She kissed him on the cheek, covered him with a light blanket, and stepped out onto his porch. She texted Evie to come get her and while waiting on his porch swing, began reading his book.

5

When daylight comes, I run outside, I want to play but I want to hide.
There is only so much time to be the child who is wild and free.~
"WHISKEY AND WATER."

"What do you mean we will have to reschedule?" Shea
tried to keep her voice even, her pitch from rising as
she stared at the lawyer's secretary.

"I'm sorry. Mr. Watson has been delayed at court and is unable
to meet with you all today. I left a message on your voice mail."

Evie pulled out her phone, showed it to Shea, and sure enough
a little red number rested above the phone icon. "When will Mr.
Watson be able to see us?"

"Let me see. Friday?"

Shea tried not to groan. She was going to have to tell Evie
what was going on. She was going to have to drive back to Nashville, have the interview, and then come back down to meet with
the lawyer. She might jinx her chance by filling her sister in, but
what other option did she have?

"We'll take it," Evie answered.

"But if something comes up sooner, could you please call us. We'd like to resolve this as soon as possible," Shea added.

"His docket is pretty tight. It's unlikely something will open up." The secretary gave them an apologetic look.

"How about the following week? Next Monday?" Shea asked.

Another look of pity from the secretary before she said, "Mr. Watson will be on vacation for three weeks beginning Monday."

Evie gave her a puzzled look before turning back to the secretary. "What time Friday?"

"Nine."

"Perfect. We'll see you then. Thank you," Evie said to the secretary then turned to push Shea toward the door.

Shea paused in the hallway, torn between wanting to leave but needing to stay and fix the appointment issue.

"What's going on?" Evie demanded once they were outside the old house turned law office.

Shea searched for the right words. "I can't be here Friday."

"I thought you didn't have a time line?"

"I have an interview in Nashville Friday."

Evie searched her face. "Interview for what?"

"To be a music writer on a kids' show."

Evie raised her brow. "I didn't know you had an interest in that."

Truth was, Shea didn't. What she had an interest in was steady work, building her name, and being a responsible adult.

"I think I'm interested. I need to be there Friday morning. I can drive up Thursday and then drive back when Mr. Watson gets back from his vacation." She liked the idea of coming back for a second trip.

Evie nodded. "Ok," she whispered.

Shea headed for the office but turned back when she realized Evie wasn't following her.

"Ev?"

Her sister burst out crying. "I'm sorry, Shea. I know it's selfish of me. Please don't hate me but I can't wait. Isn't there another solution?" She turned her back to Shea and buried her head in her hands.

"I could never hate you." From behind, she wrapped her arms around her sister and held on. If she knew one thing about Evie, it was that she hated people to see her cry.

"I can't go back to that place," Evie said between sobs.

Shea had never thought about how Evie must feel, working at the place where their momma had lived and died. Her first and only job as an occupational therapist had been at the nursing home and she chose that so she could be close to momma. Shea wouldn't want to go back either. She rested her head against her sister's and let her own tears fall.

"Then don't go back. Quit."

Evie dropped her hands from her face and held on to Shea's arms. "That's what Grady said but I can't. We have a small emergency fund and I don't want to use that just so I can quit a perfectly good job. I can't quit until I find another one but if I—" She broke again.

"If you had the insurance money you'd be able to quit and you can't get that until we read the will and you need me here so the will can be read," Shea answered for her.

Evie nodded. "I hate even thinking about using that money and asking you to stay. Can you have them push back the interview? Can you catch a plane and maybe be able to do them both? I know you're miserable here. You even get hives, but could you stay to get this resolved?"

"Actually, I'm not miserable and I don't know if you've noticed but I haven't had hives the last few days, so stop worrying about me. You've given enough to me. Now it's time to take care of you. You and Grady. I'll call my agent and see what she can do."

"I love you, you're my sister. I will always worry about you."

"I know. I love you, too." Shea hugged her sister tighter. "We're a mess, you and I."

"How so?"

"Well, aside from crying in a parking lot, I think we still live our lives waiting for the bottom to fall out. If you go back to that job and stick this money in the bank, never to be touched, momma will roll over in her grave. This is what she did it for. This is an opportunity. She's giving you security that gives you choices."

Evie nodded and sucked in a ragged breath.

"Let's go by your work so you can give notice. Come on." Shea dragged Evie to the car and pushed her into the passenger seat, and took her keys. "I'll drive, that way you can't find an excuse to chicken out."

"It'll be hard going into the building."

"Yeah, but we'll do it together."

Twenty-four hours later Leo called her. He sounded well rested and back on his game and still very excited that he'd had a breakthrough but terrified that what he'd written would be incoherent gibberish.

Evie and Grady were in the back yard grilling out, celebrating Evie's decision to quit. There was a noticeable change with Evie who seemed lighter and less worried now that she was no longer tied to her job.

Shea stepped out of the house and tucked her phone into her skirt pocket. "Do you all mind that I invited Leo over for dinner?" she asked and sat in the chair next to her sister.

"Not at all. I like Leo," Evie said.

"He's got a mean spiral," Grady added.

Life was moving on since the funeral. Maybe not like she'd expected it to. Kimberly was unable to change the interview and in that moment Shea had picked. She chose family. There were no flights that could get her to Nashville and back in time to do both appointments, even if she left today. The prospect of flying to L.A. was in discussion. Regardless, Shea was prepared to lose the opportunity. Giving back to her sister had now become the top priority. They needed to read the will to start the healing process.

Leo arrived with a watermelon tucked under his arm. He was dressed more like the guy she'd initially met, khaki shorts and a polo shirt, his hair combed away from his face.

They all made small talk at first but when Evie and Grady stepped inside to bring out the steaks and another pitcher of iced tea, Leo leaned toward her and smiled.

"What?" she asked.

"Took something from my house, didn't you?" He rested his arms across his knees.

"I borrowed a book," she said.

"Did you read it?"

"Yes, and I like it a lot. I can see why it appeals to kids."

He nodded, and then smiled. "Thanks."

"Why haven't you told anyone? You should be telling the world. Going to schools and speaking to the students."

He shrugged. "I spent a long time trying to overcome my belief that I was a stupid kid. Once I understood that I learned differently, that I had a learning disability, everything began to change. People see me as a regular guy, not a guy who struggles with reading. I like that."

She nodded because she understood. She had liked being in Nashville, away from Lakeland, because no one saw the Shea whose daddy drank too much and couldn't keep it private. No one knew that he'd died and nearly killed her momma or that she had an arrest record by the time she was fifteen for shoplifting. But she was so alone there and here she felt a part of something more, here she had history, good and bad.

"You should tell people. That's just my opinion and I'll keep your secret but you should tell." She reached out and took his hand.

"You should do the same." He laced his fingers with hers.

"What do you mean?"

"The music. You should tell your sister about the music."

The back door opened and Evie came out carrying a pitcher of tea. "Who wants a refill?" She glanced at their entwined hands but didn't say anything.

"I'll take some more, please," Shea said.

The DJ on the stereo introduced the next song and "Whisky and Water" came on.

"Grady, babe. Could you turn the station, please?" Evie asked as she refilled Shea's glass. Evie couldn't meet her gaze and when she turned to put the pitcher down, Shea watched her blow out two slow breaths and reach back to twist her hair around her fingers, something she did when she was unsettled.

Her song reminded Evie of their dad the same way coffee did Shea.

Leo gave Shea's hand a squeeze and when she turned to him, his reassuring smile gave her strength.

Shea gripped his hand and took a deep breath. "Actually, Ev, I'd like to hear it. It's not often a person gets to hear a song they wrote on the radio. Besides that, every time it plays, I get paid. I'm sorry you don't like it." That part hurt the most. But knowing why her sister didn't like her work softened the blow.

Evie sat on the edge of the deck, the tea pitcher clutched in her arms. "I knew you wrote a few songs and sold some, too, but you never said any had made it big."

"This one just took off. Caught me by surprise."

"That's how you were able to get all those flowers for the funeral, right? I was so worried that you were spending all your hard-earned cash. I knew you were working lots of jobs like the one at the museum."

"It's a cash cow. A cathartic one at that." Shea let go of Leo's hand and went to sit next to her sister.

"It's a hard song for me to hear, Shea. It's not that I don't like it. It's that it reminds me of us."

"It is us. I'll admit that at first I was hurt that you didn't like it, but I get it now." She wrapped an arm around her sister's shoulder.

"So you're famous now."

"It's gotten me some recognition." Not wanting to add to her sister's guilt, she'd told her that the interview had been changed.

"But to write this and then write kids' music, they don't seem to match."

"They don't. But it's a job that pays."

"Yeah, apparently so is song writing." Evie nudged her with her elbow. "But what about being a singer?"

Shea glanced at Leo, took a deep breath, and said, "I'm giving that up. I don't want to break into it anymore."

"You want to be a songwriter?"

Shea nodded.

"Really?" Evie whispered. "That sounds great. But you saw how much everyone loved this song. You should do more of this. If momma's money is going to be used for me to start over, why can't it do the same for you?"

Shea gave her words thought. Could she finally have one job and be a songwriter? "I dunno. I guess it can."

"Then you can write what you want." Grady chimed in.

She grinned sheepishly first at Evie and then Leo. "But I want the steady income."

"You could do that with royalties. Granted they aren't steady with amounts but they arrive in a predictable fashion," Leo said.

"And you could write songs from anywhere. Like here for example. You could use the insurance money as a cushion." Evie added.

"I could live here. See you all the time," Shea said, considering the idea for the first time.

"I would love that." A tear fell from Evie's eye. "More than anything I would love that."

Shea wrapped her arms around her sister, the tea pitcher between them, and held on.

Grady reached between them and took the pitcher, opening up the space for them to have a proper hug. "I think this is what your momma meant when she used to say 'good grief,'" Grady said. "Because even in all the hurt good things happen. Like a sister coming home. You're welcome to stay as long as you like, Shea. Should you decide to stay."

She looked between the people who were her family and now her community and nodded. Life was about the day to day, and how those days added up. Until now, her numbers had been equating to a negative balance. If she went back to Nashville or even LA there would be no family and little laughter. Maybe she'd begin to feel like she belonged somewhere when she was at work but that was work. That could end on a dime. What she had in front of her was far more than that.

"I'm staying," she told them and a cheer erupted from the small crowd.

Once dinner was over, Shea walked Leo to his car. They leaned against it, their shoulders pressed together as they angled into one another, their hands brushing.

"Now your secret's out but I'm still holding on to mine." Leo played his fingers with the tips of hers as they both looked at the crescent moon.

"I'm not sure I understand why it's a secret to begin with."

He looked down and toed the ground, so she wrapped his hand in hers and squeezed.

"School was hard. I was lucky because my parents got me tutors and lots of support but I had a teacher tell me I'd never be what I wanted to be because reading and writing was so difficult. Sure, I had lots of other teachers tell me the opposite but it's easier to hear the negative than the positive. So sports became my outlet. It felt good after a horrible study session to go hit several balls with a bat and stats were something I could memorize and have conversations about. But my mom would read to me. She always did, since I can remember. I'd get lost in those stories and want to be those characters and, in class, when I didn't understand what was going on, I'd daydream. Make stories up. Then I'd come home and tell my mom and she'd help me write my ideas down."

"Your mom sounds amazing."

"She is. Both my parents are. They told me I could do whatever I wanted and helped me achieve it."

"And look at you now."

"I don't tell anyone because I like who I've become and..."

"But who you've become is a part of who you were. I'm not saying you should take out an ad or anything. I'm just saying you are the perfect person to tell another young boy or girl that they can beat the odds. I'd have liked to hear that when I was a kid."

The silence that lingered was a comfortable one. A simple night among friends and family had become the moment to start fresh. To start building her home.

"I like you," he said.

"I like you, too."

"I'd like to kiss you again."

"Just once? You'd like to kiss me again just once?" she teased.

"I'd like to try one right now and see where it goes." He turned toward her and slid his free arm around her waist, his other tucked snuggly with hers, and gently pulled her up against him.

"I might not be able to stop at one," he whispered.

"I might not want you to." She stretched up on her toes and brought her lips to his. They came together with a soft caress, each savoring the moment until Leo growled and pulled her tighter, deepening the kiss. When they came apart both were out of breath and grinning uncontrollably.

"I'd like to take you out. On a date."

"Ok."

"Good, I'll call you." He gave her a light kiss before stepping back, his fingers trailing down her arm. "If I don't go now I'm not sure I'll be able to go. I could stand out here and talk to you forever."

"Forever is a long time."

Leo stood with his driver side door open. "Emily Dickinson said, 'Forever is composed of nows'. Night, Shea."

"Night, Leo."

She stood on the porch and watched him drive away. In the small beam of the front light, she looked at her hive-free arms. With Leo and Evie, and her friends for that matter, she'd not had any issues with hives. Only when faced with her actions as a teenager, or rather her fear of people remembering her antics, did she experience hives. Aside from Mr. Hubbs, one old man with a grudge and maybe some guilt about how he raised his own kid, those antics appeared to have been long ago archived.

At the funeral, Lorelei said momma had wanted to her to fly. Shea reckoned now was as good a time as any, as she stood on the precipice of change, to make the leap into the familiar unknown.

EPILOGUE

SIX MONTHS LATER

When I slip, he lifts me up. When I falter, he pulls me along. There's no walking in circles, just a strong hand guiding me home.~
"FINDING HOME."

Shea looked through the index cards and back at Leo, puzzled. "I don't think I understand."

"It's a treasure hunt. Each place the people go will give them a clue and lead them to another place. It culminates at my parents' ice cream shop."

"I understand what a treasure hunt is. What I don't understand is why we're going to great lengths to make this 'treasure hunt' work when it's only referred to in a small section of your fiction book. No one will be going on the hunt."

"What? Are you kidding? What if the kids of this town read my book, which I think one or two might, and want to reenact what they read? I have to make sure it's safe before I send these edits back and the book comes out."

Shea rolled her eyes. "Funny, I understand that as well. The great lengths to which I'm referring is this is our third dry run on this hunt and—"

"All right, I get it. I'm being anal-retentive. Humor me." He crossed his arms over his chest in defense.

Shea leaned into him and placed a gentle kiss on his lips. Ten months together wasn't a long time but they'd taken each day slowly, learning about each other and how to be each other's friend as well as lover. Being with Leo filled her so completely that she never imagined people could be this happy. She'd been the one to think bliss was hyperbole. But Leo, he was bliss. Walking away from the interview had been the best thing she'd done. She'd never looked back and had since sold a handful more songs, two more breaking into the top ten.

"I love you. Anal retention and all," she whispered and slid her hands down his arms.

"I'm counting on that. I love you." He pulled her into a tight embrace, bent her back, and kissed her hard before setting her back upright, swatting her on the rear and then walking away. "Come on, let's go find a treasure," he said, holding the door open for her.

"At least there'll be ice cream at the end," she mumbled.

The first three stops were fun, but by the fourth stop Shea found her "fervor" waning, and the cool air conditioning of the car far more appealing than the triple digit summer temps.

Leo pulled in front of the city library and idled. "I suppose you're right. I'm stalling."

"It's time to have faith and set the book free. Babe, kids are going to love it."

"I hope so. I guess there's no real point following the path the characters in the book followed. We've done it before—"

"Three times."

He turned to her and smiled. "Yeah, three times. I guess we can just call it a day and head home."

Home. She loved it when he said that to her. As of two weeks ago, they'd made a home together. Albeit sometimes a messy one when he was heavy into the story or she was working on a song, but it was theirs and it was everything she thought home should be: comfortable, safe, fun, and shared with people she loved.

"Wait, while we're here maybe we should get a fish sandwich. We're in short supply of groceries at home. I was planning on swinging by the store after I met up with Evie and the baby." She grinned, knowing he would tease her for being addicted to the fish sandwiches she'd made a staple in her weekly diet.

"Fish sandwiches sound awesome." Leo's stomach growled to echo his point. He parked the car in a shaded spot and together, her hand in his; they ran across the street to the little fish stand and placed their order.

"Want to sit in the park and eat them?" she asked.

He shrugged. "Sure, find a shaded bench." He led her back across the street and followed her to the same bench where she'd played the banjo and teased him about ninja unicorns.

She came from around a large tree and stopped short before sitting on the bench. She gasped, her hands coming to her mouth. She turned to him with tears in her eyes. Painted on the bench were the words "Marry me, Shea Barker. Be mine forever."

Leo was on one knee, an emerald engagement ring extended out toward her.

"I don't know when I fell for you, exactly. Maybe because I feel like I've loved you my entire life. With you, I've found the last part of my missing pieces. Because of you, I am whole, complete. Please say that you'll let me spend the rest of my life loving you."

She nodded, tears streaming down her face. "Of course I'll marry you."

He was up off his knee in a flash and had her in his arms, kissing the tears from her face.

If life was full of small moments like this, moments where Leo held her, laughed and loved her, then she'd take those little snapshots of time because when put together that reel was a big picture she'd be proud of. Finding him was finding herself. It was finding home.

HE'S THE

&A Coming Home Short Story&

ONE

KRISTI ROSE

Vintage Housewife Books

PO BOX 841

Farmington, MO 63640

www.kristirose.net

Book Layout © 2014 BookDesignTemplates.com

Cover Design © 2015 Paper and Sage Designs

Edited by CMD Editing

He's the One/ Kristi Rose. -- 1st ed.

❀ Created with Vellum

DEDICATION

This book, in particular, required consulting with experts in several areas.
I like to recognize them and say THANKS for their patience as I asked awkward and/or sensitive questions.

Dr. B. - Who, as she tried to address my own healthcare issues, patiently answered my book questions and never once thought I was a nut job. Or, at least, didn't make me feel like she thought I was a nut job:-)

Rachel- Who tolerated lots of questions on a very sensitive subject matter that takes women on an emotional trip. XO.

Dee- Who's journey was an inspiration.

Rachael and Justin- who answered lots of fire questions on the fly.

My friends who tolerated Facebook pleas for help and answered insurance questions: Marin, James, Scott, Shawn, and Jamie. Awesome, you all are.

THANK YOU <3

A forever optimist, Melinda Bane practiced the belief that if life didn't work out like she'd expected, and frequently it hadn't, she'd find a silver lining somehow. When life handed you poop, use it for compost.

Now, she had this.

Her poor house! The beautiful back sunroom, the space she loved the most, was gone, and with it her refuge, burnt to a state of smoking remains and scorched walls. She wasn't sure how to spin the loss into something positive. If that was even possible.

After moving back home ten years ago to buy into her family's diner, Melinda had driven by the 1930s Craftsman, fallen instantly in love, and bought it. The first act of her much needed life do-over. Something about the quaint neighborhood with the picket fences had said "home," and the purchase had rejuvenated her. Melinda had found her footing and left her two ex-husbands and her impulsively-made, poor-decision life firmly behind her.

"The fire's out, but you're gonna need to tarp the area, at a minimum." Shawn, the fireman, was tall, but then most guys were tall to her since she barely reached five-foot-three inches in her stocking feet. She had to focus on his mouth in order to process what he was saying.

She nodded, looked away toward the horizon, noticed light was creeping into the dark sky, and made herself count to fifty. Maybe the fire was a sign. Maybe she was going about things all wrong once again.

She would not cry. She would not cry.

Her lawn was soaked from the fire hose, and the chill of the water seeped into her slippers. The pungent aroma of charred wood permeated her senses, and Melinda wasn't sure if it was the smell, the ruined room, or the loss of her dream that made her want to empty her stomach into the hosta plants she had placed along her property line.

Every dime she'd saved for the last five months was likely going to go into repairing her house. She rubbed her empty womb and felt the impact of the fire at her very core. Two failed attempts at inter-uterine insemination had been demoralizing, each with a depression that had lasted for weeks. But the loss of this third attempt was going to set her for months emotionally, and the fire would do the same financially.

Melinda swallowed the lump in her throat then sucked in a ragged breath.

All those additional hours at the diner, cutting out cable TV, sacrificing little extras like going to the movies, dinner out, or buying new clothes, and forgoing her monthly facials had been easy when she'd first started down this path. For nearly two years, she hadn't had a vacation that went beyond reading a book in her backyard hammock, a day at Clearwater Beach, or swimming in her parent's pool. But lack of success was wearing on her, and even though time away would do her wonders, that wasn't about to happen. More sacrifice was in her future.

"You're lucky we got here before it caught the rest of the house on fire," fireman Shawn said, shifting uncomfortably. "As it is, the back wall will likely need to be replaced." He offered her a blanket.

"Yes, lucky. That's me." If by luck he meant bad, she'd believe that. Good luck would have been her putting the fire out with the large pan of water she'd splashed on it as soon as her brain processed what was happening.

She shook her head, refusing the blanket, crossed her arms over her chest, and tried to chase the chills of loss away by rubbing her upper arms.

"You're insured, right? It should cover this." He indicated to the empty space where her sunroom used to be and a large gaping hole. In the house's original state, the opening had been the back door, but was now an invitation for the out of doors to come on in.

She nodded. Yes, it would be covered, but insurance was slow, and initially she'd be on the hook for retainers and other costs, forcing her to spend her make-her-dreams-come-true money earmarked for the clinic next Friday. Her small emergency stash wouldn't even cover a fraction of what she would need to fix this disaster. Either way, her plans had just come to a screeching halt.

Normally one to seize life by the belt and drag it behind her, Melinda felt as if she'd taken a hit to the chest. One day she was going to stop being so optimistic. Stop believing that she might have a say in how her life played out, that something might go her way because, today, life kicked her in the balls.

Fireman Shawn tapped his helmet against his leg. "Are you gonna be all right here, Melinda? Can I call your mom and dad for you? I hate seeing you like this."

How long had she'd known him? Since kindergarten for sure, maybe even before that. If memory served, she'd spent seven minutes in heaven with him at one of his famous parties in high school. "How are your kids?"

"Fine. A handful. Crazy how opposite they are. Thanks, by the way, for scoring those Comic-con tickets. You made my little Star Wars fan a happy guy that weekend."

Melinda shrugged. It had been a no brainer to pass along the tickets someone had given her. She had no interest in the event but knew Shawn's youngest son did because that was all he talked about when she'd see him at the diner.

"But I was asking about you. You don't look so good."

"I'm ok. I'll call my—"

"Holy hell, Melly. I don't know if I brought enough tarps."

Melinda turned and, through the glow cast from the neighbor's porch light and beams from the fire truck, watched Jared Calhoun cross her yard.

"What? How?" She squinted her eyes at him. "What are you, construction's version of an ambulance chaser?"

Jared laughed. "I'm a volunteer firefighter. You know that. I heard it on the scanner and recognized the address. Shawn." He held out his hand to the tall fireman.

"Jared. You got this under control?"

Jared pulled a hammer from his back pocket, flipped it over before catching it with one hand. "I can get it tarped before the sun is fully up." He turned to Melinda. "But I'd worked faster if I had some coffee."

She stared at the smoldering building. The parallel to how her dreams had just gone up in smoke nearly caused her to burst out in laughter. Her emotions were on a spin cycle and, in seconds, she went from being simultaneously angry and sad to being bitter and desperate.

She couldn't get sucked into the negative what-if's. She needed to pull strength from her reserves and focus. This was only a setback. Her baby goal was certainly worth all the sacrifices and would continue to be.

"Melinda?" Jared said.

"What?" She looked at him and blinked away her pensiveness, "Yes, coffee. OK." She turned to the fireman. "Thanks, Shawn. Tell the family hi."

She cinched the belt on her pink silk robe and began the walk to the front of her house, her matching silk, pink mule slippers sinking into the wet earth with each step. By the time she stepped onto the porch of her beloved, traitorous house, the fur trim on her slippers was matted and drooping, much like her spirits.

Once inside her foyer, she slipped off her mules and tread the rest of the way in her bare feet. From the sanctuary of her kitchen, she could almost pretend that everything was as it should be. Almost, but the acrid residual smoke made her eyes water and, as she leaned over her sink and looked out through the window at the brightening sky, blinking back tears, she considered bailing. Moving to another city or state and starting over.

Maybe this was the universe's way of threatening her, telling her to get out. She'd long come to terms with being unlucky in love. She'd given it her best shot, repeatedly, and had finally looked past the idea of Mr. Right, two-point-five kids, and a dog. She had the house with a picket fence but now with a burned backside and the irony of that made her laugh out loud. She shook her head, refusing to give in to such internal histrionics. She'd had plenty of setbacks before. Today would be no different. She'd get past it and somehow figure out a way to keep to her plan. Hopefully. Because any other option would simply not do. No, sir.

The banging of Jared's hammer echoing through her house caused her to jump. Pulling herself from her pity party, she brushed her eyes with her sleeve, then turned to fill her electric teapot before setting it to boil. On autopilot, she measured out the scoops of coffee for her French Press and poured scalding water into it, all while forcing her head back in the game and trying to construct some sort of contingency plan.

She'd have to cancel her appointment and, though she could now predict her ovulation to within a day, stress was going to play havoc with her cycle. She couldn't assume it would be as predictable as it currently was. Melinda groaned in dread. She was back to taking her daily temperature, a task she'd long come to believe a necessary evil. If she had to wait for a third try, she needed to ensure the margin of error of around her ovulation cycle was next to none. She couldn't afford to lose the opportunity over complacency.

She set two mugs on the counter and checked the coffee. To pass the remaining minutes of brew time, she called her father to tell him she wouldn't be in and why. After at least fifty "No, I don't need your help," she went into her office to find her policy and the company's number.

A long term pro at self sufficiency, Melinda inhaled a deep breath through her nose and exhaled it slowly through her mouth, squared her shoulders, and shuddered back the tremors that were threatening to overcome her.

After calling in the fire to the claims department, she poured the coffee, added creamer to Jared's, and turned to take it to him, only to find him standing in the kitchen doorway, staring at her feet.

"That should hold you for now, but I don't like that you're exposed. I'll send a crew out as soon as I can to get a temporary door in place so you can lock yourself in the house." He reached for the mug; dark smudges of soot were on his hands and face. The knees of his pants were damp, and his hammer hung from a belt loop.

"Thanks," she said.

He rubbed a hand over his shaven head, leaving a streak of soot in its wake. "Here." He pulled out a chair from her small kitchen table. "You need to sit. You're in shock."

"I'm OK."

"Your eyes are bigger than the mug you're holding, and you're pale. Really pale. Sit."

"Jared—"

"Sit." He pushed the chair closer to her. "You can yell at me all you want but not until you sit."

On a huff, she plopped into the chair and promptly burst into tears.

"Hey, hey." He put his coffee cup on the floor, took hers, and placed it next to his, then squatted in front of her. "It's all fixable. Insurance will replace everything. What's important here is that you're safe, and once I get a temporary door on there, you'll be even safer. You're lucky you caught it in time." Crouching beside her, they were eye to eye, and he wrapped his arms around her.

She rested her head on his shoulder. "I was awake."

"I'm sorry…what?"

He stroked her hair and Melinda closed her eyes. "I was awake. It sparked from the outlet and traveled up the wall. I tried to put it out, but I couldn't get water to it fast enough."

"You don't have a fire extinguisher?"

His voice was low and soothing, but that didn't stop her from becoming defensive. She pushed against him and straightened up. "No, Jared. I do not have a fire extinguisher. But you can be assured that I will have one from now on."

"Hey, I'm not faulting you. If I had known you didn't have one, I would've got one for you."

"It's not your job to take care of me. I take care of me." She used the heel of her hand to wipe her tears. The last thing she wanted was to become dependent on him more than she already was. Over the last ten years he'd slowly become a greater part of her life, their friendship cementing with time. The number of guys she'd dated had dwindled, and her time with Jared had increased so much these past two years he'd become a staple in her life. She enjoyed the days when he came into the diner for breakfast or popped over on Wednesdays with takeout after his builders' meeting. Looked forward to them, actually. She missed him when she didn't see him, and if he started buying her safety equipment and doing husbandly things like checking her tires, she'd be in a heap of trouble. One day he might be someone else's husband, and then where would she be?

"Melinda, when are you gonna realize that I'm here to help? You're family."

"I was married to your brother for forty-three days over four-

161

teen years ago. We were stupid kids. That doesn't make me family."

"But once a Calhoun, always a Calhoun."

Stupid, stupid man. With stupid words that twisted in her heart. If he called her family one more time, she was going to hit him where it hurt.

She sighed with exhaustion. "I appreciate you coming by, Jared. The insurance people are sending someone in a few hours, so I guess I should get ready." She leaned against the back of the chair.

Jared rolled back on his heels, sat on the floor, stretching his long legs before him, and picked up his mug.

"I'll wait here while you shower and get ready. I'm not OK with you doing those things with a tarp as your only barrier."

"You really don't have to—"

"Yes, I do. Now go. You mind if I make something to eat? I'm starved."

Melinda shook her head and eased out of the chair. She stepped over his legs and walked as quickly as she could to her room to grab clothes. After closing herself off in the bathroom, she turned on the shower, then sat on the floor and waited for the water to get hot. Sucking in deep breaths, she forced back her tears.

Living with regret was inevitable if one chose to actually live their life, and Melinda had done just that. She made no apologies for it. But, if she could undo one thing—just one—it would be her marriage to Jared's younger brother, Lance. Not because she regretted her time with him. No, they were both young and stupid and caught up in the moment of thinking they knew it all and deserved the world. She would undo it because, more than anything, she wanted a nice guy to share her life with. And the nice guy she'd come to picture was the one that had knelt before her, rubbed her back, talked about buying her a fire extinguisher, and called her family.

2

———————

S tunned, Melinda stared at the insurance guy. "But I had the house inspected before I bought it, and they said the electrical was all to code."

"I'm sorry, but not all of it is. Looks like this room was built without a permit and the wiring was piggybacked onto the old system. Not to code at all. If they did that here, then any other room that was remodeled by them is likely at risk, as well."

She looked toward the updated kitchen and laundry room add-on that had been so appealing when she purchased it, but now might spark a fire at any moment.

"What do you suggest?"

"Getting a contractor in here as soon as you can to get it fixed. I have to put it in our files that you have faulty wiring. Send in the proof of permits and work, and we'll update everything." He ripped off a check from his pad. "Here, this should help get you started. I'm sorry to be the bearer of bad news."

She took the check. "I understand. You're only doing your job."

With a handshake, they ended the meeting. Processing what he'd told her, Melinda watched the insurance man walk away. With the check flapping lightly in the breeze, she wondered if she should let the place burn down if it were to light up again. Start over. Get something newly built. It would be far easier than tackling this obstacle.

Melinda wanted to kick herself. It was that mentality that had ruled most of her twenties and led to poor relationship decisions. Starting over might seem easier, but the payback was always two-fold, and she wasn't getting any younger. Her baby-having days were limited as they were. Starting over would only postpone that further.

A crew of three guys snapped her out of her reverie when they came around the corner.

"Hey, Melinda," called Keith, Jared's youngest brother.

"Hey, Keith. What are you doing here?" She opened her arms and pulled him into a hug. She'd always liked Keith whose child-like mind managed to stay innocent no matter how old he got.

"I'm helping the crew today. I'm the supply runner." He showed her where a variety of tools hung from his belt.

"Sounds like a busy day for you then."

"Jared said for you not to worry. We'll get you fixed up real good."

"I have no doubt, Keith. No doubt." She squeezed his arm then glanced at her watch. "Hey, would you mind keeping an eye on things. I'm going to take this check to the bank."

"Sure thing, Melly. We'll make sure everything is locked up tight when we leave."

"Thanks." She leaned in, kissed his cheek, then chuckled when she saw the hint of a blush follow.

She made good time to the bank and decided to swing by her diner's competitor, Two Chicks and Bacon, for a cup of coffee. Sure, she could get a mug at her place, but then she'd have to deal with her father and his cronies that hung out there. At Lorelei and Andee's diner, she might actually have a moment of peace. Besides, they closed in a couple hours, and their traffic should be decreasing, whereas at her place the lunch crowd would be coming in.

She pulled in to the lot and took a moment to admire the cute gingham awning and the way the logo was painted on the large picture window. If Melinda were solely in charge of their diner, it would be cute like this. Where Lorelei's place was boutique in nature, Melinda's was most decidedly a greasy spoon, a quality, money-earning greasy spoon that embodied the concept of diner in every sense of the word.

She took a seat at the counter and waited for someone to notice her. Coming here was not a custom of hers. Like all diners, Two Chicks and Bacon had their regulars. Many were friends of the owners.

"Should I be worried that you're here? Lorelei asked as she leaned against the counter. Her baby bump was the first thing Melinda noticed.

"No, I just need a good cup of coffee and a quiet moment." Melinda flipped her hair over her shoulder, and then pulled out a menu. "And maybe something to eat, come to think of it." She hadn't eaten all day, and her day had started before the crack of dawn.

"I heard about your house. I'm sorry. Breakfast's on me," Lorelei said.

"What? No. You don't have—"

"I know I don't have to Melinda, but you've had a shitty day, and I want to." Lorelei's look dared her to protest. For the second time—the first being when Jared hugged her—she felt the tightness in her chest ease.

"Thanks. I'd love some blueberry pancakes." She put the menu back in the holder. Heavy comfort food might help ease her anxiety and tilt the balance back toward her status quo.

"Watch out boys, she'll chew you up. She's a man eater," Andee sung as she came around the counter. "Oh, hi Melinda. I didn't see you there."

It wasn't the first time people, usually girls, sang the Hall and Oates song around her. She knew people called her a man-eater behind her back—that and a host of other things. Melinda wanted to tell them all their gossip mongering only added more intrigue to her reputation, and contrary to popular belief, she'd never fooled around with a married man or even entertained the notion, never broke up a marriage, and no man had ever died while keeping company with her.

"Give it a rest, Andee. She's already been kicked in the face once today," Lorelei said.

"Oh man, sorry Melinda. I forgot about the fire. I just—"

"Hold it against me that I kissed Buck once back in high school?"

Buck was Andee's husband. Andee laughed and poured Melinda a cup of coffee. "No, girl. I should thank you for that, actually, because once you were done with him, he kissed better. Of course, I taught him everything else he knows." Andee laughed again. "I just like teasing you like I do everyone else."

She didn't know if being teased about her reputation was a compliment, but the fact that Andee was treating her like she did all her other friends spoke volumes. Andee and Lorelei had been friends since they were in diapers and hung in a tightly knit closed-off circle. Even the hint of being considered part of their fold blew Melinda's mind.

Andee leaned across the counter. "Can I ask for a favor?" Her voice was a whisper, and her eyes darted around the room.

Melinda leaned forward as well. "I'll admit that I'm nervous to hear about this so-called favor, but damn if I'm not curious."

Andee's lips twitched with a smile. "I need some help with women stuff."

"Please tell me we aren't having the period talk."

Andee smacked her on the side of the arm. "I need help with the...uh...art of...um."

"Conversation?"

"Seduction," Andee whispered, and sweat broke out above her brow.

Melinda sat back, stunned. A second later she leaned forward again, her brain racing. "Andee. You're beautiful. I can't think of a single thing I could show you that would make any improvement."

Andee smiled and played with her fingernails. "You walk into a room and people stop and look. I've seen you make grown men blush, and not from embarrassment but the sincerity in your flattery, and I don't think I can learn any of that in this lifetime, but maybe if you helped me pick out some clothes, taught me a few things about how to wear them, I might, you know, be able to apply them in a constructive manner."

"Are we talking about Buck here? Appling these new things to your husband? I know it's not any of my business, but—"

"Of course we're talking about Buck. What kinda woman do you think I am?"

Melinda stared at her, one brow arched, and bit her cheek to keep from smiling.

"Sorry. I guess I did kinda set it up wrong," Andee said.

"Kinda." She toyed with the handle on her coffee cup, waiting for Andee to continue.

"Listen, you're really good with clothes. You have really big..." She pointed to Melinda's chest.

"Boobies. So do you." Melinda pointed back. "But they're hidden under this tent of a shirt." She tugged at Andee's oversize peasant shirt.

"I know, and I think that's part of the problem. We've been together seventeen years, married ten, and he doesn't look at me like he used to. I figured since Bucky really likes my, you know, I could start there."

Melinda laughed. "They're breasts, honey. Boobies. Tits. It's OK to say it. We're grown women and they're a part of who we are."

Andee's cheeks were pink. "So are you in?"

167

"Why don't you ask Lorelei? She is your BFF."

Andee rolled her eyes. "Please. I want to va-va-voom my wardrobe, not turn it into beach-bum wear. That girl has more pairs of capris than should be legal. Call me crazy, but I don't think capris say 'sex me up.'"

Melinda laughed. She wasn't a capri girl, either. Melinda looked around the diner, uncertainty giving her pause. She might have known Andee most all her life, but they weren't part of the same crowd.

"What? Afraid to be seen with me or something? Not cool enough for you?"

Melinda snapped her eyes back to Andee. "Are you kidding? What will people say about the two of us suddenly hanging out and shopping?"

Andee pursed her lips. With an arched brow, she said, "Likely they'll say nothing, but wouldn't it be cool if they said we're having a secret affair. Oh, wait—maybe they'd say you, Buck, and I were, you know, having one of them ménage à trois. That would be awesome. No one ever says anything exciting about me."

Melinda smiled. "I'm not going to teach you to dress like me." She flipped her hair over her shoulder in an exaggerated gesture and ran her hand down her wine-colored wrap shirt. "Only I can pull that off, but I can help you find things that'll make you feel good about yourself, not uncomfortable if someone other than Buck looks at you. Which will happen, I assure you." She winked. "Yeah, I can definitely help you draw Buck's attention."

Andee pushed back from the counter and clasped her hands together in delight. "Can you go this weekend?"

"Sure, unless something with the fire hangs me up."

"Great. Thanks, Melinda. I'll drive. I have a big truck so there'll be plenty of room for us, our big boobies, and your ego."

Melinda laughed and waved her away. "Go away so I can eat my food in peace." She used her haughtiest tone while watching Lorelei deliver her pancakes.

Melinda swirled the butter around the top pancake, letting it soak in before she poured on a healthy serving of maple syrup. Just as she was about to dig in, the diner door swung open and in walked Jared. He didn't see her at first and called out greetings to Lorelei and Andee. He was about to slide into the seat three places down when he noticed her.

"Uh…" He straightened back up.

"What are you doing here?" She smiled, knowing she had him trapped.

"I came to check on you."

But Andee had already filled a mug of coffee for him and placed the creamer next to it. She knew how he drank it.

"I believe I'll call bull crap on that."

"Question is, why are you here? Don't you own a diner down the way?"

"I can go wherever I please."

"So can I."

"So much for the whole 'we're family' nonsense you were talking about this morning. If I went to another construction company, you'd lose your mind."

Briefly, Jared hung his head. When he looked back at her, his eyes twinkled. "Would you buy that I believe in supporting small businesses?"

She wanted to continue with the ribbing, but to be honest, the mood was gone. Who was this guy that hung out at Lorelei's diner? How often did he come? Enough that Andee knew how he liked his coffee.

Everything she thought she knew about Jared suddenly seemed wrong. Yes, being upset with him was stupid and unreasonable. He wasn't hers. He wasn't hiding a secret life or anything. Yet, when she looked into his laughing green eyes, it was obvious she'd been naive where Jared was concerned. She'd been a fool to believe she was a large part of his life like he was hers. She wanted to bang her head on the counter for being so stupid to think she knew all of Jared. That the times he'd come around her house or the diner or the Sunday dinners she still shared with his family was the sum of his life.

"It doesn't matter. I'm just giving you a hard time." She turned the conversation back to business. "When I left this morning, your brother and a few other guys were fixing the door to the house. Thanks."

He slid into the seat next to hers and turned to face her, his hand resting on his upper thigh. "I'll come by later to make sure it meets my standard. Did the insurance guy come already?"

She nodded. "Apparently, the back room was wired improperly, and so it's likely the other rooms that were updated were as well."

Jared gave a low whistle. "I'll get my electrician out there at the latest tomorrow. He'll figure it out, and then we'll know what to do."

Melinda could only stare at him, words of disapproval stuck in her throat. She simultaneously loved and hated it when he used the plural "we" when referring to her life. She wanted him to stop, but couldn't bear to tell him that.

"That's if you want my company to do the work. I'm giving you a good deal since you're family and all. But I can respect your need to get a second opinion."

She shook her head. "I'm good." It was such a relief not to have to juggle the construction aspect, as well. She'd held off canceling her inter-uterine insemination appointment in hopes that something might go her way, and coping with that alone was taking all she had.

"Good. You should eat those hotcakes before they get cold." He plucked a berry off the stack and tossed it in his mouth.

"Thanks, Jared," she said, tears threatening to break free.

He moved his arm to rest along the back of her chair and leaned over, placing a soft kiss on her temple. "I got your back, Melly. Let me take care of you."

Lord knows she wanted to lean into him and let him carry the burden. Even for a small amount of time. But her head told her heart to stop being so foolish. That depending on him made her weak and gave people the wrong idea about them. The last thing she wanted was for the gossips to natter on about her going through the sons of the Calhoun clan. Jared, or Keith for that matter, didn't deserve to be talked about like that simply because they were friends with her.

Reeling from it all, afraid her need for him and desire to be rescued was written across her face, Melinda asked for a box for her food.

"You leaving so soon?" Andee asked as she loaded the pancakes into a container.

Melinda nodded. "I have a lot to do. Call me about this weekend, Andee."

"Sure thing, hon." Andee said with a wink. "Lorelei made a to-go bag for you already." Andee placed the container into a cute brown sack with rope handles and handed it over. Melinda peered into the bag loaded with a plethora of comfort found in bakery items.

"Hey. You all right?" Jared grabbed her hand.

She looked at his hand covering hers and gave his a squeeze. "I'll see you tomorrow." She slid her hand from his and left the diner.

With nowhere else to go, she was forced to head home and face her current crisis once again. As she inspected the makeshift back door, the soot-covered back wall of her house, and the water damage, it took every bit of discipline not to eat the entire contents of the bag Lorelei had sent with her. Chances were high she'd follow up the bingeing with a good cry and end it by rocking in a ball.

Instead, she pressed a fresh batch of white coffee, shipped from the Pacific Northwest, turned it into an iced delight, and curled up on her porch swing with a good book. She didn't want to go inside and turn on a light, afraid she'd ignite another fire. She didn't want to think about everything that needed to be done or Jared's offer to help. In all her days, the highs and lows of marriages and break ups, she'd never felt as alone as she did at this moment. Yes, she had her parents, and even Jared's parents, but she didn't have that one person who would hold her when the sun went down and love away her fears.

H e was a fool. Actually, he'd always been one when it came to Melinda Bane, and the older he got, the more foolish he became. One simple remark from his may-not-be-bright-but-astutely-observant brother, Keith, about how sad she'd looked today, and Jared had jumped in his truck and drove to her house. He'd use any excuse to rescue the overly self-reliant woman, and this was the best opportunity to show her she could count on him.

Never mind he had bids to finish or that he was balls tired and had been looking forward to watching a game on TV. Nope, if there was even the slightest chance he might get Melinda to see him as something other than Lance's brother, he was going to take it. He'd always had a predilection for blond buxom bombshells, and Melinda was no different. Oh hell, who was he kidding? His affinity was for Melinda only—all the others were just poor imitations.

Jared pulled his truck along the curb a few houses down from Melinda's and watched her sit in the fading sun, staring out at nothing.

Thankful he'd had the wherewithal to assemble a game plan of sorts, he'd managed to interrupt his mad drive over with a stop at a Chinese takeout. Grabbing the bags of food and a fire extinguisher he'd picked up earlier, he then made his way to her porch.

"You do know that you can turn on the lights. The house isn't going to explode." He rested one foot on the first step and hoped she'd hear the jesting in his voice.

She didn't startle, just swung her weary gaze to him. "You don't know that. I thought the same thing last night when I turned on the light to the sunroom and sparks shot out of the outlet."

"I brought protection." He held up the extinguisher. "Come on, let's go live dangerously."

"That's not funny. This is my house, Jared. I don't want it to burn down." She didn't even raise her voice.

The fight in her was gone, and that's when Jared realized things were worse then he had thought. Emotional toughness was a part of who she was. Determination was what he'd come to expect from her and admired. Hell, it was one of the things he loved about her.

"Melinda, if you want, I can turn off some of the lines that feed into the part of the house you're worried about. My gut would be the laundry room and maybe your bathroom. But you've got enough natural light in the day to not need it, and tonight we can set up battery-operated lights to get you by. My electrician will be here tomorrow to get to the bottom of it."

"Would you, please? I'd feel better."

He nodded and climbed up on the porch. "Here, feel like some food? You can get this set up while I take a look at the fuse box."

She jumped up and smiled. "Thanks."

It took less than five minutes to power off her areas of concerns, and when he came into the dining room, she'd set the table with small hurricane lamps, dishes, and the food.

"You're OK with candles? Open fire?" He gestured to the lamps.

"Yeah, I feel like I can control those. Want a beer?" She was smiling, and he was immensely pleased he had something to do with that.

"Sure."

"Have a seat," she called from the kitchen. She came back into the dining room carrying two beers in each hand. She set all but one down, twisted off its top, and handed it to him. Damn, she turned him on. Had since the first day he'd laid eyes on her in high school. Then his fool-ass brother had to get his hands on her, initially to piss Jared off, but then Lance had realized she was the right sort of accessory—a pretty girl and a hard worker, and he needed both of those to support his Hollywood dream.

"I didn't realize I was hungry until I started putting this out. It smells so good. Thanks for bringing it." She plopped into a chair, pulled herself up to the table, and crossed her legs Indian style. With a sigh of pleasure, she reached for the first carton.

Jared took a swig of his beer and tried to keep his eyes from wandering to her legs or the way the seat cupped her cute ass. He was overcome with a strong need to place a languid kiss there.

Heat flooded his body as desire fought with common sense for control of his decision-making skills. He knew he couldn't kiss her, but man oh man, he really wanted to.

"I have to wash my hands." He stepped toward the hallway.

"Did you turn that fuse off?" she asked over her shoulder, dumping sticky rice onto a plate.

"Yeah."

"It'll be dark in there. There's a flashlight in the cabinet below the sink. Right side." She dipped a spring roll into sweet and sour sauce.

Jared found the flashlight, then closed the door behind him. He stood staring at his reflection, the limited light accentuating the bags under his eyes. His desire to be around her was growing each day. He loved her more today than yesterday, and the frustration of having to balance their friendship with what he really wanted was keeping him awake at night. The subtle yet dull throb in his temples told him a headache was coming on. All this repression was going to give him a stroke.

Opening the medicine cabinet, he searched for aspirin. His heart skipped a beat as he read the label on the second largest bottle. *Prenatal.*

They weren't the store bought ones either. These were prescription.

All the air in the room went still as a chill of dread ran down his spine. Jared wracked his brain trying to remember if he'd seen Melinda out with anyone or if she'd mentioned any dates. Whoever he was, Jared would kill him. The question was, slowly or quickly? Why wasn't he here? Why wasn't he in her life?

Maybe he didn't exist. Maybe she wasn't pregnant and taking the vitamins because that was something women did. Jared smiled and almost laughed out loud with relief. That had to be the answer. Never mind how moody she'd been. He could attribute that to the fire, and rightly so.

For good measure, he decided to look in the bottom cabinet. He didn't know what he'd find, but a reassurance that his assumptions were accurate would be nice. A giant box of those tampon things would go a long way. Tucked behind a roll of toilet paper was a book about the forty weeks of pregnancy and life after delivery.

Jared sat on the floor and stared at the picture of a baby in the womb. He placed the book back in the cabinet next to an ovulation kit and closed the cabinet doors. He definitely needed the aspirin now. After he used the counter's edge to pull himself up, he had to lean against it to wrestle off the childproof cap. After dumping two tablets in his hand, he placed the bottle back on the shelf while simultaneously knocking a thermometer off. Putting the thermometer back, he closed his eyes, refusing to see anymore. He tossed the pills into his mouth and swallowed them dry, then turned off the flashlight and placed it on the counter. With no light to guide him, he felt his way out of the bathroom, staggering into the light like a man who'd been in the dark far too long.

Melinda was shoveling food into her mouth, pausing only to take a swig of beer.

"I know you like to live on the edge, challenge life, but don't you think drinking is taking it too far?" He walked up to the table and snatched the beer from her hand.

"Hey! What in the hell? What are you talking about?"

"You have someone else to consider now."

Confused, she looked around. "Um…"

"The baby, Melinda. The baby. Do you really think you should be drinking while you're pregnant?" He slid into the dining chair next to her and took a long pull from her beer, finishing it off.

"Jared—"

"Whose is it? Why isn't he coming around?" He put her empty bottle on the table, then reached for his. He tossed it back, finishing it in three swallows. His gaze wandered to the two unopened bottles she had brought out earlier.

"I'm not pregnant." She reached for a bottle and twisted off the top. "But I want to be." She took a long swallow, her eyes still on him.

Jared's mind raced, dividing her remark into manageable bite-size pieces. It made sense she'd want a baby; most of their friends were having them. But he still couldn't figure out all the logistics.

"You got someone special on the hook that you're wanting to be the father of this baby?" This was what he really wanted to know, needed to know.

She sat back in her chair and snorted with what sounded like disgust. "Don't be such a knuckle dragger."

Yep, it was disgust.

"I don't need a someone special to have a baby."

"Melinda—"

"I can have a baby all by myself."

"Well, maybe science has changed since we were in school, but last I knew, you needed a man to contribute to the process."

"Exactly. Contribute, yes. Be present. Nope."

Jared was shaken. "Are you saying...?"

She leaned forward in her chair and put the bottle on the table. With both her hands free, she took the empty bottle from him, set it aside, and then cupped his hands in hers. "I know I've shocked you. That's why I haven't said anything. But I'm talking about inter-uterine insemination. I bought sperm from a bank."

"Melly..." He wanted to cover his ears, make her stop talking.

"It's hard for someone like you, Mr. Tradition, to wrap your mind around someone purposefully being a single parent, especially when you come from a family like yours."

"What's that supposed to mean? And what does it have to do with this?" He was pretty sure she'd just insulted him.

"You know, your mom has always been a stay at home mom. Doesn't she still do your laundry?"

"No." He pulled his hands from hers, then crossed his arms. Truth was she sometimes did.

"What I'm saying is that you don't know anything other than having two parents. One that worked all the time and one that was home all the time. In my situation, I'm purposefully assuming the role of both those people. That's something I'm sure doesn't align with your traditional values."

"Wow, that's the second time tonight you've referred to me as primitive. You come from the same type of family. How're your parents handling this? Or haven't you told them, either?"

She laughed, and the grip on his hand eased. "Funny enough my momma's torn between being appalled and overjoyed at potentially having a grandchild. I think the grandchild idea is tipping the scales because last week she emailed me an article about food that helps fertility."

"I don't know what to say." He searched her face. The vixen that he'd always associated her with being, a man's temptress, was not staring back at him. Instead, he saw a pleading earnestness in her expression, her beautiful face soft and vulnerable. Maybe even a little uncertain, and Melinda had always been all things confident.

"Say that you understand. That you'll still be friends with me when I'm cranky because I'm hugely pregnant or overly tired."

"You don't want to go about this in the typical way?" He tried to ask the question as delicately as he could without getting called a Neanderthal again.

"Yes, because I've been so successful at marriage in the past. I've tried the traditional route. I've dated so much that the folks of this town call me all kinds of names, and you know I'm right. What's the latest? That I'm a black widow. Any guy who stops and talks to me is having an affair with me. Women don't talk to me. There's no one in this stupid ass town left for me to date."

A thousand remarks threatened to escape, but the one repeating on loop in his head was she *hadn't* dated every guy in this stupid ass town. She'd overlooked him.

"What about other towns. Orlando? Tampa?"

"I've been on all the online dating sites. I've kissed more toads who stayed toads than I care to count. They stereotype me based on my looks. Think I'm vapid and without brain cells. That I don't know all those accidental brushings of their hands against my breast isn't their cheap shot of trying to feel me up. I've never been one to let life happen to me, and I'm not about to start now."

"But this is a baby."

"Yeah, I'm starting my own family. Plenty of women do it, and I aim to be one of them. Can't you understand, or try to understand, where I'm coming from?"

"Why does it matter if I do or not?"

She answered without hesitation. "Because you're my friend. Your opinion means a lot to me."

Removing his hands from hers, he stood and looked around the room, his eyes settling on Melinda. His friend. Horseshit. It was all horseshit. They had a friendship built on what exactly? What would she think if she knew he came around because he was looking for something from her, and it wasn't freaking friendship? Jared scrubbed his hands down his face, the dull thud of his headache replaced by a louder pulsing, stabbing pain. "I should go."

She gave him a doe-like blink. "OK."

"I'm going to check the back door first." He shuffled out of the dining room and made his way in the dark to the back of the house.

Melinda followed. "I feel stupid being intentionally in the dark."

"Yeah, I know what you mean," he mumbled.

"Jared—"

He swung to face her. "I think you need to wait a bit and think it through some. What if the kid has needs, needs like Keith. That hasn't been easy on my folks, you know."

She shrugged. "Then I'll do the best I can. It would be no different if I had a baby and the dad took off. That happens, too."

"I wish you'd wait."

"Your wish has been granted. The money I was going to use will now have to go to getting these repairs started."

"But insurance should cover it."

"Insurance will piecemeal the payouts and cover the fire. Not the electrical. That pushes back my baby-getting plan until this project is done." She sounded very close to tears.

Jared checked the durability of the door and the security of the lock. His crew had done a good job.

"This will hold. It's not a long-term solution, but I'll take another look in the daylight. Maybe we can make it work for a while so you don't have to postpone anything." He couldn't believe the words coming out of his mouth. Hadn't he just asked her to give it more thought? Now he was an enabler. He shook his head in disgust. His love for her was the bane of his common sense.

"I can only hope." She pressed her hands together as if attempting to contain her optimism.

"I'll see ya in the morning," he said and waited for her to precede him to the front of the house.

"What about the food you brought?"

Her flashlight lit up the dark hallway, but once in the front room, the brightness of the lamps made him squint.

"I'm good. Mainly, I wanted to make sure that you were doing OK and that the door was safe enough. I've done that. I'll see you in the morning." He gave her a nod and turned to leave, tripping over one of her ruined mule slippers.

This woman with her flaxen hair, heart-shaped mouth, and hourglass figure, who haunted his dreams, had now just blown his mind with her desires for hearth and home.

Not that he was surprised by that. Quite the opposite, in fact. He just thought perhaps he would have more time to make her see she might want those things with him. Clearly, he'd never even been a consideration.

4

She awoke early, having tossed and turned through most of the night, her conversation with Jared on a loop. Determined not to read into anything he said, she decided that any, likely all, his reactions had been based on shock.

The idea that a chance, albeit a small one, might exist, and she could achieve her targeted plans filled her with new energy. She didn't care that she had showered in the dark or had blown her hair dry in the foyer using her hall mirror. She had hope.

She arrived at the diner as her dad was setting up the tables and Chuck, the short order cook, was prepping the kitchen.

"Hey, darling," her dad, Bert, called as she stored her purse in a cabinet in the kitchen.

"Hey, Pops." She kissed his cheek, then took the large saltbox from him and moved to the next table to continue his work.

"Stopped by yesterday and saw the damage. We're telling your momma it was a small electrical fire that was contained to one area so she won't worry."

"That's basically true."

"Right," he said, pointing at her. "But I don't know how long I can keep her away so the sooner you get it fixed the better."

Melinda paused, wondering if she should share her dilemma with her father. "Jared's already come by."

"Good. Good."

"But it might take a while. The electrical needs to be looked at."

"Hell, that's no good. Your momma might want you to move home until it's all taken care of. You know how she worries." He placed full ketchup bottles on the tables, working around her.

Moving home, even temporarily, was not an option. If she had to sleep one night in her childhood bedroom, a room her momma had left intact from her senior year seventeen years ago, she'd need at least ten more years of therapy. Hands down. It was her momma, after all, who set her up to believe she was a princess, and all things ahead of her would be shroud in glitter and rainbows. Learning the truth had been a hard lesson.

"I'm opening up, darling," her dad said as he flipped on the neon *open* sign and turned the locks. "Here comes the crew."

Without fail, many of the local delivery guys and gals came in for breakfast. Their schedule so predictable Melinda knew who was on and off by the day of the week, and she found comfort in the regularity. The morning passed quickly, and Melinda got lost in the mechanics of transitioning the diner from breakfast to lunch.

"Woohoo, baby." The shrill call of her momma's voice put Melinda's instinct to flee at conflict with etiquette. Part of her wanted to duck and commando crawl out of the dining area and into kitchen, and the other part of her wanted to cover her ears and pretend she heard nothing. That trick had worked when she was a kid.

Instead, she turned to accept the hug she knew would be coming her way. "Momma." She kissed her cheek, using the action to stifle the groan that wanted to escape when she set eyes on her aunt who trailed behind her momma.

"Aunt Glory." She waited for her mother's older sister to indicate whether she wanted to hug or kiss. One could never be presumptuous. When her aunt presented her cheek, Melinda obliged, pressing a light kiss for fear if she'd press with too much force she'd get the old windbag going.

"Sweet child," Glory said with a dismissive pat.

"Melinda, honey. Glory and I are going to Orlando to do some shopping. You should come with us." Her mother took a seat at a table for four and placed her oversize purse in the chair next to her.

"I'm working, momma." She flipped over the coffee cups on the preset table and poured each a cup.

"You can skip out early, can't you?" Her momma bat her large blue eyes, a strategy she'd used most of her life to achieve her goals.

Melinda would rather have the worst kind of fungus on each of her shellacked nails, rendering her weekly manicures off limits, than go shopping with them. "Not really. Besides, there're things I need to do with the house. Clean up from the fire."

"Yes, but honey, just throw a rug over it or hang a picture. Out of sight, out of mind. It'll still be waiting for you when you get home, and maybe while we're out you might find the perfect accent piece."

"To accentuate the fire?" Melinda turned to glare at her dad. Downplaying the fire had been his idea after all, and now her mother thought it was something so small and insignificant a picture could cover it up.

"To help you get over the fire. Something to cheer you up."

A baby would cheer her up, tremendously, but she kept that thought to herself. Her sunroom miraculously being built by a benevolent do-gooder would be nice, as would Jared finding no further electrical problems. Heck, Jared suddenly falling in love with her would set her right for eternity. A knick-knack would most definitely not cheer her up.

"I'll think about," she said.

She made a mental note to slip away before they were done

with their meal, but the diner had a different agenda. Midweek was typically steady, but today, likely due to some event happening in town, the diner was packed. She was trying to concoct an exit strategy since her mother and aunt were nearly finished with their breakfast when Jared came in and stood by the counter.

"Hey." She searched his face in hopes to ascertain how the conversation might go considering last night's talk. His text this morning asking her to leave a key under the mat had left her with endless questions. If she were the type to waste energy on running endless scenarios, she'd have surely done that. But, to Melinda, that was time better spent elsewhere, and the answer would only be known when he told her how he felt.

"Hey." His smile was slight, but at least he met her gaze. "The electrician finished, and I thought we could talk about what he found and some of your options."

"OK. I'd rather do it outside of here. That OK?"

He nodded. "If you agree to the idea I have then we might need to go pick out a door, so that sounds fine with me."

"Can I grab you anything to eat?"

He shook his head. "Why don't I take you somewhere to grab some food? We can talk about all the options."

"OK." She smiled and stepped back, her gaze holding his. There was something new in the way he looked at her, something tender, or perhaps it was something hungry. She wasn't sure.

One more step back and Jared continued to watch her. Did all the talk of babies open up his eyes and paint her in a new light? Maybe he was seeing her for the woman she was and not his kid brother's ex-wife, or a flirt, or what she secretly feared—a risk and not marriageable material.

She flashed him a quick smile before scanning the diner for her dad. "Excuse me."

Popping her head into the kitchen she said, "You have every-thing under control here? Jared says the electrician is done, and we need to talk through some options. I was hoping I could split. I can come back to help with the dinner service."

He waved her off. "Go take care of it. I have a fishing trip scheduled next week, and if your momma gets her mind set on you moving in, I can see that trip going down like a sinking ship."

"Thanks, Daddy." She kissed his cheek.

"But tell your momma you aren't going shopping."

Melinda groaned. "Do I have to?"

When her dad raised one brow, she sighed in defeat. Grabbing her purse from under the counter, she pushed through the swinging doors from the kitchen and reentered the diner. Jared was talking to a guy she recognized as the local pool man. Likely, he and Jared did business together, and when her eyes met Jared's, he smiled and winked.

Lord, this man. He never stared too long at her chest and always laughed at her jokes, sincerely laughed, not the I-want-to-get-in-your-pants laugh. He always gave her first pick of the fortune cookies when they shared takeout and refused to let her open a door. Jeez, she was crazy about him.

She stopped at her momma's table. "I have to go with Jared to work out some details about the fire. Sorry. Maybe next time I can go shopping with y'all."

"Melinda—"

"Momma. I really need to take care of this. Please try to understand." She leaned down and kissed her mother's cheek, then did the same to her aunt. "Y'all have a good time."

She'd no sooner turned her back and took a step toward Jared when her aunt's voice carried across the diner.

"Maybe if you unbuttoned one of those top buttons on your shirt and leaned over the counter more you'd find yourself a man. You wouldn't need to be getting that sperm from the bank and could get yourself in the family way honestly."

Jared rubbed his hand over his head, and she knew he was

searching for the right reaction. She spun on her heel. "Momma, how could you tell her my business?"

"Oh, honey, you know me. I get one glass of wine in me, and nothing is off limits."

Melinda stared at her aunt, a million biting remarks ready to be spoken, but the challenging look on her aunt's face stopped her. What was the point of a verbal spat with a bitter old woman?

"Melinda?" Jared said from behind her.

She turned to leave.

"Good idea leaving with him," her aunt called from behind her. "Maybe the older brother can accomplish what the younger one couldn't."

Dignity was the point.

She looked around the diner. Some people stared, while others looked away, embarrassed either for her or by her. Did it matter?

She faced her aunt. "Aunt Glory, I make no apologies for who I am or what I want. I'm no different than most people. Sure, I've been unlucky in love." She gave a short laugh. "We can all agree on that, right? But I've never used a man, and I certainly won't start now, and what you suggest is...is... You owe Jared an apology."

"Hey, let's just leave and get something to eat." Jared touched her elbow, his fingers gently pressing in, coaxing her to walk away.

She stared at her aunt, daring her to say something more.

"Yeah. Let's." She turned her back and lifted her chin. She could feel the diner's crowd watching her. With her eyes forward, she allowed Jared to guide her from the diner and to his truck.

They drove in silence for about a mile before Melinda pressed the button that lowered the window. With the air cooling both her flushed face and her temper, she tried to gather her wits.

"Are you ok?" He didn't know what to say. He was reeling from the foreign desire to punch a woman in the mouth. Damn that mean aunt of hers.

"I don't think I'm hungry. Could you just take me home?"

"Melly, don't let her get to you."

She gave him a small smile. "I'm not actually. Just a tad embarrassed that she aired my business and brought you into it. That's all. I prefer to be the one to share my affairs. Let's talk about something else. Tell me about the electrician."

Not looking at him once, she continued to stare out the window. The wind lifted and twirled strands of her hair and, without belaboring the decision, he took her hand. It was a good sign when she didn't pull hers away that she was letting him in.

He wanted to do more, hold her and reassure her through touch. He wanted to see her rage or swear or do something more than simply stare out the window.

"Well, I'm sorry to say that the wiring is faulty. There were even signs of a different small fire in your attic."

She turned to face him, and then closed her eyes and rested her head against the seat. "Of course, there was."

"I think that should be your first priority. While he was checking the electricity, I was looking at the back of your house. That wall isn't as damaged as it looks. With a little bit of work, a small expense, and a new door, I can get that up to code. It'll meet my standard of personal safety and look good, too. You won't have a sunroom, but you can build that on at any time. Like they did, but better, of course."

"It still puts off my plans." She didn't even open her eyes.

"Yeah, maybe. But I think we should go after the inspector for all the cost. He's bonded, and there's no way this should have passed inspection. We can even go after the electrician. You'll get this covered and then some. It's a short wait, but then what's the rush?"

Jared pulled his truck along the curb next to her house and cut the engine. He knew as soon as he'd said the words they'd been the wrong ones to say. Melinda turned her stony expression toward him.

"What's the rush?" she yelled as she unbuckled her seatbelt and pushed the door open. She jumped out, turned to look him square in the eye, and slammed the door as hard as she could.

He followed her. "Melly…" he said to her back.

She swiveled on her heel and pointed a finger in his face. "I make no apologies for who I am."

"Nor should you."

"I've made mistakes," she said, tapping her chest. "Sure. We all have. Mine, I suppose, are just more fun to talk about and poke fun at. This…this baby thing will just be something else for them to say about me, but I don't care. I don't care."

"Melinda—"

"Yeah, sometimes I've been more forward, more open and less coy, but bullshit games like that piss me off. Everyone I've ever hit on has been a consenting adult, and I like sex. I like it a lot. It's especially good when shared with someone you have an emotional connection with. I'm not going to apologize for that either because I haven't broken the rules. I don't steal husbands. I'm not a cheater."

He wasn't sure what she wanted him to say, if anything. But at the mention of sex, his mind had taken a slight deviation, forcing him to rein it back in.

"But let me tell you what the rush is. The rush is that I'm tired of waiting. I'm tired of trying to do everything by the book, hoping people would say something nice about me for a change. But like my daddy says, 'I can shit in one hand and hope with the other and see which one fills up first'. I'm tired of shit. I want a baby. I want a family. I want a house that doesn't catch fire when a light is turned on, and I want a sunroom."

She turned back on her heel and stomped up the front porch stairs and into the house.

"We all want that Melinda," he said, following her in and slamming the door behind him.

"Yes, but you can get it anytime you want. Just ask any girl out, and they'll follow you to hell and back. People like you Jared. They like that you took over your daddy's business. They like that you don't baby Keith and you make him work, which builds his self-esteem. You're a citizen they're proud of."

"You think I wanted this life? You think I wouldn't want to be out there chasing my dreams like Lance? I never wanted to run a construction company. But ever since we were kids, my dad pounded into us that this was our legacy. Our destiny. Hell, the day I was born he painted Calhoun and Sons on all the work trucks. But process of elimination left me holding the bag. I wanted to be an architect. Build skyscrapers or colleges."

"At least, it's sorta close," she said, her voice soft. He knew she was trying to find the silver lining, but now he was pissed off, too.

"So if I bring you a puppy and tell you to mother it—that it's sorta close—that'll work for you? That'll fix this insane need to have a child by yourself?"

"Fair enough," she snapped.

He followed her into the kitchen and nearly ran into her back when she stopped short.

"What's that?" She pointed to the oversize silly elephant slippers he'd brought over this morning and left sitting on her kitchen table, a pink bow tying them together.

"I bought you some slippers. I noticed yours were ruined, and I couldn't find any like them so I got these. I figured they might make you smile. You've had a crummy week."

She pulled them off the table and hugged them to her chest. With eyes closed she asked, "Why?"

"Because I want to see you happy."

"Because I'm family?"

For the first time, he realized calling her "family" might not be helping his cause, but if he put it all out there and she rejected him, well, he didn't know what he'd do. "Maybe if you were happier, you wouldn't need a baby?"

Melinda's eyes snapped open. "And it starts with slippers?"

"It starts somewhere."

"I don't understand why you're acting like this. Why you're so resistant. This doesn't affect you."

"But it affects the man in your life."

"What man? From where I'm standing, there's a paucity of eligible men. Look around you. There's no man, and not one trying be in my life. If I keep waiting, I'll end up like my Aunt Glory." Her face was flushed, and her eyes glistened with unshed tears.

He stood firm, arms locked across his chest. "So you're quitting. You're all done with men. Never mind that you might find someone next week or even tomorrow, you're just going to eliminate the guy now. Why bother when you can go to a bank and get all your needs met."

Melinda snapped. "Might find someone?" she screamed. "I've been waiting as patiently as I can. I've been flirting and trying and again I ask you, what guy?"

She dropped the slippers, then shoved him in his folded arms, pushing him back on his heels. "What guy? I have no one, Jared. It's just me."

Her chest heaved with controlled anger, and Jared knew this was the moment. It was time, for lack of a better phrase, to fish or cut bait.

He bent close to her before saying, "This guy. Me. I'm talking about me. I'm been trying to be a part of your life since high school. Trying to show you that not all Calhouns are created equal. Hoping you'd not judge me based on my stupid ass brother. I think I've been a pretty good friend to you, tried showing you I was trustworthy—"

"Why didn't you say anything? Back then, why didn't you say anything?" she whispered.

Jared hung his head, staring at his shoe as he gathered his thoughts before returning his gaze to hers. There was not point telling her now that Lance's initial interest had been less than honorable, and all because he'd had a crush on her.

"I'd already lost you once to my brother. Then again to what's his name. When you returned home, bought this house, I hoped my luck had changed, and then it seemed like the timing was never right."

"And it's right now, the timing?" She took a step toward him.

He shrugged and leaned against the wall. "I want to have babies with you. It's selfish, but if you think you might being able to like me like that—"

She wrapped her hands in his T-shirt, then jerked him toward her and planted her lips on his. Touching her left him hungry and wanting more. A lifetime of more.

She pressed her body against his, and her arms slid around his neck. He decided to stop wasting time and, with one swift movement, she was in his embrace, and he was finally kissing her neck as he had longed to do. To hell with all his fantasies of her. The real experience was far better than he'd ever imagined.

EPILOGUE

EIGHTEEN MONTHS LATER

Melinda pressed the button on her key fob to open the sliding passenger door on her minivan. Not once had she regretted her decision. Being the practical person she was, the precious cargo waiting for her in the back of the van was proof positive her determination to have a baby was the right thing to do.

"Are you all ready to get out of those awkward car seats? I bet you are. I bet someone has a stinky diaper." She was pretty sure someone did because the stench on the last mile had been powerful.

Melinda released the latch and swung a car seat from its base. She smiled down at her son and tickled his chin before she set him on the grass next to her. Stepping into the van, she reached across, released a second latch, and heaved the seat supporting her daughter up and out of the van.

Say whatever about her not losing all her baby weight and how she'd packed it on, but toting two car seats with fat twins had made her upper arms buff as hell. The better to slug someone with was what she told people. Not that she had actually hauled off and hit anyone, but flexing them came in handy when people got mouthy.

She heard Jared before she saw him. His whistling a jaunty tune told her he was around the corner working.

Holding a carrier in each hand, she started toward him.

"Hey," he said and tossed a hammer in the air before catching the other end and tucking it in his tool belt.

"What are you doing here?"

"Working on the sunroom." He pointed to the spot where he'd just hung a birdfeeder on her newly built and absolutely gorgeous sunroom. It had far exceeded her expectations.

"I mean, I thought you had a meeting in Tampa."

"It was cancelled so I came home to see my family." He stepped close, took both carriers from her, then leaned forward and pressed a slow kiss to her lips. "Hi, babe. How was Lorelei's?"

"Fun. She's pregnant again. So is Evie Duke. So it was full of baby talk and good food."

Jared smiled and kissed her again. "Not everyone can have two kids out of the gate like us. They're just trying to keep up."

Melinda smiled. "We still got 'em beat."

"Thankfully, it's not a competition."

"But if this next baby has a twin then they'll never catch up."

Jared's laughter was cut short. "What? What next baby? You're talking about the one we might have in a year or so, right?"

"Or if all goes well, thirty-two more weeks."

"How...? What...? Where...?"

Melinda wrapped her arms around his waist and snuggled close. "Don't you remember, babe. You were there. I'm not making these babies on my own."

"I thought you couldn't get pregnant if you were nursing."

"Apparently, you can."

"Sweet Jesus. We're gonna have to build out the second floor. Put in a bathroom."

Melinda laughed and pulled open the door to her new

sunroom. Things had sure moved quickly for them, not that she was complaining. She glanced over her shoulder at her husband who was asking their six month olds what color they wanted their bedrooms and laughed when he told their daughter he was going to install bars on her windows.

Some people had all the luck, and Melinda was glad she was one of them. She swore that day, just as she had every day before, that she'd never take luck for granted. If it hadn't been for a small spark that started a fire, she and Jared might still be waiting for a sign.

KISS ME

⇒ A Coming Home Short Story ⇐

AGAIN

KRISTI ROSE

VINTAGE HOUSEWIFE BOOKS

PO BOX 841

Farmington, Mo 63640

www.kristirose.net

Publisher's Note: This is a work of fiction. Names, characters, places, and incidents are a product of the author's imagination. Locales and public names are sometimes used for atmospheric purposes. Any resemblance to actual people, living or dead, or to businesses, companies, events, institutions, or locales is completely coincidental.

Book Layout © 2014 BookDesignTemplates.com

Cover Art 2015 Paper and Sage Design

Kiss Me Again/ Kristi Rose. -- 1st ed.

❀ Created with Vellum

My Anya Monroe and Eryn Carpenter~ who are willing to brainstorm via skype, google hangout, or whatever it takes. #thisisfriendship

A successful marriage requires falling in love many times, always with the same person.

-Mignon McLaughlin

With a final, forceful tug, Andee Swift pulled the jean skirt over her hips and nearly fell over, catching herself at the last minute by thrusting her hand out to grab the edge of the bed.

"Are you ready yet?" Buck called from the other room.

She heard the fridge slam closed and the telltale signs of her husband twisting the top off a beer, tossing the cap onto the counter, and letting it dance across the space--where it would come to a rest nowhere near the garbage can, and would likely sit until she, or Janice, their cleaning lady, helped it make its way to the trash.

"Throw the cap away, "Andee yelled and rolled her eyes.

She sat on the edge of the bed and attempted to pull on her knee-high black boots--wench boots, Buck called them--but the band on her skirt cut painfully into her stomach, forcing her back upright.

All this for love.

Correction. She had love.

What she wanted was to be *in* love again. That heady rush of anticipation before Buck kissed her, the pinpricks of pleasure that followed lovemaking. She knew he missed those things, too, and it was her goal to make them recapture those feelings. Before they were so far gone, they'd never find them again. Before he found them with someone else. Even if they had to go to extremes to get there. No cost was too high to save her marriage.

She needed something to calm her nerves.

"And get me one, too." She certainly didn't have any room for a beer, much less food or air, but her nerves were shot and her anxiety was off the charts. "Take a step out of your comfort zone," the books advised. "Try something new," suggested online sites. Heck, what they were about to do could be considered a giant leap.

"That was the last one. I'll pour some for you in a glass," Buck called.

Andee leaned back against the bed to ease the pinch of her stomach. How many beers had he had today? This week? She wasn't sure, but it was definitely more than normal. Buck was not himself. Hadn't been for--if her math was correct and she were to be completely honest--over a year. It started with an impatience and edginess he'd never displayed before and was now comple-mented with increased drinking and limited touching. Yes, it could be worse but she didn't want to see what that looked like.

She pushed her worries aside, intent on focusing on today and not the disaster that was their relationship. They hadn't fought this much since . . . ever.

After much struggling, which resulted in heavy breathing and sweat beads on her brow, Andee was finally ready to go. She stood, smoothed the old skirt before trying to stretch the band to give her more room, and then made her way out of their bedroom to the center of the house--a kitchen and great room combination.

Buck gave a low whistle. "Sweet mother of God, those boots are hot." He handed her a small glass of beer. "You don't look comfortable."

"It'll be fine. It's the skirt. It's tight." She chugged the beer and fought off a burp born from carbonation. Ugh! This was so not the start she had pictured for this night, their night out. It should not start out with beer, burps, or farts. Could anything be less romantic? She was trying to get him to fall back in love with her, not be one of the guys.

"Why don't you wear a different one?" Buck squinted and leaned in to take a closer look at the skirt.

"Because I wear those other ones to church or family dinners and there is no way--No. Way--I'm wearing a church skirt to a sex dungeon. I'd have to burn it afterward."

"Is there writing along the bottom there?"

Andee covered the ink marks that dotted the hem with her hand. "Maybe."

"Does it say Andee hearts Buck? Lorelei and . . . Andee . . . B.F.F.?" He looked at her, puzzled. "Is that skirt from high school?"

"Maybe." Andee shrugged.

"That skirt's what? Twenty years old?" Buck laughed then took a pull from the beer. "You still have clothes from high school?"

She swatted at his arm. "Stop. And it's about seventeen years old. Thank you very much. Look at you. Those pants are about the same age."

"Hey," he cried indignantly and pointed to his well-worn camouflage cargo pants. "These are my hunting pants. They're good luck. I figured we could use all the luck we could get." He finished his beer and set the bottle on the counter.

What did that mean? Did he think they were going to need luck to get turned on by each other? That arousal might require more than a highly charged sexual ambience and the person you loved? Unsure of how to respond, she went with sarcasm.

"Yeah, that's why you should wear the pants that you spray with deer urine every year. Because that's hot. It's a sex club, Buck. We should try for sexy." Andee picked the bottle up and walked to the sink to rinse it out. She dropped it into the recycling bin before returning to the fridge to get two bottles of water. It was a bit of a drive to where they were going.

"It's sexy to the deer."

Andee turned to hide her eye roll and immediately regretted her impatience. "Did you put the overnight bags in the car?"

"Yup." Buck took the water bottle she handed him.

Grotte d'Amour, also known as the Love Cave, Tampa Bay's finest BDSM dungeon, was their destination and over an hour away. Andee had felt it best they get a hotel nearby. Should everything go as planned, fingers crossed, she hoped they'd be too revved up to make the drive home, too desperate for each other. A hotel would be the icing on the cake. Besides, she'd already had plenty of sex with Buck in a car and they were long past high school lovemaking, forced to be creative with their intimacy. This was to be a new experience, something spontaneous and fun. One of the relationship books she'd read had given her the idea, and she was still bowled over that he'd agreed to try.

"Are you ready?" Buck asked. "You sure you still want to try this?"

"Are you having second thoughts?" She played with the lid on her water bottle.

"You said you wanted us to spice things up. This is sure a deviation from what we're doing."

Dreading where a response might lead, Andee searched carefully for the right words. "We're in a rut, Buck. Marriage does that to couples, and we don't have the excuse, or luxury, of blaming it on children. Research shows that the seven-year itch really happens at ten years. Happiness in relationships declines."

They'd be celebrating ten years of marriage next week. But what worried Andee more was that they really had seventeen years together, having been high school sweethearts. Andee couldn't bring herself to look at the statistics on those dynamics. The ten-year itch numbers were disturbing enough.

"If you say so."

"Look," Andee said and pointed to the large thermometer she'd created in Excel, blown up to over two hundred percent and hung on their fridge. "We've worked really hard to save money for the last ten years. Which is great. It's starting to pay off. The article I read about the ten-year itch says that spontaneity is lost to forward planning. We are awesome at forward planning." She tapped her finger on the picture she took great pleasure in updating every month to mark their progress. They were one month out from achieving their goal: to buy a vacation home. Every time Andee looked at the picture, she wanted to clap her hands in glee and dance around the room. That was until she had read that article. Seeing the confusion on Buck's face, she finished with, "Which means we have no spontaneity."

"And apparently too much forward planning means the balance is a sex dungeon." Buck pushed up the sleeve to his white T-shirt to scratch his bicep.

"We're trying something new."

"Aren't we though," he said with a shake of his head.

Andee pulled scissors from the kitchen drawer and held them up. "The instructions on the web site say the theme for Friday nights is sensual. To come as your alter ego. A hunting man is not your alter ego." The list of suggestions she'd read in the women's magazine listed both BDSM and costume play. Doing both in the same night gave her a double win, made her feel victorious.

She gathered up his sleeve to his shoulder hem and began cutting. When she'd finished both sides, a quick look told her she needed something more. Ignoring his sighs, she cut strips length-wise down the front giving the shirt a shredded look.

She dropped the extra fabric in the garbage. Looking down at her plain attire, she wondered if she could cut something from her shirt as well. Maybe a hole in the middle to expose her stomach? But she couldn't see wasting a good T-shirt for these purposes and instead grabbed the bottom edge of the shirt, pulled it up and over the center of the collar under her chin and tugged the edge downward, cinching the fabric. The look exposed her midriff and cupped her large breasts nicely. In fact, the pull of the fabric helped tug her breasts upward, a position they'd struggled to maintain in recent years.

"Now I see the theme. I kinda look like a homeless redneck and you look like a redneck cheerleader." Buck stared at his exposed arms. "I think we should have gone the leather route."

"The only leather we have is your letterman's jacket." Andee pulled her waistband up, hoping to minimize the red marks it was creating from the constant pressure.

"We really suck at this." He held out his shredded shirt and raised a brow. Turning his wrist slightly, he glanced at his watch. "I guess we should go. It's almost ten."

Andee stifled a yawn.

Buck slid a riding crop belonging to their fifteen-year-old niece who rode dressage off the counter. "We could forget this and just go to bed."

There was no tease in his remarks, no suggestion of what they might do if they stayed home versus trying out this dungeon.

"Are you scared?" Andee poked, knowing his triggers. Truth was she thought she might be. Just a little.

"Shut your mouth, woman. Nothing scares Buchanon Swift." Buck waved the crop over his head before bringing it down for a light slap against her thigh, the cattail catching her exposed skin right below the hemline of her skirt.

"Ow," Andee cried, tears springing to her eyes. "Wow. That really hurt." She rubbed vigorously against the already red and raised skin.

Buck rushed to her. "I'm sorry, babe. I didn't even swing it that hard. Flicked it, really." He pulled her hand away to look at the welt and hissed upon first inspection. "You should put ice on it."

Blinking back the tears, Andee looked at Buck. "Maybe this is a really bad idea. How can we go to a place like this Love Cave and even consider participating when I can't take a slight flick from the crop?"

"I'm not real big on pain either. I don't even like watching my brother spank his kids."

Defeated, Andee let her shoulders slump. Who was she kidding? They weren't swingers; they didn't even like to double date unless it was Cole and Lorelei. She unfastened the snap on her skirt and took her first deep breath since pulling it on. "Truth is my stomach was starting to hurt." She rubbed at the red marks circling her waistline. "We suck."

"Nah. We just need to rethink it. I've got an idea."

Andee waited for him to finish.

"I saw some Easy Cheese in the pantry. I think we have bourbon and sugar cubes left. How about we get into some . . . other clothes, turn on some Mad Men. I'll let you pick the season. We can break out our sixties food, make each other an Old Fashioned, and dream about being able to drink on the job. Or at the very least, walk out whenever we want."

"What about the hotel room? We'll have to pay anyway."

"There's our spontaneity. See, we're reckless with money." Buck made a check mark in the air and laughed. "Check that off the list."

Andee laughed with him. "Reckless with money wasn't on the list."

It was good to see him smile, to share a moment and feel connected to him again.

"Work with me here." He rubbed her arm.

"You'd rather marathon-watch a series we've already seen than go to a sex club?"

Buck shrugged. "Maybe this isn't the right type of club for us."

It was not lost on her that he didn't suggest going straight to bed.

Andee sighed. At least they had this. He seemed to enjoy her company when they watched TV. "I think there are some 100 Grands in the freezer. I'll pull up Netflix. You make the drinks."

"Atta girl." Buck swatted her on the bottom. "Go change."

"I think I'll have to cut this skirt off me to get out of it."

"I'll meet you on the couch," he called.

Though she was relieved to be staying in and getting out of the torturous contraption, staying home only fed into her insecurities about the state of their marriage and their sex life. If they didn't have wild, reckless sex tonight, would the days after be more of the same?

Andee miraculously managed to get out of the skirt without having to cut it then changed into one of Buck's old college shirts and a pair of elastic-waist running shorts--also known as her daily lounge wear. Pulling her hair into a low ponytail, she looked at herself in the large mirror over her dresser. When had she stopped spending time on her appearance? Was it before or after she and Buck got into this rut? How long ago was that? Three years? Maybe four? Even tonight, she'd barely added to her makeup regime, thinking the dark eyeliner was sexing it up enough.

What made it worse was that as a couple they might be experiencing a dip, but lately she'd hit a low on a personal level as well. Sure, a routine was inevitable, and the fact was that she and Buck had been creating routines together for many years, so it was remarkable that they hadn't fallen into a lull like this before.

But they were most decidedly in a rut. They could call it what they wanted. Dress it up under the guise of familiarity and comfort and try to convince everyone that only couples who had something so solid could obtain such a thing, but no one ever talked about a car hitting a pothole or getting stuck in a groove as a good thing.

How could marriage be any different?

It wasn't, and no matter how she looked at it, she and Buck

were not experiencing a good thing. Once his interest was gone, would he move on toward something newer and fresh? Upgrade?

It was the term her father had always used when he'd move them to yet another house he was planning to remodel. "Everyone wants something better, something more," he'd tell her. This point of view was even reflected in her mother, who continually changed her look and style.

Andee groaned and stared at her closet full of clothes older than her marriage.

They clearly needed a dose of *better*. Especially in the sex department. Ugh. It totally sucked. It wasn't that they didn't have sex. In fact, they'd had sex a few nights ago. Only it was just the same old sex every time. The same moves. The same length of time. The same quick cuddle afterward. Lately, when it was over, Andee was left feeling more alone and less loved than at any other point in her day, week, or life.

She was sick of the same, and though she'd never subscribed to her father's philosophy, it was a long time coming for her to start mixing things up. Yes, something was off between them. If she waited any longer, that something could grow into a big monster and destroy everything dear to her. There was no way she was about to let that happen, things had already gone too far. It was time for a new season in the life of Andee and Buck.

Buck didn't peel out of his father's parking lot. He didn't even feel the urge to do a doughnut or make an obscene gesture. He just got in his truck and drove away, with a smile so large he thought he might look a bit maniacal. It wasn't every day a person got fired and was excited about it.

If his father had one thing going, he was consistent. Unfortunately, he was consistently a ball buster. Ever since Buck could remember, his father had ridden him about grades, or football, and now the job. Ridden him? Nah, that sounded like something normal parents did. Buck's father was nothing more than an aging bully and he was tired of it. A son shouldn't dislike his father as much as he did. Buck was a grown-ass man, for Pete's sake, and he lived for his days off and time away from his old man. Being near him was walking a tight rope and depending on a vindictive person to set up the safety net. The stress of being always tense and on edge was wearing him down.

As if on autopilot, he drove toward home but got distracted by the empty lot near the mall that he'd fallen in love with. OK, maybe love was a strong word. He didn't actually love the unturned earth.

His phone chimed. A glance at the screen showed his father calling, so Buck ignored the call. Instantly a text from his brother showed up.

Where R U?

Buck looked around the busy strip mall and randomly picked a spot.

Beef O'Brady's. Having a beer. Celebrating, he answered.

On my way was Cal's reply.

Buck groaned. Now he was stuck actually going to have a beer with his brother when he should be heading home to lower the boom on his wife.

Of course, one beer wouldn't hurt anything, and it would give him time to figure out how he was going to tell Andee that he was changing the game.

He pulled out of the empty lot and gave it one last look. It was a blank slate that he could do something with. A dream he was finally coming to terms with. But this foundationless piece of earth had the potential to bring down everything he held dear. Normally, changes weren't a concern for him and his wife because they were usually in sync with each other. Both determined and driven by opportunity and goals, they made a formidable team. Unexpected change like he was planning was going to no doubt disrupt their lives. More importantly, it was going to push Andee out of her comfort zone and into a space where he knew she'd sworn she'd never live. Together, they'd spent years cultivating their path and now he'd be asking her-- pushing her actually--onto a new, less organized and possible extremely unstable path. A path with potential financial disaster and incredible stress lining the way. Marriages were destroyed on less. But for Buck, the time to begin his entrepreneurial venture was now. As he saw it, staying with his dad carried just as much risk. It would break him, and how long could she stay with a broken man?

The drive across to Beef's took no time and he was seated at the bar with a beer in one hand and an order of wings arriving at any minute when his brother slid onto the stool next to him.

"Dude, dad's been trying to call you. What number is that?" Cal nodded toward Buck's beer before waving for the bartender to come over.

"It's my first, and I don't care that he's been trying to call me. It's bullshit, Cal, to fire someone and then call them up and yell some more, because you know that's what he wants to do." Buck held the beer with one hand and picked at the label with the other.

The bartender placed the platter of wings before Buck, who pushed the plate halfway between himself and his brother.

"It feels like we're breaking the law having a beer midafternoon on a work day," Cal said.

"You going back today?"

"Nah, I told him I'd talk you off the ledge."

Buck snorted with disbelief. "What ledge? Man, I feel free. I feel alive." He raised his bottle. "To kissing that toxic job and the asshole we call dad good-bye."

"Don't be like that."

"Why do you stay?" Buck asked, turning to face his brother.

Cal took a long pull from his beer before answering. "I tried to leave once. A few years ago. But the offers were lower and the upward mobility sucked. Michelle was pregnant with Colby . . ."

"So you stuck it out." Buck shook his head in disbelief. Man, they were a dysfunctional group.

"Back then I had two kids and one on the way. I didn't have much choice, and I still don't." His brother wouldn't look at him.

"That's why he owns you, Cal."

"What do you want me to do? Let my family go without the things they like? No more trips to Disney because Dad can't ignore his own father. One day he'll be out and we'll be in charge."

"You'll be in charge. I'm out. If I had kids, I'd have left long ago. There's no way I'd come home feeling this angry all the time. It's bad enough Andee has to deal with it, but kids? No way. You know, over the last year, we've been shorter with each other. Fighting."

Cal clasped him on the back. "That's marriage, bro."

Buck shook his head. "Not my marriage. I don't want to do anything. Not even hunt. I dread family dinners on Wednesdays. It puts me in a foul mood for the rest of the week. That's no way to live."

Cal shrugged. "I don't know what to tell you."

"I'm sorry you're going to be stuck with him on your own." Part of Buck hated that his brother would be on his own but a greater part was stoked to finally be free.

"You're really not going back?" Cal's pushed his beer away and stared at his him. "Even though it's your weekend to cover the store?"

Buck shook his head. "I'm sorry but no. I'm not going back."

"Man, he's gonna be pissed," Cal said before finishing his beer.

"Hey, brothers Swift. Mind if I join you?" Jared Calhoun sat on the stool next to Buck.

"Jared." They shook hands. "What brings you out to Beef's on this fine Friday afternoon?"

"Had a taste for some wings." Jared leaned back to rest his hand on his upper thigh and turned his attention to Buck. "I think our girls are out shopping together."

Buck grinned. "You and Melinda dating?"

Jared nodded, a wide smile consuming his face.

"It's about time," Cal said. He and Jared had graduated high school together and had run in similar crowds.

"Beer for my friend here," called Buck to the bartender while holding up his own.

"Guess some things just need time to percolate." Jared leaned across Buck and snagged a wing.

"And a fire to accelerate it," Cal added, referring to the house fire Melinda had experienced a week ago. Jared's construction company was handing the cleanup.

The bartender set out three beers.

"To the future," Buck toasted and the three raised their beers.

"I'll drink to that," slurred a man behind them. Sitting at a two-top table was Kevin Norman, another graduate from their high school, but from Buck's year.

"What's your deal, Kev?" Jared asked.

"I'm a free man, boys."

"You quit your job, too?" Buck asked.

"Nah." Kevin leaned back in his chair and raised his bottle. "I'm getting divorced. No more nagging wife. No more requests to pick up milk or bread. Just me and my freedom and the hot young thing I'm dating. She doesn't even know what the Disney Channels is." Kevin toasted himself and took a swig.

"Don't be so sure. You said she was young, right? She probably grew up with Hannah Montana," said Cal, who would know as he'd often complained that his oldest made him watch every episode.

"That'll make her good at twerking." said Kevin with a hooded wink. "Know what I mean?" He winked again and swayed. "It's great, fellas. Freedom."

Jared laughed. "Yeah, it tastes good now. Let's see what you say when you see Lisa out on a date."

Kevin scoffed and sat back so quickly he swayed in his seat. "Ha, she'll never date. She's too busy with the kids. They're her world." He said the last bit in what Buck assumed was a poor imitation of Lisa.

"Until it's your weekend to keep them and suddenly she's got forty-eight hours to herself. Lisa's a looker. She's got that take-care-of-you, make-you-feel-good vibe about her." Jared fanned the flame. "She won't last long on the market."

Kevin jumped up, bumping the table, which spilled the beer he'd set down only moments earlier all over his pants. "You shut up, Jared Calhoun. Keep your hands off my wife."

"Your ex-wife," Jared said as he stood. He was at least three inches taller than Kevin, and while Kevin's football muscles had gone soft from years behind a computer, Jared's had grown from years of owning a construction company and working outside.

Kevin pointed a shaky finger at Jared before he scuttled off to the restroom.

With a laugh, Jared sat back on the stool. He held up his beer. "Here's to never being as shortsighted as that moron."

Buck surely hoped his hesitancy to change his comfortable life wouldn't change the way Andee saw him. That it wouldn't leave her with doubts as to how much he valued her or their relationship. Even if the last year had been rough. He needed to pull his head out of his ass and simply tell her what was on his mind, and he'd do that right after he had another beer.

3

Andee was good at several things. She was punctual, great with numbers, brilliant with organization, cheerful in the morning as well as late at night, could hold her drink, knew how to hook up a winch to a stuck truck, and was a loyal friend.

What she was not good at was waiting. Well, she was OK at waiting for most things like standing in line, watching her garden grow, and listening with endless patience to a long, drawn-out story. Where she really sucked at waiting was when there was a grand prize at the end of the wait. Like when her sister was going into labor, which she seemed to do every couple of years. That kind of waiting was hard.

Much like the waiting she was doing right now.

She ran her hands down the side of her shirt, feeling the way the new outfit highlighted her curves, and suppressed a giggle. It had been over six years since she'd had a shopping spree, and even then it had been to look for clothes that would work with the diner she and Lorelei were opening. This trip was all about wooing her man.

She pushed aside the curtain and strained to see if she could make out Buck's headlights coming up the drive, but all she saw was darkness. Pitch black nothing.

Seven days since their failed attempt to spice it up. One week and they'd had sex once. Well, she supposed she should give them credit. They had changed it up by doing it on the couch. That's what happened when people drank too many cocktails and watched a show about people having sex. But sex on the couch was much like sex in bed, with the exception that the space was smaller and the cuddling didn't last as long, due to the fact that it was virtually impossible to stay in a sandwiched position and actually breathe in nurturing amounts of oxygen.

It had been a stroke of genius to enlist the help of Melinda Bane, sexpot extraordinaire, to help her create a new look. The woman was gifted when it came to fitting clothes to body shapes and, let's be honest, with attracting men. If Andee could bottle just an ounce of Melinda's confidence or even her best friend, Lorelei's, she'd likely not be in this mess. She'd have nipped it in the bud early on.

But she hadn't, and now it was damage control time. Buck was going to walk in and find a new woman. A hot woman. His hot woman. Melinda had seen to that. His mouth was going to hit the floor and all thoughts of anything outside of her would evaporate from his brain. At least, she hoped he'd have a strong reaction. She needed him to have some reaction, or else her greatest fear, that Bucky was no longer attracted to her, would be actualized, and her father's over-simplification of human proclivities would apply--on some level--to everyone. Specifically to the person who meant the most to her.

She glanced at her watch; he should be home any minute. When he ran late, he always sent a text, at the very least, and there was no text waiting on her phone. An earlier text had said he'd had a crappy day at work and was stopping by the local sports bar for some wings and a few beers.

How would he react when he saw her? What would he think?

Andee walked away from the window, refusing to look in the mirror she passed, and into the kitchen to pour a glass of iced tea. What if she'd gone overboard? What if her new look was more what Melinda preferred and less what Buck did?

Not willing to muss her artfully applied, shiny pink lipstick, she decided to use a straw, which gave her an idea. If by some chance he didn't like her new look, and she could keep from falling apart, she could at least use the confidence it gave her. She spent the next three minutes practicing how to suck from the straw in a suggestive way, hoping Buck wouldn't be too dense to pick up on her hints. For the next few minutes, she tried out several poses, hoping to find one that look natural yet showed off her cleavage, but then she got distracted by the thick locks of her newly straightened hair She liked the way it fell around her shoulders all slick and glossy, a drastic change from her usual bouncy curls. She felt styled instead of windblown.

This must be what glamorous felt like.

Andee caught a glimpse of her silhouette from a shadow on the wall. Melinda had been right--she'd been in serious need of a proper bra, and the change in figure was remarkable. Her small waist, once lost in the oversized shirts she wore to accommodate her substantial chest, was now accented. Also, though her boobs were large, they didn't look overly huge--like Dolly Parton's--in her new fitted bra. They looked . . . good. She looked good. She looked curvy and fit and felt seductive and much like she imagined a temptress would feel.

If this was how Melinda felt every day then it was no wonder she attracted men like bees to honey. This feeling was heady, powerful, and addictive.

The flash of headlights pulled Andee from her thoughts and pushed her into motion.

Buck was home.

Nervous flutters filled her, and she pressed her hand to her stomach to settle them, but was unsuccessful. As if the flutters were transferred, Andee's hands began to shake as well. Having never settled on a pose, she quickly pressed her body up against the counter and then, for good measure, put the straw in her mouth.

She felt like an idiot.

Damn it! Why hadn't she researched ways to present herself? Her mind could only think of stupid poses she'd seen in magazines and posters. She quickly discarded them all, mainly because she didn't have a fainting chaise on which to recreate most of the poses she pictured and didn't want to be on the couch as that was what he would be expecting.

Giving up, she huffed, spit out the straw, and decided to greet him at the door. But halfway there, she changed her mind and turned to sit. Before she could lower herself into the overstuffed wingback, she changed her mind again, instead walking quickly to the kitchen, where she snatched up the mail and started sorting through it.

Buck came into the house with a bang, by both shoving open the door and slamming it shut right after. He stumbled before straightening back up and shuffling to her.

"Hey, babe," he slurred then attempted to kiss her cheek but missed and caught her jawline instead.

"Are you drunk?" The answer was obvious.

"I had a helluva day." He tossed his ball cap at the bar stool next to their island, missed, shrugged then stumbled the ten feet to his favorite recliner, where he fell, slumped into it, and then extended it out to the fullest.

"You had a bad day before or after you started drinking? Did you drive home?" Andee tossed the mail on the counter and picked up the ball cap. She placed it on the island's counter. A tight coil of disappointment mixed with apprehension had replaced her nervous butterflies.

So much for wowing his pants off.

"Nah, Cal drove me home. He followed me to the bar. Suck

up." Buck rubbed his hands over his face, which made the last part come out muffled.

"What happened?" She sat on the arm of the couch and faced him.

"I got fired. My old man is a piece of work. You know that?"

Andee sighed. This was not the first time Buck's father had fired him. Usually they would disagree on a sales strategy. Conflicting opinions would lead to angry words and raised voices. Cal, Buck's brother and the quintessential yes man, would always take their dad's side, which inevitably inflated her father-in-law's ego to the point where he'd fire Buck. Usually by the end of the day, he'd call, demand an apology, and tell Buck to report back to work the following day. Who knew people could get so heated over tires and how to sell them?

"What happened this time?"

Buck's eyes were closed, but he raised his brows. "Cal told him we were looking into buying a vacation home. That we're a month out from beginning our search."

"And he fired you for that?" Andee leaned forward and rested her elbows on her knees.

"No. He fired me because he wants us to go in on a family vacation home. Something in Montana or somewhere where the guys can hunt." He opened his eyes and shifted in the chair to lift his hip up to pull folded papers out of his pocket. He handed them to her.

Red flashes of warning went off in Andee's head. Their vacation home and hunting were two things she'd been dead set against combining There was no point going away with Buck if all he was going to do was hunt. For Andee, relaxing with a man who'd spent long hours in the brush, smelled like animal urine, and didn't shower, was not the image of vacation she had in mind. It certainly wasn't a way to steam up their sex life, either.

After unfolding the papers, she eyed the printouts. "What in the name of all that is good and holy is this?" She held up a picture of a cabin. Well, the word cabin was being generous. Maybe lean-to was more appropriate. "Or this?" Another shanty. "A vacation home in Idaho, Montana, or Wyoming? Are their deer really that much different?" She shuffled through the pages. Before her brain further exploded into a thousand bright and angry pieces, Andee wanted to make sure she had all the facts.

"Dad wants to hunt bigger game. Elk, moose, maybe even bear."

"What happened to the whole 'eat what you hunt' philosophy? When did your family start eating bears?"

"I dunno, Andee. It's stupid, and I said so. I told him no. That you wouldn't be interested in a cabin--"

"Are you interested in a cabin instead of a vacation home?" She stood up, flinging the papers onto the couch.

"What I'm interested in has no bearing in this conversation." He squinted at her before breaking into a laugh. "No pun intended."

"What the hell does that mean?" Andee planted her hands on her hips.

Suddenly, Buck looked at her. His eyes narrowed, or tried to, as much as they could in his current state. "What's different about you? Did you get stuck in the rain? Your hair looks like you just got out of the shower but . . . not." Buck hiccupped and tried to sit further back in the recliner. As if distance would help his vision and perception.

"No. I did not get stuck in the rain. I straightened my hair and had it colored. Look, no more gray." She leaned over him to show him her roots, the touch of gray hidden beneath streaks of chestnut and caramel.

"I can't see past your boobs." He leered. "The twins look good. But I'm not crazy about your hair like that. I like it all fluffy, like a big ball of out-of-control yarn. That's your hair. It's glorious."

"My hair reminds you of yarn?"

Buck tried to sit up but gravity was too much. Instead, he

pointed to her shirt. "What's that on the side of your shirt? Come here. Let me touch it."

Andee hesitated, questioning her ethics. Could she seduce him? If he rubbed her shirt, would his hand move upward? Should she stop him or see what happened? He was drunk, after all. There was no telling how the rest of the night was going to turn out. Shrugging, she stepped toward him and turned so the side of her shirt was closest to him, as was her right breast.

Buck rubbed the leather panel that joined the front and back of her shirt. The panels pulled the fabric in and helped accentuate her figure. Buck scratched the leather with his nails.

"What's this? It looks like the underbelly of a dragon," he said and followed it up with a belch.

"You're disgusting."

"You're disgusting. Hurting poor, harmless dragons to make a shirt. I bet they're on the endangered species list." He laughed, clearly more impressed with his joke than she was.

Andee tried not to let the disappointment overwhelm her. Tears pressed against her eyes, begging to be free. This night had not gone even a fraction as she'd imagined, unless she counted the one comment he'd made about her boobs.

"Oh hey, guess what I found out?" Buck said with a snap of his fingers, only his snap was weak and quiet. His attention was drawn to his fingers as he tried to make his snap louder.

Andee clapped her hands together in a loud boom. Buck's head snapped up, his attention on her.

"You were saying?"

"I was?"

"You were saying you found something out today."

"Oh yeah. Guess who's getting divorced?" His expression was smug; he knew he was beating her to the scoop.

Andee was suddenly very interested. "Who?"

"Kevin and Lisa Norman."

Andee froze, panic wrapping a cold hand around her as she

struggled to grasp what Buck said, but could only focus on one thing--Kevin and Lisa's relationship was nearly identical to hers and Buck's. The guys had graduated together just like the girls had, and they'd been together just as long. They never seemed to fight, were always laughing and hugging. Was it Lisa's need to always sport some new jewel or that she lived at the gym? Was it Kevin's receding hairline? Andee covered her mouth. They had three children, and she couldn't help but think of them. No one had ever expected them to split up. Ever.

"Are you kidding me? What happened?"

Buck shrugged. "I heard he has a little honey on the side."

Andee pressed her hand to her heart and took in a shallow breath, fighting the urge to hyperventilate. Kevin and Lisa were at the ten-year marriage mark as well.

Fear rippled through her as she tried to think about life without Buck. It was impossible to imagine, as they'd been together for half her life. She didn't know any other man. She didn't want to.

"Bucky," she said. "Come to bed."

But he was already asleep, soft snores coming from his open mouth. Andee covered him with an afghan his mother had made them and walked slowly around her house, turning out the lights, and touching items they'd collected over the years. Mementos from vacations together, memories attached to each piece, but her mind was on the Normans and trying to not compare how much they had in common with her and Buck.

In their room, she washed her face without seeing her reflection in the mirror before her, instead focused on what was in the past. Snippets of their life that might have contributed to the crappy state their marriage was currently in. The rift between them looked small, innocuous, but she was quite certain if she peered over the edge, she'd find the depth greater than she'd thought. There was more going on here. Buck getting fired and drunk? That wasn't him. Fired happened at least twice a year and was inevitable with a misanthropic asshole like his father for a boss.

But to get drunk knowing he would have to face his father again tomorrow was only borrowing trouble. Something she herself could not avoid, as she tried not to think about his reaction to her--or lack thereof. What man preferred his wife to look like she'd been cleaning toilets all day versus looking as if she'd sex him up in a hot minute? A man who wasn't romantically interested in his wife, that's who.

Both mentally and physically weary, she fell into bed and refused to give in to her tears. But sleep eluded her as she lay on her side of the large bed, Buck's side empty. Her mind continued to drift to the Normans, trying to imagine what Lisa was going through. Eventually, after she'd lost the war and succumbed to her tears, she fell into a fitful sleep that was heavy on dreams of a bleak future.

4

B ecause she was co-owner of a breakfast diner, Two Chicks and Bacon, Andee had to be an early riser. It was her job to grab the papers, fresh vegetables, flowers, and other essentials that she and Lorelei used each morning. The next morning was no different, with the exception that her hair was straight, her clothes new and better fitting, and she'd spent more time on her makeup. She'd needed to in order to hide her red, puffy eyes.

Cleaving tightly to what she perceived to be the threads of her marriage, she banked her disappointment and fears in hopes of clearing her head so she could find a solution. She desperately needed a plan. Forward motion had to be better than this whirlpool of inactivity, just circling around the issue.

Andee started the coffeepot for Buck, but she didn't kiss his cheek to wake him nor did she set out the fresh orange juice that he liked to drink before he went on his regular morning run. She assumed he'd be in no state for the physical activity and would likely wake up at the last minute and rush to work. She wondered if she should make him a Bloody Mary--hair of the dog if you will--to help fortify him for the battle with his father. But eventually she decided the last thing he needed was more booze in his system.

By the time she arrived at the diner, carrying her stock in a large crate, her brain still had not produced an inkling of an idea, and her mood had gone from proactively determined to foul and scared. She kicked the door closed behind her and wished she could kick it again. Lorelei stood in the kitchen, a large bowl resting in the crook of her arm, the whisk hovering above it.

"Morning. You look pretty. I like your hair," Lorelei said quietly.

"Really?" Andee's voice was heavy with sarcasm. "Bucky likes my hair frizzy. Says it reminds him of yarn."

Lorelei's mouth made a small "O" but no sound came out. She placed the bowl on the counter, whisk standing up in the batter, and faced her friend.

"You wanna talk about it?"

Andee shook her head. "In his defense, he was drunk, but if I think about it I might start crying." She slid the crate onto the counter.

Lorelei had been Andee's best friend since elementary school, but how did one tell a blissfully happy, almost-newly married woman about the dark side of marriage? Besides, Lorelei was known for her temper, and being six months pregnant and hormonal only increased the odds that if she heard everything, she might punch Buck in the junk the next time she saw him.

Lorelei reached out and pulled her into a hug. "OK. I'm here whenever you're ready."

Andee nodded and swallowed past the lump in her throat. She hated pity parties, especially when she was the center of one, but darn if she just couldn't get herself out of it.

"Are you still up for the interviews today?" With Lorelei's baby due in four months, they needed to hire someone to replace her while she was on maternity leave. Truth was the diner was doing so well they could afford to hire enough additional people that both Lorelei and Andee could take more time off. Andee had dreamt about spending that time in her new vacation home, the thought of which brought a sense of calm to her chaotic state of mind.

"Yeah, I'm still good for that. The sooner we nail that down, the sooner we can move on to the other things we want to do."

Lorelei sighed. "It'll be hard not coming here six days a week. It's all I've known for eight years. But a break will be nice."

"I'm not sure a baby is much of a break," Andee said with a laugh.

She went through her morning set-up routine in a haze, full of questions about what her next action should be. What if he didn't respond like she expected yet again? If she tried one more time, and he didn't notice, could she survive the blow to her esteem? To their marriage? Clearly, he was underwhelmed by her new look.

What had started out as an attempt to bring them closer had only succeeded in building one more obstacle for her to overcome.

Andee flipped the sign to open and unlocked the doors, greeting the regulars as they made their way to their favorite tables.

"Don't you look pretty," said Mr. Jenkins, her former drivers-ed teacher, now retired, as she filled his coffee. "You do something different?"

"My hair's not curly. I straightened it."

Mr. Thompson looked at her hair and shook his head. "Nah, I think it's more the way you're carrying yourself. That color looks nice on you."

Even with all the weight of her home life pressing down on her, Andee couldn't help but feel pretty in the new outfit she'd picked out with Melinda. The fact that Mr. Thompson, a man, had noticed . . . Well. Andee pressed her lips together briefly before letting the words tumble free. "You noticed the color? I thought that was beyond men."

"Girl, I've been married nearly fifty years. I've learned to notice color." He finished his sentence with a wink.

A million questions begged to be asked, but Andee surveyed the crowd and held her tongue. Maybe an opportunity to pick his brain would arise at a later date. She could only hope.

After returning to the coffeemaker, she set the empty carafe on the hotplate to be refilled and grabbed the full one, ready to replenish cups at the counter, stopping short when she saw Melinda Bane sitting there, her hands wrapped around a mug.

"So?" Melinda wiggled one brow.

"So nothing." Andee refilled her cup.

"Oh, come on. Don't hold out on me. I need details."

Andee leaned across the counter and dropped her voice. "Seriously. Nothing. He had a bad day at work, came home drunk, and thought my shirt was made of dragon skin . . ." She shrugged instead of bursting into tears.

Melinda slapped her hand against the linoleum and leaned back in the chair. "You have got to be kidding me," she said in a loud voice.

"Shhh. Keep it down."

Melinda leaned forward. "I never thought of Bucky Swift as a buffoon, but hey, wonders never cease. What about your hair?"

"He said it looked like it did when I got out of the shower. He did not prefer it. He did, however, like my breasts."

"Well, that's something. I think you look very pretty."

"Great. Then you and I can get married." Andee leaned against the counter and slapped the edge repeatedly with a tea towel. "Oh my word! Did you hear?" She bent closer toward Melinda.

"Hear what?"

Andee looked around the diner at the guests. She knew gossiping wasn't friendly, but this was more about panic and learning from other's troubles. Regardless, she didn't want to offend anyone. "Lorelei, come here a sec." Andee waved her friend over.

When the three were together, Andee closed the space between them and lowered her voice. "Kevin and Lisa Norman are getting divorced."

Lorelei gasped but Melinda sat back in her chair.

"Good for Lisa," Melinda said. "That butt face has been careless and disrespectful. If a person is in a relationship they should end it before starting one with another person." Melinda sat forward "You know, he cornered me about a month ago and propositioned me. As if I do that sort of thing. As if I don't know his wife or hadn't just served his kids breakfast." Melinda owned a greasy spoon that would be Two Chicks' competition if the menus were even remotely similar.

Melinda continued, "Just because I'm divorced doesn't mean I'm easy, like he implied. Of course he did this after I caught him out with some young girl, looked fresh out of college. And I'm being generous here."

Andee couldn't believe her ears.

"He was out in the open with another woman?" Lorelei asked.

Melinda nodded. "He didn't care who caught him."

Lorelei narrowed her eyes. "I hope she skins him alive."

"She won't." Melinda shook her head. "I saw her the other day, and she asked me if I was happier once I got divorced. I told her I was just relieved. She looked like she could handle a bit of relief."

"What am I---I mean what is she going to do?" Andee asked.

Melinda grabbed her hand. "This is not you and Buck. Listen, men are morons. They don't always put the pieces together. You have to show him how this new look benefits him."

"She's right," added Lorelei.

Melinda adjusted her shirt, exposing her ample cleavage even more. "I got this new shirt today. You like it?" She leaned forward.

"No, you didn't. You got it yesterday when we were shopping."

Melinda smacked Andee on the side of the arm.

"Ow," she said, rubbing it. "Oh, I see what you just did. I get it."

Tell them without actually telling them. Sneaky. "You think I should try again."

"Um." Melinda rolled her eyes. "Yeah. I think you should try again until you get the results you want."

"What if I never get the results I want?" Andee whispered, partly to herself. "What if he wants a new honey? He's been acting weird."

"Impossible. Buck loves you. Always has. Always will," Lorelei said.

Melinda nodded her agreement.

Yeah, but it wasn't Buck's love she doubted, just his desire for her. Everyone knew those were two different things. Men who had affairs were men who loved their wives, usually, but somewhere along the way the passion for them had turned into friendship and companionship. The shift in marriage went from turning them on to tuning them out.

Andee saw that coming like a freight train about to jump the tracks. Not that she thought Buck was a cheater, but he was a redblooded, horny man, and the last time they'd tried a position outside of missionary, the president had been campaigning for reelection.

The jingling of the front door bells indicating a new customer stopped her from further sharing her fears with her friends. Andee turned to find Buck walking into the diner dressed in his typical, not-at-work, weekend clothes--a T-shirt, cargo shorts, and his favorite ball cap--which was puzzling He pulled his ball cap off and ran his hand through his hair before he folded then tucked the hat in his back pocket.

"Hey," he said when he came to the counter. "Melinda. Lorelei." He nodded to them. "How are ya? How are the repairs coming on your house, Melinda? Heard Jared's company was fixing it up." He returned his gaze to Andee, Melinda's recent house fire already forgotten.

"Can we talk?"

"Now? Why aren't you at work? Isn't it your Saturday?" She knew it was his once-a-month weekend to cover the store. She straightened her shirt and pushed back her shoulders.

"Can we take this elsewhere?"

Andee scooped up a set of dirty dishes and dumped them into the bin for the dishwasher with a clatter, tossing a plate over them for good measure. Perversely, she took pleasure in his wince.

"Buck here tied one on last night," she told the girls. Frankly, she was tired of this state they were in. Tired of trying to figure it out while he avoided it through work or TV, and drinking.

"Why don't you all go into the kitchen," Lorelei said and pushed the dishwashing bin toward Andee.

Andee snatched up the large plastic box, gave it a good shake, and nodded her head toward the back, indicating Buck should follow her.

With more force than she intended, Andee slid the wash bin onto the table and began loading it into the dishwasher, tossing the plates and mugs haphazardly into the machine.

Her fear of what Buck was hiding and frustration over her repeated failures to draw it out of him had morphed into simmering anger. There was no denying that she was scared, but she'd finally hit a place where she simply needed everything to be resolved so she could move forward. Living with no understanding about what the hell was happening was eating her alive. Doubt was now consuming logic.

If Buck was no longer turned on by her and wanted someone else, then as her father would say, "It was time to fish or cut bait." This sentiment applied to whatever else might be eating away at the underpinning of their marriage.

Slamming the door of the dishwasher closed with her hip, Andee grabbed a pen and paper and began taking inventory. She heard the swinging door whoosh open and slide closed and turned to face her husband.

"Babe?" He took a step toward her.

"What's going on, Buck? Why aren't you at work?" She crossed her arms, pen and paper gripped tightly in her fist, and shifted her body away from him.

Stopping, he rested his hands on his hips. "I got fired. Remember?" He met her gaze.

"You get fired at least twice a year. Why is today any different? Put on your uniform and go to work." Why was he suddenly so resistant to his job? Where was this coming from? From what she'd read, it was too soon for Buck to be having a midlife crisis, but damn it if it didn't look like that might be what was happening.

Buck shook his head and stood firm before her. "I'm not going back there."

She watched him search her face, trying to read her. Good luck, *she* couldn't even get a good gauge on how she felt. She slapped the pen and paper on the counter and planted her hands on her hips, ready for a faceoff.

"What do you mean you're not going back there? Where you going? What are you doing? You've worked for your father since you were fifteen. You've never work anywhere else-*ever*- but today is the day you've decided to change that." She tossed up her hands in amazement.

Buck briefly scrubbed his hands over his face. "Yeah, that's the plan." He scuffed his foot against the cement floor and met her gaze.

"You're just walking away?"

His mouth opened, then closed before opening again, the words apparently unwilling to come out. Andee almost took comfort in that. Almost.

She looked away to gather her racing thoughts, but panic had disabled her coping skills and left her in a heightened state where she was working from her gut. "So what? You're going to go work for Publix now? I thought you swore you'd never be like the masses here and work for a grocery store. I don't understand,

Bucky. Help me understand why everything is changing." She fought to keep the hysteria from her voice but failed.

In anticipation of what she was about to inevitably hear, she gripped the counter with one hand and waited. What would he say? What would it change? Would the eventual outcome be something drastic like divorce or just change the structure of their marriage? The possibilities were endless. Truth was, she might be able to handle almost any of the scenarios with the exception of someone else.

"Your dad always says to follow your heart--" The ringing of Buck's phone interrupted him. After pulling it out, he looked at the screen and pressed ignore. He switched the tone to vibrate.

"Oh my God." Andee moaned and covered her eyes with the palms of her hands, "Do not quote my father. He's a person who is never content with what he has." She dropped her hands and watched him ignore the call, "Was that your dad?"

"Just listen. Your dad did what he wanted and he was happier for it."

She sliced her hands through the air to emphasize her point. "And my mother was stressed out because of it. Trying to figure out how to feed us when he was between jobs. Trying to keep up the appearances he expected. My dad is a selfish asshole who moved his family every six months to a wreck of a house. He made us live in a construction zone nearly every day of our lives all so that he could make more money. Money that he does nothing with. Just hoards it. "

"Oh, come on. It was never that bad. I've heard the stories. I was even there for part of it, and you never went without." Buck crossed his arms over his chest.

"I bet my momma would tell a different tale." Her voice hit a new high.

The low hum of vibration filled the pause between their words.

Buck's volume met hers. "We should ask her because she seems pretty happy to me." Following a sigh, he reached into his pocket and silenced his phone a second time.

"Why are we even talking about my parents? What does this have to do with anything?"

"It has everything to do with what I'm talking about." He moved away, turning his back to her, and she watched his shoulders rise and fall as he took in a deep breath.

She closed her eyes and quietly said, "I get that my parents are much nicer than your dad, but you didn't grow up with my dad. His life wasn't as rosy as he always made it look. I know working for your dad is much like facing a bully. But you're going to own those stores one day--"

"I don't want to own them." The terse tone of his words snapped her eyes open and she saw him facing her, his face drawn and angry. "I don't want anything to do with it. I'd rather be a beggar on the street than give him another day of my life. I'm sick of him pitting Cal and I against each other for bonuses and promotions--that rarely come through, need I remind you. I'm tired of him trying to hijack my life. For the love of God, Andee, he wants to take our vacation home money and use it on a hunting cabin. That alone should piss you off."

"We had a plan," she yelled. "Now, suddenly that's no longer good for you? I don't know who--"

"You're so focused on your ten-year plan that you can't see what's going on around you." He met her volume and took it a notch higher.

Andee gasped. "You come home drunk, tell me you've been fired, and now you're telling me that you're not going back? What else are you gonna surprise me with?"

Buck pulled out his phone and shut it off. He tossed it on the counter. "Do you not see how unhealthy this relationship is?"

Andee paled and wrung her hands. Had he been avoiding his issues with her just like he was avoiding his father's calls? Could he really think they were unhealthy or was he talking about his father? A cacophony of thoughts, most heavy with fear, crowded her mind making logical reasoning impossible, "Is that him that keeps calling? Aren't you going to tell him your plans?"

"I'd like to tell you first, but if you don't care--" He stood with one hand on his hip and the other pointing at her. ·

"I never said I didn't care, but it's kinda rude to let him hang like that--" Andee folded her arms around her, squeezing her arms tightly, hoping to hold herself together. If he could treat his own father with such careless disregard, how would he treat her?

"He fired me!" He stepped toward her and shouted, "Do you not hear what I'm saying? Are you unable to hear me?"

"But have you even told him what your--"

"He. Fired. Me." Buck yelled again. "I don't owe him anything."

"What about me? Do you owe me anything because you've made all these changes without so much as a hint as to what is on your mind-" She hollered.

"I'm trying-"

Their voices escalated as they continued to talk over the other, not listening, instead trying to get the other to see their side. A years worth of stress, confusion and its mounting strain spilled out through their words and in the pitch of their voices.

"You can't even tell your father you're done-" she said over him.

"I told him yesterday-"

A shrill whistle made the argument come to an abrupt stop. Lorelei stepped between them.

"Now. There's nothing I want more than for y'all to work this out and put it behind you. But I reckon you might not want to do it here, with everyone out in the diner privy to the conversation."

"Jesus," Buck said and stepped away.

"Was it bad?" Andee asked Lorelei.

She nodded. "Everyone out there is tuned in. I'm sure the gossips have phoned their counterparts and word is spreading as we speak."

Andee slumped against the counter, her head resting in the palms of her hands.

"We'll just work this out at home," Buck said and started to move away, but Lorelei snagged him by the elbow and pulled him back.

"No. I've known the two of you my entire life, and I've never seen you all like this. From what I can gather this fight is two different conversations. Neither of you can see that. My folks are in town and my dad's doing a marriage retreat of sorts at the church this weekend. It starts in a few minutes. I called him and he's expecting you."

"I don't think so, Lorelei." Buck shook his head.

Lorelei stepped closer, and though she lowered her voice, Andee heard her say, "Yeah, Bucky. You're going. Do you know that Andee thinks you don't find her attractive anymore?"

Part of her hated that her friend had outed her but another part felt relief. She'd been too afraid to say the words, afraid his confirmation would follow them.

Through her tears, Andee saw Buck stare at her. Yet, he made no move to comfort her or ease her fears.

Lorelei turned to Andee. "You all rarely fight. And now, when you need to do it to work out some stuff, you're no good at it. You two don't know how to fight. You need a mediator. That's my dad."

"What about the interviews?" Andee stalled.

"You're just gonna have to trust me. I'll hire the one I think works best. Can you do that?"

Andee nodded and wiped her eyes with a tea towel.

Buck sighed. "Why can't you do that for me, Andee? Trust me like that."

Before Andee could respond, Lorelei cut her off. "Not here. Take it to dad."

"What about closing up?" Andee twisted the tea towel in her hands.

"Kylie is coming in. She'll help through the weekend. You all just focus on each other. Melinda said she'll help out until help gets here."

Andee started to stay something, but Lorelei pulled her into a hug. "Focus on your marriage," she whispered.

Andee nodded and let Lorelei wipe her face clean with the towel.

"Do you want to ride together?" Buck asked.

Andee shook her head. "I need a minute to gather my thoughts. I'll follow you there." She pulled off her apron then bent to pull her purse from a crate on the floor. If there was one thing from this whole experience that Andee was certain of, it was that if Buck Swift no longer wanted to be with her she likely wouldn't have the strength to knock some sense into him. That the idea of him moving on would break her in two.

F rom the moment he walked into the diner and saw the tired but frustrated expression on his wife's face, he felt pretty confident there was no chance his actions from last night would blow over.

He was tired, his head pounded, and his gut told him that this was not the time or place to have the conversation they needed to have. But now that his plan was in motion, he didn't want to waste another day and had already put a call in to the realtor who was selling the empty lot he'd come to covet.

Now, as he waited to walk his wife to her car, he banked his frustration. The last thing he wanted to do was air his business in front of more people, including Reverend Parker, a man Buck had always wished was his father instead of the ballbuster he'd gotten. But he'd go to hell and back to never again see his wife look like she had a moment ago. Her face ravaged from tears and fear. Even if hell looked like couples counseling with the guy who used to be his youth pastor, who had married him and Andee, and who threw a football like a laser.

While Buck held the diner door, waiting, a line from an old

movie played on repeat in his head. "Dead man walking," it screamed, all the way to the church.

He parked beside Andee, and together they walked in silence to the large building. Usually they'd hold hands, but today he worried about touching her. Afraid she'd start crying again. His intense need to ease her pain and guilt for knowing he was wrecking her ten-year plan almost made him reconsider going back to work for his tyrannical father. Almost.

He'd known this was going to be hard. Andee came from a large family that was always on the move, changing plans, and forgetting about little things like deadlines, routines, and sched-ules. It had made his little type-A planner crazy back in high school, and she was only able to manage it now because she could leave her family's nonsense behind for the comfort and structure of their home.

Andee needed predictability and it was his job to see she had it. That's why dropping this bomb on her without time to prep her was going to be hard. Real hard. And it was all his fault because he hadn't figured out the best way to prime her for his news back when he knew the change was coming.

They entered the front of the church, and immediately his eyes were drawn into the chapel, down the long center walkway that ended at the altar where Jesus hung from the cross.

"God is watching," His wife whispered.

"Pardon?" Her words caught him off guard.

"God is watching. It's something momma used to say when she thought we were lying. It always got us to confess. I suppose that's the point of this exercise." she mumbled the last bit.

It was do-or-die time. There'd be no skirting the truth in order to avoid what needed to be said. There would be no white lies to save feelings.

It wasn't that he believed God would smite him down or anything like that. He knew that he was to blame for the state of their relationship. His hesitation and concern with rocking her boat, for increasing their risk, had made him drag his feet too long. Andee deserved better.

Reverend Parker came out from an annex room and smiled at them. "Come in. Come in. We're just getting started, held the introductions until you arrived." He gestured for them to precede him.

Andee looked to him, something she always did when she was nervous and moving into new territory. He gave her a reassuring nod and, sensing her hesitation, stepped forward.

"Reverend. Thanks for letting us come last minute." Buck extended his hand and the two men shook, the reverend clasping Buck's hand between his.

"I'm glad you're here. It's good to see you both. I wish it were under different circumstances, but this'll be a good thing. Trust me, son. I'll take care of you."

They released hands and Reverend Parker clapped him on the back as Buck moved to wait at the door for his wife to precede him.

Reverend Parker opened his arms to give Andee a hug.

"Have faith, sis," Reverend Parker said, using the nickname he'd given her ages ago, back when she was a child and, like Buck, was at their house more than at home.

Buck held the door open for her and followed her into the small annex room. Inside, he counted three other couples. A small gasp escaped Andee and he swung his gaze to the direction she was looking and saw Kevin and Lisa Norman.

Kevin look like Buck felt. Plowed down by a truck. Kevin had certainly had far more to drink yesterday than Buck had and the pallor of his skin reflected just as much.

Reverend Parker closed the door and asked everyone to take a seat. "Let's begin with introductions and why you're here." He indicated to a couple who appeared to have many seasons together behind them. They were smiling and holding hands.

"We're Fred and Milly Brown. We've been coming to couples

therapy for the last twenty years. After our kids moved out, we suddenly found ourselves alone, together. A lot. It was rough. Instead of throwing in the towel, we gave this a try. We've been coming every year since for a tune-up." Fred told the room while Milly nodded in agreement.

Buck and Andee shared a look but she quickly looked away, likely because she remembered she was mad at him. Not about to let the moment go, he leaned toward her but made it look as if he was adjusting in his seat. "Show offs," he whispered.

She pressed her lips together to hold back her laugh and gave him a slight nod to tell him she agreed.

"Hi," said a perky, young blonde sitting next to a stick of a guy. "I'm Tiffany and this is Tyler." She pointed to the stick, who waved.

"Hi," Tyler said.

"We're getting married in four months and this class was recommended before we actually tie the knot." She rubbed her knees, in nervousness or excitement. It was hard to tell.

"Yup," said Tyler, clearly bored and only there because he was told to be.

Reverend Parker pointed to the Normans.

Lisa was sitting slightly turned away from Kevin with her arms crossed. "I'm Lisa Norman. I'm married to this jackass--sorry Reverend--and I'm here because we have children, and we promised our families we would come."

Kevin nodded. "I agreed to come."

"If you don't want to be here, Kevin, don't. It'll be a waste of my time as well as yours. It's OK to leave. God won't strike you down as soon as you walk out of the building." Reverend Parker leaned against the wall, hands in his pockets.

"I wish he would," Lisa mumbled.

The reverend could stare a person down in under five seconds. His gaze was penetrating, as if God was watching from behind the same blue eyes he shared with Lorelei. He was giving that look to Lisa right now and Buck had to look away.

"Sorry again, Reverend," she mumbled.

"I know you're hurt, Lisa. But let's try to keep this aboveboard."

"Yes, sir."

Reverend indicated to Buck and Andee that it was their turn.

"You talk," Buck whispered.

"Hi. We're the Swifts. I'm Andee and this is Bucky . . . um, Buck . . . and ah . . . We're here because your daughter made us come," she said the last bit to Reverend Parker.

He tossed back his head and laughed. "So she did. She's bossy like that. But I think it might have something to do with the fight you all were having. Am I wrong?"

Buck shook his head. "No sir. We were certainly having a fight. But is that so unusual?"

"I don't know, Buck, is it? Do you and Andee always fight in public?"

Buck shook his head again. "No sir. Actually, we don't usually fight." He glanced at his wife. "Not since you taught us, back in youth group, how to wait and listen. To pause before we react."

Reverend Parker smiled. "I'm glad some things stuck from back then." Everyone in the room laughed. "If my memory serves, I believe you two were also in those classes." He looked at the Normans.

Kevin planted his elbows on his legs and buried his head in his hands, his nod barely perceivable.

"OK, let's start with a prayer and get to working on making each other happy."

Everyone bowed their heads, and Buck could see Andee's lips moving. He wondered if she was adding her own little silent prayer at the end of the group's.

"OK, first assignment is to take eight pictures. " The reverend pulled a stack of paper off the table. "I'll give each of you one of these. You're to answer the questions by using a photo. I assume you all have smartphones. I know the Browns have done this before, so I ask that they try to reach deep for more thoughtful answers." Reverend Parker walked around the room and handed out one piece of paper per person. "Do not share your list with your spouse or soon-to-be spouse."

Desperate for a lifeline, a way to ease his wife into what he hoped would be a successful journey they would share, Buck said his own prayer before opening the paper and reading the instructions.

Be creative. Use pictures, screenshots, or any other sort of image that answers these questions with only one picture. Be prepared to explain it. You have thirty minutes.

1. Where did you go on your first date?
2. Where did you go on your last date?
3. What's one thing your spouse loves more than anything?
4. What's one thing you love more than anything?
5. Where was the last place you shared a laugh?
6. What is your spouse's goal?
7. What is their dream?
8. What is your dream?

GO!

R eady to escape a room heavy with confusion and uncertainty, Andee jumped up and looked around the room. Reading the word GO had prompted her fight or flight system into action. It was do-or-die time, as Buck would say, and she was torn on what to do. She should fly away and hope to avoid the issue. Maybe she could live with the missionary position the rest of her life. It wasn't that the sex was bad or anything. Oh, who was she kidding? There was nothing wrong with their missionary sex; it was the feeling of being shut out of his life that had her knees quivering. Watching him avoid his father made her scared he'd do the same to her.

Or did she fight? Truth was she couldn't live with this Buck who wasn't talking to her.

The Browns were already scrolling through their smartphones. The soon-to-be-weds looked like they were surfing Facebook, and the Normans weren't even moving.

How did Lisa feel? Did Kevin seem like a stranger to her? Or worse, did she know him so well that his betrayal cut even deeper? Did pictures only remind her of what was lost? Perhaps she didn't know him at all and that was why he'd strayed? One thing was for certain, Andee didn't know the answers and likely wouldn't even after a weekend spent with them at this event. She turned to see what Buck was doing and saw him scrolling through his photos.

"I'm going outside. I can think better out there," she whispered to him.

"Good idea." He stood and followed her out of the room. "I think I'll sit in the chapel," he said before breaking off.

"OK." She tried not to read into his actions. But her first thought was to wonder if he needed to sit in the chapel and ask for forgiveness before he delivered a lethal blow. Had what she thought was a simply a rut in their sex life really been the indicator of something far worse? Did he regret not sowing his oats more? Had his taste changed so that he no longer preferred girls like her? What if he now found their easy and predictable life mundane and boring? What if he was ready to upgrade?

She sat on the concrete stairs of the church, shivered, and slowly sucked in air, trying to steady her racing heart and not think the worst was about to descend upon her. Wasn't it a good thing that her husband wanted to chill out and binge-watch TV with her? That he loved to make these marathons themed to align with the show? Just a couple of weeks ago, he'd only spoken to her in a British accent for three solid days while they'd marathon-watched Sherlock. Andee wanted to slap herself upside the head. She'd thought it was fun and cute and quirky, but was it really a sign of doom for their relationship? Were they more roommates than lovers?

Andee glanced at her car. Could she get away with running? With a bone-weary sigh, she unfolded the paper and got down to the business of answering the questions. A couple of the searches for items made her laugh and remember moments such as when they went fishing and she caught a bigger fish. Or when they dressed up like Hans Solo and Princess Leia for Halloween, which also hadn't resulted in any wild sex afterward as Bucky got sick off Jello shots.

Now she saw his avoiding sex as a symptom of something much deeper and not knowing what flared her anger. When had they stopped talking? She scrolled past a picture of her ideal vacation home, a screenshot she'd not only put on her phone but on their fridge and in the encouraging emails she'd sent him about staying focused. Was it around the time she became single focused on a stupid house?

Andee shook her head, hating where her thoughts were going. Weren't they stronger than that? Could a house be the root of their problems? A terse laugh escaped her. She could guess and worry and plot a quick get-away but none of these would answer the bigger question. Nothing but facing him with an empty agenda and a willingness to hear. She glanced at her watch and stood up to go inside. Now, if she could only put her new determination into practice.

The last one to enter the room, Andee pulled the door closed behind her. Buck looked up from his phone and gave her a sweet smile.

Don't read into it!

"All right. We'll let the Browns go first since they are old hats at this. Fred, Milly." Reverend Parker gestured toward them. Fred stood and faced his wife.

"I tried to come up with something different from last time, but I'm afraid only the last date and last laugh changed. Oh, and the thing you love the most. I was going to put your new sewing machine, but I think the grandkids trump that."

Fred and Milly laughed together as they stared at each other, and Andee wanted to barf or cry. She wasn't sure which was the stronger reaction.

Milly's was much like Fred's, and Andee decided she wanted to cry. She'd give her right arm to be like them after one million years of marriage.

"Andee, Buck. You're up next."

"I'll go first," Andee said and stood. She might look like a fool after he went, but at least the gossipmongers would know that she'd given it her all.

"Why don't we try it a different way? Why don't you go at the same time?" Reverend Parker offered.

Andee looked at Buck, who nodded and stood so they faced each other.

With a deep breath to draw in courage, she said, "I'll start. My number one was where we went on our first date." She found the picture on her screen and turned it so Buck could see. "This is a picture of us at a Buc's game, last year. We took one of my nephews and a girl he's interested in. Our first date was at a Buc's game. I went with you and your family," she explained to the group while looking at Buck.

Bucky showed her his phone. He had the same picture. "I remember. I had to ask your dad for permission and promise that my folks were going. Taking your nephew and his girl reminded me of when we went. It was a good day. Both times."

They smiled at each other. Andee wanted to touch him. Any part of him, his arm or whatever. For just a moment, the connection between them felt strong, and she wanted to hold on to it.

"Why don't you go next, Buck," said Revered Parker.

Buck looked around the room. "Bear with me. I had to improvise here. My number two was our last date. This is the web site of the furniture store where we bought our couch, and this is our couch. Our last date was last week when we stayed home and watched Mad Men."

Andee guffawed. "That's not a date. That's what we do all the time."

"Not all the time. Sometimes we just watch TV, but these times are different."

Andee shrugged. She wasn't so sure she agreed.

"How so?" asked Lisa Norman. She put her hand up in defense.

"I'm not trying to challenge you. I'm just curious as to what makes it a date and not just watching TV."

Buck looked at Andee with pleading eyes, but she returned his gaze with a questioning one.

Buck sighed. "Oh, all right. Because we really get into it--make food from that region or time, talk with accents or whatever. It's an event. Not just channel surfing."

"Wow, you need to turn in your man card," said Kevin bitterly.

"Really? I'd like to stack my behavior next to yours and see which one of us hasn't been acting like a man. You up for that?" Buck challenged with a square of his shoulders.

"All right. Settle down. This is a good time to remind everyone that what is said here stays here. Everything here is confidential and should be treated with respect and courtesy. Or God will smite you." Reverend Parker smiled. "OK. That part might not be entirely true. But you never know." He winked at Andee. "Your turn, sis."

Andee held up her phone. "This is a picture of Texas Cattle Company. We went there for dinner a few weeks ago. That's what I picked for our last date."

Buck leaned toward her in disbelief. "That wasn't a date. That was an obligatory dinner with my folks so my dad could talk down to me even more."

"But we dressed up and went out. Remember, we went to the movies afterward."

"Because I was in such a bad mood. I didn't want to go home and fight with you because my pain-in-the-ass dad makes me want to punch a wall. Time in the theater gave me a chance to cool off."

Andee stepped back and searched his face. How had she missed that? How had she not known how upset he was? She was so used to his father and his autocratic ways, she'd just assumed he was as well.

"I'm sorry. I should've paid better attention."

"It's just that lately he's been getting to me more and more." This time Bucky extended his hand, tucking hers in his. "If we were to go on a date out in public, I sure wouldn't include my dad."

"Why are you two here?" Lisa asked them, her voice thick with annoyance.

"Because people can forget how to communicate, and they can forget how to listen. Because sometimes fear of change makes people act . . . unusual. I suspect there's change on the horizon for them," the reverend answered. "Next question."

Andee reached forward and took off Buck's ball cap. "Number three is his favorite possession. He loves this thing more than anything. Has had it almost as long as we've been married. It's been washed and reshaped and is falling apart, but he refuses to give it up."

Buck snatched it back and put it on his head. "It fits perfectly, and I think it's beautiful. I'll get rid of it when it disintegrates in my hands and not a moment sooner. But you're wrong. This is the thing I love the most." He held up his phone and showed a picture of her and Lorelei, arms around each other, laughing. It was the night Lorelei and Cole had told them they were expecting and asked them to be godparents.

"You love Lorelei?" Andee couldn't help but ask. She knew it was silly, but the fact that he'd picked her made her knees weak.

"Yeah, but not like I love you and certainly not as much. Not that you're my possession, but I can't help but feel like you're made for me," he said with a shrug, staring into her eyes.

Andee responded by promptly bursting into tears. It felt so good to hear him say how much she meant to him. Being called a possession might be an outdated idea, but she was OK with it. Knowing this made her feel treasured and wanted.

"Then what is happening to us?" she asked him.

Buck took a step toward her, but Reverend Parker stopped

him. "Let's keep on track. I think you'll have your answer soon enough. Buck, what is the thing Andee loves the most?"

He held up his phone, and the picture was of her sitting outside by a campfire with her family. "Andee loves her family the most. This includes her friends. This includes me. That means everything to me." He placed his hand over his heart as he told the last bit to the group.

Andee continued to cry softly in her hands, pausing to take a breath when Kevin Norman tossed her a box of tissues.

"I need a moment. Can you do the next one?" she asked Buck.

"Sure. The last place we laughed is the same picture from the first question. Our couch--or rather, our house. Same night from last week."

Andee thought back to when she'd cut the arms off his T-shirt and laughed through her tears. "I'd forgotten about that time. I put the movie we watched after dinner with your parents. We laughed at the movie." Her voice raised an octave. "But your answer is so much better than mine." She grabbed another tissue and sobbed into it.

"Andee. Why don't you go next?" the reverend suggested.

She nodded, sucked in some shaky breaths, and scrolled through her phone. "My spouse's goal? I think he has a few, but I selected this. It's a shot of a twelve-point buck. He'd love to bag one of those."

Buck nodded in agreement.

"Is that your goal, Buck?" asked Reverend Parker.

"It's one of them. Sure."

"But is it your immediate goal? Is it the thing you think about all the time?" He held up his hand to stop Buck from talking. "Think about it for a second. I'll come back to your answer. Why don't you show us what you said was Andee's goal."

"OK. Well, Andee's easy as she has her goals outline by decades. Her goal for ten years is to buy a vacation home, in twenty years is to retire early, and thirty years is travel a lot." His picture was of the goal thermometer she kept on their fridge.

"What's that?" Lisa asked, leaning forward to get a closer look.

"It's my goal chart. It keeps me--I suppose us--on track."

"That's a lot of pressure," Kevin said.

"Yeah, and we all know how you handle pressure. You lose your job, and I go back to work. We switch roles and you go crazy on me. Crazy," Lisa said, pointing her finger at Kevin.

"It's hard staying home with kids all day. It's not for me." Kevin crossed his arms in defiance.

"No. Responsibility isn't for you. Being a grown-up isn't for you. Working as a team like Andee and Buck--that's clearly not for you."

"OK. Time-out. It's not your turn yet. But this is good stuff. Last question, Andee. Buck. What are your dreams?"

Andee put her phone on the floor and stood up and faced Buck. They were going to get to the root of what was going on between them. "I don't need a picture--"

"My dream is to make Andee happy. Even if that requires sacrifice on my part."

"And has it?" asked Kevin.

Buck stared at Andee. She could see he was searching her face while seeking words, but the hesitation was all the confirmation that she needed.

"I would never want you to give up on a dream just to make me happy." She took a step toward him.

"But you've worked so hard to get to this place, and you desperately want a vacation home. You and Lorelei have worked every day for six years. You deserve a reward." He leaned toward her, reaching out to brush her arm.

Andee pressed a finger to her chest, pointing. "I deserve you being honest with me about what you want. If you don't want a vacation home then we'll regroup. Because what I 'desperately' want is you."

"So, Buck, let's go back to what your goal is. Does that have something to do with this? What was your fight about today?"

They answered the question at the same time.

"Buck was keeping something from me." She crossed her arms.

"She wants me to go back to work for my father," He said flipping his hand toward her.

"What?" They said in unison, searching each other's face.

"I heard you when you said you didn't want to go back to work for your dad. But you never said why. You've always said you put too much blood, sweat, and anger into that job to walk away so easily. I thought you wanted to take over the business. Then today, all that's changed."

Buck shook his head, and pressed his thumb in the space between his eyes. "Let Cal have it. I'm tired of hating every day when I go to work."

"How long have you felt like this?" She stepped toward him, wanting to offer him comfort.

Buck shrugged. "I think forever, but over the last year it's gotten worse."

Over the last year, *they'd* gotten worse. Could this be the why? Since when did Buck feel like he couldn't talk to her? With this realization, her heart broke all over again.

"Why didn't you ever say anything? How am I to know what you want if you don't talk to me? Keeping how you really felt from me made me think you were hiding something."

"I wasn't sure what I wanted or what I was going to do about it. So I sat on it."

"And went around like everything was normal. Except you were constantly grouchy, started drinking more, and you didn't sleep. When you say you aren't sure what you want to do, it scares me. What if what you want is what this guy wants?" She pointed to Kevin.

"I said I wasn't sure what I wanted. I'm sure now."

"For the love of God, Buck, then tell me," Andee cried.

"I want to open up my own business," he said with a shrug.

Andee clasped her hand over her mouth and sank to the floor.

"It's not that bad, really, Andee. I got it all figured out--"

"It's not that," she said, shaking her head. "I'm so relieved. I thought you wanted someone else. I thought you were bored with me and my frumpy style and frizzy hair. The fact that I still wear clothes from ten years ago, and I'm not very spontaneous."

Buck came down on his haunches and reached for her. "Babe, I love you. You're my life. My best friend. If I start my own business, you're going to have to give up the vacation home. Shoot, you'll have to give up vacations, and a whole lot more. I'll be gone a lot and work even more than I have in the past. Then there's the risk. It'll change a whole lot."

Andee fell into him and wrapped her arms around his waist, pulling him close to her. "I'll shred that stupid thermometer as soon we get home. We'll make new goals. New plans. You sacrificed all that when Lorelei and I opened the diner. Why would I do less for you?"

"Because I'm supposed to take care of you," he answered.

Andee pushed away from Buck, the force knocking him back onto his rear. "Said a Neanderthal man from the sixties. I thought we were a team." For good measure, she punched him in the shoulder. "You know the timing of this is perfect. Lorelei and I are hiring additional staff so I'll have more free time. If we aren't going to have a vacation home to go to, I could use a new project to keep me busy. Lorelei and I have been talking about a second business, a food truck. But with the baby coming, she doesn't have the time. I might be able to help you with your new business if you're interested."

Buck rubbed his shoulder and smiled. "Really? Because that would be awesome."

Andee smiled. "I'd have to see your numbers, of course."

"Of course." He opened up his arms and she moved into them,

loving how she felt wrapped in his embrace. "It's such a relief to finally tell you," he whispered in her ear.

"I'd feel pretty confident in saying that once the doors of communication are fully open and the channels are safe--even when the discussion is a hard one--areas of your life that might also be suffering will get better as well," added Reverend Parker.

"I think he means you should wear your hooker boots to bed tonight," Buck whispered in her ear.

"All right. Let's move on to the Normans. Lisa. Kevin. You all ready?" Reverend Parker picked up the box of tissues Andee had been using earlier and handed them to Kevin, who, Andee noticed, was hiding his face in his shoulder and looked to be crying.

"I'm a terrible husband." He sniffed.

"And father," Lisa added.

"OK. Let's not attack anyone," encouraged Reverend Parker

"This is going to be awful," whispered Andee.

Buck nodded and held her tight.

EPILOGUE

TWO YEARS LATER

With a gentle push on the shovel's handle, Buck scooped up the sandy soil and tossed a soft mound into the wheelbarrow. He smiled at the photographer from the paper and waited for him to snap his picture.

The small crowd clapped and Buck caught Andee's eye then winked.

"Mr. Swift," the reporter called and waved him over. "A few questions, please."

"Sure." He watched Andee walk toward him, her heels sinking in the soil, laughter on her lips as she made the journey.

"Three stores in two years. That's incredible growth. This fourth store is the first outside of Lakeland. Care to share your secret for growth?"

"Behind every good man is a better--and likely smarter--woman. At least, that's the truth in my case. When I told my wife I wanted to open the first Swift Oil and Auto, she pulled out her accountant's hat and mapped it out for me. She saw potential in ways I hadn't and knew when to take a risk when I hesitated. That's my secret. That and providing a quick, quality oil change and auto needs to people with busy lives. That's the goal of Swift Oil and Auto."

"Thanks for your time," said the reporter, who ended the conversation with a handshake.

Andee came up from the side, grabbed his arm for support. She lifted one shoe and tried to shake the dirt off the heel.

"You look awfully hot in that skirt," he told her.

Andee slid her foot in the shoe and pulled her blouse away from her chest, shaking it back and forth in hope of getting air movement. "Next time you break ground on a store, do it in winter."

Buck slid his arm around his wife's waist. "That's not what I was talking about."

Andee blushed and swatted him lightly at his chest. "Oh, Bucky."

"But since you mentioned it, my pickup is right around the corner. It has A/C. We can go there and fool around. It'll be like old times. Like we're back in high school."

"Or like last week when we did that after we walked the lake." The flame in her eyes matched the fire that burned inside him for her. Seventeen years with the same girl and he wouldn't change a thing. He was hers for life. She was his turtledove.

"Kiss me," he said craving to taste her.

She leaned into him, pressing her length to his and delivered a soft, sweet lingering kiss. When she pushed away he admired how sexy she wore her new business suit. But more than anything he loved the look she was giving him now, an open smile and inviting eyes.

"Give me your keys," she said holding out her hand. "I'll meet you there in five minutes."

"Deal." He passed over his keys, and when she turned away, he gave a light slap to her rear and pulled her back toward him. "Kiss me, again."

CARE TO LEAVE A REVIEW?

Dear Reader,

I am so honored that you took the time to read my book. If you feel so inclined, I would appreciate it if you left an honest review. You don't have to say much. Put the stars you feel it deserves and a few words. Some folks don't even put words. Reviews go a long way in helping authors in all sorts of areas including marketing.

Thanks again. You're a rock star!

Click the link to go to book page and select where you want to leave the review: Book page

Have a great one.

Kristi

ABOUT THE AUTHOR

Kristi Rose was raised in central Florida on boiled peanuts and iced tea. Kristi likes to write about the journeys of everyday people and the love that brings them together. Kristi is always looking for avid readers who are willing to do beta reads (give impression of story before edits) and advance readers who are willing to leave reviews. If you are interested, please sign up for her newsletter. Aside from her eternal gratitude she also likes to do giveaways.

Come hang out with Kristi at any of the following:
www.kristirose.net
kristi@kristirose.net

www.ingramcontent.com/pod-product-compliance
Lightning Source LLC
Chambersburg PA
CBHW020553180626
46810CB00007B/2490